More praise for
Stuart Kaminsky
and LIEBERMAN'S FOLLY

"The Kaminsky protagonist is irresistible. . . . Featur[es] characters you can almost touch, streets you can almost walk on, and—something we don't see all that much anymore—an expertly plotted story."
The Philadelphia Inquirer

"Presents one of the most 'surprise' endings in recent murder mystery history."
St. Petersburg Times

"[Kaminsky] outdoes himself in this smartly observed Chicago procedural. . . . A beautifully assured performance. Don't miss this one—and pray a series follows."
The Kirkus Reviews

"He's about as crafty and soul searching as a crime writer can be."
Booklist

Also by Stuart M. Kaminsky:

BURIED CAESARS
A COLD RED SUNRISE*
DOWN FOR THE COUNT
THE HOWARD HUGHES AFFAIR
THE MAN WHO SHOT LEWIS VANCE
YOU BET YOUR LIFE

Inspector Porfiry Rostnikov Mysteries:

DEATH OF A DISSIDENT*
BLACK KNIGHT IN RED SQUARE*
RED CHAMELEON*
A FINE RED RAIN*
THE MAN WHO WALKED LIKE A BEAR*

*Published by Ivy Books

LIEBERMAN'S FOLLY

Stuart Kaminsky

IVY BOOKS • NEW YORK

Ivy Books
Published by Ballantine Books
Copyright © 1991 by Stuart Kaminsky

Library of Congress Catalog Card Number: 90-49309

ISBN 0-8041-0924-9

This edition published by arrangement with St. Martin's Press, Inc.

Manufactured in the United States of America

First Ballantine Books Edition: May 1992

Cover photo © Marc Pokemper/Tony Stone Worldwide

To Joe Perll

Prologue

The tavern was called Babe O'Brien's. No one named O'Brien had ever, in its twenty years of business, owned the place. In fact, no one even remotely Irish had ever owned Babe O'Brien's. The name had been chosen by Juan Hernandez De Barcelona, who had never been to Barcelona and whose ancestors had almost certainly never been to either Ireland or Spain.

Juan Hernandez De Barcelona was a black man about the size and shape of a two-door refrigerator. He had earned his money by working on the docks of Port au Prince. As a boy he had loaded and unloaded ships. As a young man he had loaded and unloaded drunken sailors. And as a man he had unloaded pistols more than once into the bellies of people who annoyed the Baron Duvivier, a colonel in the Tonton Macute who sometimes found it expedient to employ the services of an outside broken-bottle man like Juan rather than one of his own troops.

It was the Baron, whose business was not always that of the country, who advised Juan Hernandez to add the "De Barcelona" to his name. Although Juan would one day kill the Baron with his bare hands and steal the money the Baron wore in a money belt under his brown uniform, Juan Hernandez always respected the memory of his mentor and the advice he had been given.

When he reached New Orleans after taking the place of a black American sailor named Jerris Simms who had had an unfortunate encounter with a machete, Juan Hernandez considered investing the deceased Baron Duvivier's money in a whorehouse, but the competition in New Orleans was more than Juan was yet ready to deal with. Instead, he moved to Corpus Christi, Texas, because he liked the name, and put his capital in a tavern formerly named the Blue Ridge. It was in a neighborhood changing from poor redneck to poor Mexican and a smattering of blacks—mostly Jamaicans and Haitians.

Juan Hernandez named the place Babe O'Brien's because he wanted to be an American success and in a movie he had seen the name over a tavern owned by a short fat character played by an actor whose name he didn't recognize.

Juan Hernandez was a killer but he was also a romantic: He believed in the American dream. The bar was not even the beginning.

The real business of Juan Hernandez was women. The bar, Juan told potential employees, was just a front, like the front of the house in *Gone with the Wind*. To his disappointment, one of the Mexican whores had told him that the house in the movie was just a big flat painted lie propped up by boards.

But beyond the end of the bar was a door behind which was the real business of Babe O'Brien's. Here Juan himself sat night after night drinking slowly and passing judgment on those who wanted to enter that door. Behind that door, the flesh was fresh, young, and reasonably well paid. The women and girls were black, white, brown, and yellow. They were Indians, Chinese, Mexicans, Creoles, French, Haitians, Jamaicans, and even one Russian or, at least, one blonde with an accent who claimed that her name was Ludmilla and that she was from Leningrad.

Juan Hernandez dealt only in cash and he kept no books except behind the bar, for the drinks. The only tax paid was on the bar and, strangely enough, the bar turned out to be profitable, not the kind of profit that Juan Hernandez felt was sufficient, but profitable still. For twenty years, Juan had suffered little inconvenience at the door at the rear of Babe O'Brien's. In his third year of business, that entrance had acquired the name Heaven's Portal. It had been so named by a skinny drunk who had come only once. The drunk had paused and sang to Juan Hernandez De Barcelona, "You are my lucky star." And moments later he added, "You opened heaven's portal here on earth for this poor mortal."

In the next seventeen years there had been three robbery attempts in Babe O'Brien's, one by a trio of brothers named Valenciana who were gunned down by Zetch the bartender before they got near Heaven's Portal. Juan Hernandez De Barcelona had sat watching the event unemotionally.

The second attempt fifteen years later was better planned. It was conducted by a pair of black men from Alabama who had heard about Babe O'Brien's. One of the black men was named Lowell Caldwell. The other had only one name that anyone knew, Toggle. Toggle was even bigger than Juan Hernandez De Barcelona. He and Lowell approached Heaven's Portal about 3:00 A.M. on a Tuesday when business was dead slow. Toggle and Caldwell had grinned at Juan Hernandez De Barcelona, who at that time wore a trim little goatee and his hair slicked back. Lowell pulled out a small gun and shot Juan. Toggle got behind Juan and put his arm around his neck before he could rise. Zetch the barman hesitated but Juan did not. He was simply moving slow. He grabbed Toggle's hand, grunted, and pulled down, snapping the giant's right arm. Lowell, who was murmuring "No, no, no," took another shot at Juan. The bullet entered his stomach just above the navel. Juan took enough time to turn and smash Toggle's head against the concrete pillar near the door. Ten seconds later Lowell Caldwell had died in a manner that even Zetch, who had been an homicide investigator with the Cleveland police before he lost his left leg, did not like remembering.

Juan Hernandez De Barcelona had not spent even a night in the hospital as a result of this incident. A doctor who was well paid to keep the incident quiet removed the two bullets on a bed recently vacated by Ludmilla the Russian. Juan was back at his table near the Portal the next night, bandaged, playing solitaire, and pocketing cash. What was left of Toggle and Lowell Caldwell was dumped in front of City Hall. The story was all over the newspapers and on TV. Juan Hernandez De Barcelona had become a local legend.

No one had bothered Babe O'Brien's again until a year previously, and then it was only by mistake. Two rednecks with accents so thick that Juan could not understand them found Juan funny. It could have been the bottle of cheap bourbon they had shared or their inbred bigotry fueled by each other's prodding, but the men, Cal and C.C., decided that they were going through Heaven's Portal and that they would pay only when they came out and only if they were satisfied and no "Buddha Nigger was gonna tell them ought else."

"Hell," said C.C. "You should pay us for coming in here."

"Yeah," said Cal, who had a scruffy white beard. "Why not? How about you pay us?"

Cal pulled out a fairly large handgun and C.C. said, "Hot damn if you ain't one mean gator." And C.C. pulled out an even larger handgun.

Having learned from his last encounter with Toggle and Lowell, Juan Hernandez De Barcelona had rigged a surprise under his table. The shotgun was bolted to the table facing the space between Heaven's Portal and the bar. It was also rigged so that it did not require a pull of the trigger, only a sudden upward thrust of Juan's knee.

As pellets rained across the intruding duo, both Cal and C.C.'s guns fired. One bullet took off Juan's right ear. The other killed Zetch. At almost the same instant, both C.C.'s head and Cal's gut were torn apart by Juan's shotgun blast. The cleanup had been swift and the police well paid. Juan had not bothered to go to a doctor for his ear. He put ice on it, let Ludmilla bandage it, got slightly drunk, and came back the next day to look for a new bartender.

Juan considered these attempts on his life and property a reasonable part of the risks involved in running a business. In truth, Juan Hernandez De Barcelona, who by 1979 was forty-three years old, had saved close to one million dollars. He could have quit and lived comfortably for the rest of his life, but two things stopped him. First, while

Juan had always wanted to be an American success, he had no thoughts at all about what he would do when he was successful. He liked sitting in the bar and watching the customers. He liked talking to the girls, hiring new ones, breaking them in, firing the old ones and giving them nice bonuses. He liked watching old movies on television. There was nothing else he wanted to do. Besides, he would not consider himself a success until he had an even one million dollars in the cans in his house on Buena Grande Street.

And so, in a way, it was the American dream that killed Juan Hernandez De Barcelona, just as it had killed many another ambitious immigrant.

On this day, as he sat at his table drinking a Coke and watching his new night bartender serve the drinks and fill the till, he heard a scream beyond Heaven's Portal. Screams seldom penetrated that thick door. About five years earlier he had had to fire a tiny Korean girl named Tina for screaming in mock ecstasy loud enough to be heard in the tavern. Occasionally, a client would go a little too far and a girl would let out a cry of pain. More often it was the clients themselves who would scream, but this was different.

Juan Hernandez got up from his table, waved at the new bartender, and caught the rifle the man threw him. Juan had seen someone throw a rifle to John Wayne like this and had waited for this moment. He went through Heaven's Portal, rifle in one hand like the Duke or the Rifleman, and moved toward the scream. He didn't bother to open doors on the way. He knew which ones were occupied and which girls were working. The sound had come from one of the Mexican girls, the Madera sisters. They were a duo, special price. They had worked at Babe O'Brien's longer than any other girls.

As he strode down the corridor like an improperly armed samurai in a baggy gray suit and no tie, Juan decided that he would give the girls a big bonus and fire them. They were too smart. Smart girls were trouble. These girls were good for business, but they were, like right now, trouble.

He kicked open the door and aimed the rifle at the bed. A naked man lay there. Juan remembered him. Juan never forgot the face of a client and he had not read trouble on this one. Even now he did not read trouble. He saw fear. And where were the girls? The man's head did not turn but his eyes looked behind the door through which Juan had come.

Before Juan could turn, he was shot in the neck. Even shot and choking on his own blood Juan spun and faced the two naked young women who stood together, each holding a pistol. They fired together and Juan Hernandez De Barcelona died thinking that America had been a goddamn mistake.

Girls were screaming in all the rooms now.

The man on the bed was named James "Skettle" Harte, who claimed to be a grandson of Bret Harte. Skettle had told the Madera sisters that he had a record and had done hard time in both Alabama and Illinois. Skettle also claimed to be wealthy and influential. The Madera sisters had not bought that part of his story. For them, Skettle was just the client the girls had been waiting for. One of the girls, Estralda, had placed the barrel of her pistol in his ear and ordered him to scream. When he hesitated, the other sister pushed him on his side and inserted the barrel of her weapon into another orifice. Skettle screamed.

Now James "Skettle" Harte watched as the two women, their breasts bouncing and erect, moved quickly. The older one, Guadalupe, pried the rifle from the late Juan Hernandez's hands. The younger one threw her gun to Skettle, who caught it in confusion as he was shot by the rifle Juan had brought into the room. Skettle was writhing in mortal pain with no idea what had happened to him or why.

Footsteps were coming. The sisters said not a word. The younger one picked up her sister's gun and stuffed it under the mattress; the other girl dropped the rifle on Juan's chest. The two of them had just managed to turn Juan's body back toward Skettle and the bed when the first innocent bystander filled the door. He was in his sixties, naked, thin with a big belly.

"Lord shit," he said. "I'm gettin' out of here."

Frank the bartender bulled his way in, looked at the dead

men and the frightened sisters hugging each other and said, "You got someplace to go?"

"Sí," the older sister said. "Yes."

"Then go there," he said, kneeling over to unbutton Juan's jacket and remove the money belt.

People were scrambling all over the place, grabbing for clothes, climbing through windows. The sisters put on their clothes quickly and went along the hallway Juan had come down less than two minutes before. They went through Heaven's Portal and past a pair of drunks in the corner who didn't seem to know anything out of the ordinary was going on.

Seven minutes and five blocks later the Madera sisters entered the home of the late Juan Hernandez De Barcelona.

They moved quickly, searching for the money they knew must be there. They did not fear the bartender or any of the other girls, none of whom had any reason to think Juan had his money in buckets at home. The older sister, Guadalupe, knew. She had heard him talk in his fevered sleep about the buckets on the night Doc Totaro had pulled the bullet from his gut and left him on Ludmilla's bed. Guadalupe had heard him and remembered and from that day the sisters had taken turns watching Juan when he went home in the morning and came to Babe O'Brien's the next afternoon. They watched him for months. They never saw him going to a bank. And then they had begun planning.

They moved quickly because they knew the police would come. They didn't know when, but the police would be here. Guadalupe guessed that it would take the cops at least an hour to figure out where Juan had lived and even then they might have no reason to come here. The situation, they hoped, was clear. Juan had been killed by and had killed a berserk john who the police would find had a record.

The sisters searched. The house was a mess. Piles of junk. Old lamps, broken radios, furniture. After about twenty minutes, the younger one found a can of bills inside a gutted television set. The older one found the next bucket on a shelf in the attic.

"The *hijode puta* has hidden them all over the place," she cried in frustration. "It will take us all night."

But they didn't have all night. In two hours they had found four buckets of money. They were dirty, frightened, and panting when they heard the siren. They threw the cans into a sheet and went out the back door, the younger sister, Estralda, carrying the sheet over her shoulder like a sack of laundry.

The siren wasn't heading their way, but they had no way of knowing this. Theirs was not the only felony in Corpus Christi that night. A woman named Phoebe Floyd had stabbed her husband Frazier in the neck with a barbecue fork when he changed the television channel on her while she was watching *The Sound of Music*. These sirens were for Phoebe. The sisters left the house and got out of town, never learning that more than forty cans of bills would be found by a sixty-five-year-old black cleaning woman named Clarise Rogers who was hired two weeks later by the Southern Pride Realty Company to clean the house of the deceased owner of Babe O'Brien's so it could be sold.

Clarise had quietly taken the cans home in her husband's truck at night and three weeks later moved just as quietly to Stockton, California. There she rented six very large safety deposit boxes, which she visited about once a month.

The Madera sisters discovered that they had cleared a total of $54,674. They split it evenly and began to worry about fingerprints, rumors, Frank the bartender, and what the other girls beyond Heaven's Portal might put together about what had happened.

It was agreed that they should part and not see each other again. They should part and go as far from Texas as they could get and they should not tell each other where they were going.

And so it was that Guadalupe took a bus to San Diego where she invested her money in an all-night diner. The diner didn't flop but it didn't flourish either. It just ate up the profits a nickel at a time. When the money ran out, she sold the diner and moved north to St. Louis where she went back into the business and met a man on vacation who said

8

he loved her. He took her back to Chicago with him and she was happy to go.

Meanwhile, Estralda went to Miami, where she had no trouble finding work when her money was spent. From Miami she went to Phoenix and from there to Las Vegas and from there to Chicago, where she prospered and planned and dreamed of a new future in which she would someday own a business rather like Babe O'Brien's. And for almost ten years it seemed as if her dream would come true.

But the gods had very different plans.

1

"Lieberman?" the woman said over the sound of the Cubs game from a radio.

When she had entered the T & L Delicatessen a few seconds earlier, the customers, six old men known to each other as the Alter Cockers, looked up and stopped talking.

Women of any kind were rare inside Maish's T & L Deli between the hours of ten and five, and it wasn't even two in the afternoon. And women like this just didn't happen into the place. They didn't even happen into this neighborhood. Oh yes, there were a few women who came before nine in the morning. Melody Rosen, Herschel's daughter, who clerked at Bass's Children's Shop down the street, often stopped for a toasted bagel and coffee. And Gert Bloombach, a sack of a woman who worked in a law office downtown, came by every Tuesday and Thursday at eight for a cup of tea and a lox omelette. And there was Howie Chen's granddaughter, Sylvie, a nice-looking girl with thick glasses, who came in once in a while, never ordering the same thing twice. They stopped on their way to work for coffee and a "What's new?" along with the neighborhood storekeepers, cab drivers, and an occasional cop.

The first of the Alter Cockers didn't really start coming in till around ten. The Alter Cockers were a clatch of old Jews and one old Chinese, Howie Chen. They had been given their informal club name by Maish and they bore it with pride, letting in a new member with reluctance and a long initiation.

"Lieberman?" the woman repeated to the overweight man, a somber-faced bulldog in a white apron behind the counter of the T & L Deli. Though the old men had stopped talking, the woman still had to raise her voice over the sound of an unseen radio.

Maish was too polite to stare at the woman. Besides, he had a reputation to uphold.

"Nothing bothers Maish," Syd Levan said whenever the mood struck him. "We should call him Nothing-Bothers Maish. A guy could come in here with three heads asking for lobster bisque to go and Maish wouldn't bat an eye. Nothing-Bothers Maish."

So, with the Alter Cockers looking at him, Maish had to honor his own reputation, but, the truth be told, he was bothered by this creature who belonged in a television ad for some make-up or bathing suit or diet cola.

The radio from nowhere blasted the sound of a crowd and the voice of Harry Caray as the woman waited for an answer from Maish, who seemed to have forgotten where he was. She looked around at the two old men at the counter, who smiled up at her more with memory than hope. One old man wearing a cap, none other than Herschel Rosen, nudged the other old man and said, "Which one?"

"Which one?" asked the woman.

"Which Lieberman?" said Herschel, the gnome, looking around for the approval of his cohorts as if he had made a brilliant play on words.

There were three booths. Four old guys, one of them Chinese, were in the first booth. The second booth was empty. A disembodied hand rose above the top of the third booth and motioned with a single finger to the woman.

Three minutes before the woman had entered the T & L, Ryne Sandberg had hit a double to drive in two runs in the eighth and Harry Caray had gone *meshugah*.

Abe Lieberman, as much as he usually enjoyed sitting in the heat of his brother Maish's deli, longed to be twenty minutes away in Wrigley Field, eating an Oscar Mayer, looking at the bare, tan shoulders and freckled backs of girls in the bleachers on their day off. It would have been even better to be thirty or forty years back watching Bill Nicholson or Hank Sauer swing on an underhand sidearm pitch from Ewell Blackwell and send it into the right-field bleachers.

It was no kind of August day to be in Maish's with the air conditioning out of order. Lieberman had both a fan on the table aiming at his face and a radio but the fan was tired and old and the radio sounded like it was suffering from Al Bloombach's asthma.

"I don't know about this, Davey," Harry Caray had said on the radio.

"Trillo's not a bad choice in this situation," assured Dave Nelson, who could always be counted on for a reassuring cliché.

"Not a bad choice?" Lieberman told Hanrahan. "He's the only choice Zimmer's got. He's the closest thing to a Mexican on that bench. I'm taking my grandchildren to the game Monday. You want to come? I'll get an extra ticket from MacMillan."

Detective William Hanrahan had grunted, smiled, and shook his head no. This morning Hanrahan glowed with confidence, his cheeks pink, his usually unkempt dark hair cut short and brushed back. His face, a handsome flat Irish face, was puffy. His short-sleeved blue shirt was soaked through with sweat, but his tie was neatly pressed. Hanrahan was working extra hard today to convince himself, his partner, and the world that he didn't need a drink.

While Manny Trillo was stepping to the plate, the T & L door had opened with a bang. There was no spring on the door. The unwary who pushed it too hard often found it bouncing back in their faces. The spring had been removed about two weeks earlier by a duo of repairmen who had never reappeared. Speculation among the Alter Cockers was that the duo were doorspring thieves making their way across the nation.

The woman, her red hair billowing out, had flowed past the lethal door and asked her question. Now she was standing in front of Lieberman's booth. She wore a tight white dress with little flowers or something embroidered across

12

the low neckline, over which the tops of her breasts glowed like brown moons.

"Lieberman," she said.

"Valdez," Lieberman said.

And Manny Trillo blasted one out of the park.

"Holy cow," shouted Harry Caray.

Lieberman leaned back admiring life, the Cubs, and Estralda Valdez, the classiest prostitute on the near North Side.

"Have a seat, Estralda," he said. "Can I get you something?"

"Something cold, no calories, *viejo*," she said, sitting down in the booth next to Lieberman. "Got to watch the waist."

She touched her flat stomach and looked at Sergeant Abe Lieberman, who motioned to the sad-faced man in the apron behind the counter.

Opinion was divided among the Alter Cockers as it was among the men and women of the Clark Street Station. There were those who thought the slightly dyspeptic Abe Lieberman looked exactly like a dachshund while the opposition claimed he resembled no animal more than a bloodhound, an underweight bloodhound perhaps, but a bloodhound nonetheless. Lieberman, it could not be denied, was not an imposing figure at five seven and hovering around 145 pounds. He looked a good five years older than his sixty years. Lieberman's wife thought his best features were his curly gray hair and the little white mustache, which she described as "distinguished." She thought her husband looked more like a lawyer or an accountant than a policeman. Maish, on the other hand, thought his brother looked like an undernourished Harry James. Maish had once told this to a young cop who asked who Harry James was.

"The band leader with the trumpet," Maish had explained. "The one who married Betty Grable."

"Betty Grable?" the cop had asked and Maish had given up.

Now Maish brought a pitcher of iced tea and a fresh glass

for Estralda. He filled her glass and Abe's and looked at Hanrahan.

"Another coffee," said Hanrahan.

"Hungry?" Lieberman asked Estralda Valdez.

Maish hovered.

She shook her head no and Maish slouched away.

"What's his story?" Estralda said.

"Maish? Jealousy," said Lieberman. "He's my brother. You like baseball?"

"It's OK," she said with a shrug. "I like boxing."

André Dawson struck out to end the inning. Lieberman reached over and turned off the radio. There wasn't a sound in the T & L but the whirr and clunk of the table fan. Conversation, usually loud and blustering on topics ranging from baseball to the price of pastrami to past and planned trips to Israel, had ceased while ears with little tufts of gray growing from them strained to hear what this painted vision wanted with Abe.

"Let's get on with it," Hanrahan sighed, checking his cup to be sure there wasn't a last drop at the bottom before Maish returned to fill it.

"It's a hot day and the Cubs are ahead," said Lieberman. "Let's savor the rare moment, William."

Hanrahan grunted and waved at Maish who moved toward them with a half-full coffeepot.

Lieberman was in no hurry. He was reasonably comfortable in the little booth surrounded by the smell of kosher meat on the slicer, the sound of old men talking about nothing. He also knew that what Estralda had to say was important. She had told him it was, had asked to meet him outside of her territory, someplace safe where no one would be likely to recognize her.

Lieberman had decided that a good place to meet would be the T & L, which was only five blocks from his house and where the likelihood of anyone coming in who knew Estralda was nil.

Lieberman didn't want to hurry Estralda or himself. He had stayed up late watching a tape of *Zoo in Budapest* with Loretta Young. Bess had watched with him for an hour,

14

then left, saying she was going to catch Koppel and then going to sleep. Lieberman had finished the movie and the last box of Tam-Tam crackers. By the time he got to bed it was almost one and Bess was snoring softly. Lieberman had slept four hours, a good night for him.

"What time is it?" Bess had said when he got up, rolling over and reaching for her glasses.

"Four-thirty," he had said.

"You getting up? You're taking your physical today?"

"That's tomorrow. Go back to sleep, Bess. I'll make your coffee," he said, leaning over to kiss her. She was asleep before he reached the bedroom door.

He had ground the coffee beans in the new little electric thing, put the hot water on, stuck the filter in the Melita, and read the *Tribune* while he waited for the coffee to trickle down. Lieberman liked the smell of coffee. Coffee itself he could do without.

He had called in to the Clark Street Station at six and Nestor Briggs had told him about Estralda Valdez's call. Lieberman had then called Estralda and set up this meeting. And now here he was looking at her, his most reliable informant and certainly the best-looking one he had ever had. If she had something to say, she could say it better at her own pace.

"I got a guy on the line who won't take no for an answer," she said, reaching air at the bottom of her second glass of iced tea. She played with the cubes with her red fingernails and paused. "I tell him we're through. I tell him really nice. Kiss him on the forehead. Tickle his *cojones*. Give him a good night, you know, but he's got a temper. I think he might turn up and get nuts. I'm pulling out, *viejo*."

"Give us his name and we'll have a talk with him," Hanrahan said as Maish returned with coffee. "You don't have to pull out."

"I got other reasons for wanting to get out," she said, touching her red lips with her even redder fingernails. "Besides, you don't talk to this one," she said laughing, her eyes on the fascinating rapidly melting ice cubes. "I got a deal for you. You watch over me tonight. I got money

15

put away someone's bringing me. I clear out in the morning. When I get where I'm going in Texas, I let you know where to find my book of clients."

"Including the one who's chasing you out?" asked Hanrahan, two-handing the cup of coffee.

"Including," said Estralda, "but that's one name won't do you any good. And I told you. I got other reasons for getting out."

"Whole thing won't do us any good," said Hanrahan. "No offense, señorita, but what can we do with the names of a whore's clients?"

"Could get you a big promotion or thanks, *borrocho*," she said. "You let the johns on the list know you're tearing it up and they make you both chief of police."

"I'm too old to be chief of police, Estralda," said Lieberman. "You really think this guy is dangerous?"

"I know it," she said, pushing the glass away and looking at Lieberman. "But even if he wasn't, it's time for me to get somewhere warm. Winter's not that far, you know?"

"We'll miss you," Lieberman said.

Estralda shrugged.

"I'll miss you too, *viejo*," she said. "I've put a few dollars away. Maybe I can go back home and start a fingernail-painting shop or something."

She turned and looked over her shoulder out the window. Lieberman turned to see what she was looking at but there was nothing outside but passing cars, the sky, and the empty lot across the street where they'd torn down the Walgreen's last year.

"What about Escamillo?" Lieberman tried. Escamillo Silk was a boxer, a middleweight with a big smile and a little promise if he could stay away from coke. Although he was married and living with his wife, Silk, whose real name was Leon Cascabella, liked to wear Estralda on his arm and Estralda liked to be seen in public. Since she couldn't advertise, being with Silk was good business. She had a nose for business. And maybe Escamillo had something else to offer.

"Can't count on him," she said. And she was right. "We're

16

not, like, that together, you know? Besides, I don't want him knowing I'm pulling out. I'll be gone and maybe a week from now he'll notice. You got to get to my place before midnight," she said.

She looked out the window again but this time Lieberman knew she wasn't looking at something that was there. She was seeing something or someone she couldn't shake.

"This guy gets off work at nine-thirty this week," she said. "He could come any time till one in the morning, maybe later."

"We'll be there quarter to nine," Lieberman assured her.

"There's a motel across the street with a Chinese restaurant," Estralda said. "You can see the front entrance to my apartment building and lobby from it."

"We can see better from the lobby," said Hanrahan.

"And you can be seen better," she said. "I don't want no trouble with the condo committee. I gotta sell that place. I been real careful. Cops sitting around the lobby . . . I don't need it. Besides, you can see my window from the Chinese place. You can't see it from the lobby. Just be near if I need you. Give me a call when you get there. It's OK any time before nine-thirty. You got my number."

Lieberman looked at Hanrahan, who gave an enormous put-upon sigh, and nodded. Lieberman conveyed the nod to Estralda even though she couldn't have missed it.

"Then that's it," she said, standing and giving Lieberman the full view with capped-teeth smile. "You don't believe I'll go straight in Texas, do you *viejo*?"

"Why not?" asked Lieberman.

"Maybe I won't," she said with a sigh, straightening her tight dress as she stood. "I'm all I got to sell. We don't stay young forever and don't live forever, none of us, *verdad*?"

"Lady," Hanrahan said, "what are you pulling here? We all know you could pay some street junkie four bills to have the guy knocked off."

"No," she said with a laugh and took a step toward the door. "If I went around paying to have every crazy I link with killed, I'd go broke and we'd be ass-high in bodies. Be on time, *viejo*."

17

"We'll be there," Lieberman said, and she walked out special for the Alter Cockers, slow with memories. The phone behind the counter was ringing before she reached the door. Maish took his time answering and didn't pick it up till Estralda was out of sight and the Alter Cockers were beginning their post-Estralda critique.

"We don't need her book, Abe," Hanrahan said, shifting in the booth and turning the fan so that it would hit him too. "I figure we're lucky if half that story about the john is true."

"Let's say we're giving her a farewell present. We owe her," said Lieberman.

"Abe," Maish shouted. "For you."

Lieberman got up slowly, knowing the warning ache of arthritis in his knees was inevitable after sitting in one position for an hour.

"Who's the girlfriend, Abeleh?" asked the old man at the counter in the cap.

"Maish," called Harry from the Alter Cocker table, "give Bess a call. Tell her her Abe is galavanting with Rita Hayworth's daughter, Princess . . ."

" . . . Caroline," Howie Chen supplied.

"Jasmine," said Syd Levan, who looked a little like Nikita Khrushchev.

"Abe?" came a woman's voice on the phone.

"You got me, Louise," Lieberman said.

"Call just came in," said Officer Louise Jackson. "José Ruiz's son saw Del Sol in the Chapultapec Restaurant less than an hour ago."

Emiliano "El Perro" Del Sol was known to have beaten Sylvie Estaban nearly to death with a telephone for talking while Julio Iglesias was singing on the radio. El Perro was reported to have cut the throat of one of the Varga brothers for accidentally stepping on his shoes. More than one person Lieberman knew had been in the Dos Hermanos bar the night El Perro beat into pleading senselessness two construction workers who had dared look at him while he was painfully and slowly composing a letter to his mother in Panama. El Perro was the leader of the Tentaculos, the

18

tentacles, the gang that believed it owned North Avenue.

"Thanks, Louise. We're on the way."

Lieberman hung up and nodded to Hanrahan, who slid out of the booth.

"El Perro," said Lieberman. "The Chapultapec on North."

"It's going to be one of those days, Abraham," said Hanrahan with a sigh.

"Let's hope so, Father Murphy," said Lieberman. "Maish, I'll drop back later maybe."

Maish shrugged and Herschel Rosen, buoyed by his earlier foray into the world of sit-down comedy, said, "Come back without the tootsie and Chen'll kung-fu you into the street. Right, Chen?"

"Don't I always?" said Chen to general laughter as the two cops went out onto Devon Avenue.

Lieberman and Hanrahan moved down the sidewalk to their car, a steel-gray Buick whose brakes cried when you stepped on them. They were parked in front of Hinky's Bike Shop. Hinky, like most of the Jews in the neighborhood, including Lieberman, had migrated north from the West Side to Albany Park thirty years earlier. The poor southern whites and East Indians had driven them further north to Rogers Park and now Rogers Park was starting to show signs of change. East Rogers Park, from Lake Michigan to Ridge Road, was already given up as lost to Russian immigrants, Vietnamese, Hispanics, and white dropouts. West Rogers Park, where Lieberman lived, was holding on. The Chinese and Koreans had helped to stabilize the neighborhood, but the Jewish migration continued. Skokie was still the place to go if you couldn't afford to go even further into Wilmette or Highland Park.

With each move, false memories of the good old days in Lawndale, "Jew Town," before the blacks moved in were evident in small ways in Rogers Park. The small white lettering on Hinky's sign said, "Formerly on Roosevelt and Central Park." Sam and Harry's Hot Dogs on Western Avenue had topped that. In the middle of the store was a replica of a street sign from the old neighborhood.

Lieberman drove knowing both he and Hanrahan knew

that Hanrahan wouldn't be steady till after lunch.

El Perro's offense was a minor one. He owed Sam Resnick two hundred dollars. Resnick, an old friend of Lieberman's from the West Side, owned a hardware store on North Avenue. El Perro had put a variety of tools and knives "on the cuff." The cuff was old and frayed and Resnick knew he had to collect or lose face and respect in the neighborhood and move out. It wasn't the amount as much as the existence of the debt that threatened Resnick. Officially, the neighborhood where Resnick had his hardware store was well out of Lieberman's domain. Until five years ago it had been familiar territory to Lieberman, but age had earned him a transfer closer to home if not a promotion.

"Life is hard," said Hanrahan, looking out of the window at the string of sari shops and Indian restaurants as they neared Western Avenue.

"It's supposed to be," Lieberman said. "You got a song that goes with that or are you just feeling particularly Father Murphy this morning?"

"Prices go up. Stock goes bad. People shoplift, an apple here, a can of tomatoes there. They add up to ruin," Hanrahan said. "The saints don't hear your prayers. And children? They desert you in the hour of your greatest need. When you are lying in your deathbed, candles at your head and feet, they'll be there, asking for your blessing, weeping, and you know what you should tell them? What I should tell them?"

"No, Bill, what should you tell them?"

Lieberman pushed his glasses back on his nose and headed south on Western. The smell of Dunkin' Donuts wafted through the open windows and Lieberman felt a belch coming on.

"Go away," Hanrahan said majestically. "Where were you when I needed you?"

"Which kid?" Lieberman said.

"Michael," sighed Hanrahan. "The one who lives in Buffalo. Supposed to come in for a few weeks, bring the wife, the kid. Know what they decide to do?"

"Emigrate to Australia," Lieberman tried.

"Close," said Hanrahan. "Disney World. Bunch of tin

music and robots look like zombies. Scare the kid half to hell and back. If I had anything to disown them with . . . What time you got?"

"About two-thirty," said Lieberman.

"Want to stop at Simi's on the way?" said Hanrahan, looking casually at a fascinating Pontiac showroom. "Burger and a beer?"

"I don't want to miss El Perro," Lieberman said.

"I understand," Hanrahan said softly, holding up his hand and giving a pained smile. "I understand. Why should one's friends be any more loyal than one's children. Why should obligations and promises be met? You know what today is?"

"Friday," said Lieberman.

"Seven years and six days since the dry cleaner," said Hanrahan.

"You don't know how many days, Murphy," said Lieberman.

"Give or take one or two, Rabbi. Give or take one or two."

The incident in the six-store mall had been on a routine call. Argument, shouts in a dry-cleaning shop on Petersen. Pizza shop next door had called in the complaint, said the shouting was scaring customers away. Lieberman and Hanrahan had taken the call on the way to a follow-up with a robbery victim. They'd hit the shop at a little after three, heard voices arguing inside. Lieberman had knocked. He had been ignored.

Lieberman had knocked again and someone had come to the door. The someone had a very large gun, a Hopkins & Allen .38 five-shot, in his very small hand. The gun had been pointed at Lieberman. The sight was comic. A little shaking man with wild curly hair and a big gun. Behind the man inside the shop stood a big black man in some kind of delivery uniform.

"Put the gun . . ." Lieberman had begun, but the first shot had stopped him.

He had no idea if the man had missed or hit him. All Lieberman could think of was, "I wonder who this man is who is going to kill me?"

There was a second shot but it went through the window of the dry cleaning shop, spraying glass onto the sidewalk. It missed Lieberman by a good six feet because the little man with the big gun was on his way to the floor with a large hole in his chest from Hanrahan's police special.

That was way back and this was right away, but . . .

"We'll stop at Simi's after we see El Perro," said Lieberman.

Hanrahan settled for it and spent the rest of the drive complaining about the ingratitude of friends and relatives. Lieberman tuned him out but nodded occasionally and threw in a word here or there, generic words like the guy who did Santa Claus on the radio every year and took calls from the kids. Santa Claus gave no promises, laughed a lot, and asked if the kid calling had been a good boy or girl.

Hanrahan had been drinking fifteen years ago when he and Lieberman became partners after Lieberman's first partner, Xavier Flores, had retired. But the drinking he did back then was nothing compared to what he started to do five years ago when Maureen, Hanrahan's wife, moved out on him and left him an empty house in Ravenswood. No talk of divorce. They were good Catholics. No thought of moving out of town. Lieberman had helped Maureen get a job with Sol Schuster's accounting company. When the two Hanrahan boys and their families came to town, Bill and Maureen would meet at the house, have a dinner party, and Maureen would go back to her apartment after everyone left.

North Avenue near Crawford was wide, busy, and full of parking spaces. The street was bright, hot, and heavy. A fat woman in a blue dress shifted her shopping bag from one hand to the other and talked quickly to her friend or sister, who was also fat. As they got out of the car and locked it, Lieberman smelled the sweat of the two women as they passed and it was neither pleasant nor unpleasant.

The Chapultapec was across the street. The two cops walked to the corner, waited for the light to turn green, ignored the sound of squealing brakes somewhere down the street, and crossed, their eyes fixed on a broomstick of a kid dressed in black who leaned against the darkened windows of the Chapultapec scanning the street, keeping watch for an attack, a danger. He was the proof that Emiliano was inside the restaurant. He may have been an early warning system but he was also the red flag to any enemy warriors that said, "If you're looking for El Perro, you've come to the right place."

Emiliano wanted to be protected but he made himself vulnerable. He wanted people to like him, to love him, to admire him, but he hurt those who came too close and laughed at their pain.

"Fernandez," Hanrahan said with a grin to the kid. "Get any twelve-year-old girls pregnant this month?"

Fernandez didn't smile back but he looked at Lieberman, his brown eyes starting at the top of the policeman's head and going down to his toes and back again. He nodded and the cops moved past him through the door of the Chapultapec and into the blind darkness and loud music.

Julio Iglesias was singing a song Lieberman didn't recognize.

Lieberman could see nothing but vague shapes as his eyes adjusted to the yellow-brown table lamps and the dim light given off by a Dos Equis neon sign on the wall. The smell of frying food from the kitchen touched memories.

"Look who's here," came the voice of El Perro. "The Priest and the Rabbi. Ain't your territory no more, man. Come to exorcise the devil?"

"Emiliano," Lieberman said.

"Shhhhhh," he whispered. *"No fraga me. La cancion.* The song."

Slowly Lieberman's eyes adjusted to the darkness and he began to see bodies and faces in the room. Nine Tentaculos, including Emiliano, were seated at the tiny restaurant's tables listening to Julio Iglesias. On each table was a plate of sliced meat and a mound of Mexican bread.

Emiliano smiled at Lieberman and Hanrahan and nodded to the juke box near the window. Hanrahan smiled back and stared at El Perro. It didn't do to stare too long at El Perro, whose face was a map of wild scars leading to dead ends. A scar from who knows what battle ran from his right eye down across his nose to just below the left side of his mouth. It was rough, red, and had probably taken an afternoon of stitches. The nose had been broken so many times that there was little bone, no cartilage. When lost in thought, which was seldom and most frightening, El Perro played with the flesh of his nose, flattening it with his thumb, pushing it to one side absent-mindedly. His teeth were white but uneven except for his sharp eye teeth, which looked as if they belonged on a vampire. Emiliano's black hair was brushed straight back.

Lieberman thought but didn't say that El Perro hadn't a shot in hell of being a movie star.

The song ended and Emiliano sighed deeply, pulled out a brush, and worked his hair back.

"That man can sing, *viejo*," he said. "I met him once you know."

"After that, what's left for a man to look forward to?" Lieberman said.

"Yeah," Emiliano said dreamily, brushing his hair. "I should have had my picture taken with him, right, Piedras?"

A voice, deep and gravelly, answered, "Should have had your picture took."

"Yeah," agreed Emiliano looking at Lieberman. "Well, how I look? Like Pat Riley, the fuckin' Lakers' basketball coach on TV?"

"There's a resemblance," Lieberman said. El Perro didn't look anything like Pat Riley, but Lieberman wasn't here to commit suicide.

"Fucking A," Emiliano said seriously. "Everyone says I look like him. Imagine, me looking like a Mick. What are you standing for? Sit down. Fuck, man."

The restaurant seemed even smaller than Lieberman had remembered it. It had been a small flower shop before Alfonso and Angelica Naranita took it over and turned it into a restaurant. Angelica was a good cook but the Naranitas had no ambition. Their children were grown. This was good enough for them, at least it was until Emiliano Del Sol had chosen to call it home away from home.

The place was quiet. Tentaculos waited for El Perro to tell them what to do or think in the presence of two cops.

"You heard I was here and you just came back to the neighborhood to say hello to an old amigo," Emiliano said, using a chunk of bread like a clamp and plunging it into the platter of meat. He snared a rare piece and held bread and meat out to Lieberman. "Taste this. I had Angelica add more sugar and a little more jalapeño sauce."

Lieberman took a bite. It was sweet fire. He chewed, knowing he would pay dearly for it later. Emiliano watched and smiled benevolently. Hanrahan gulped meat and bread down without chewing it.

"Good, huh?"

"Piquant," Lieberman said.

"You want a beer?" Emiliano asked, dipping the bread back into the meat for himself. Before Lieberman could answer a dark hand with a scorpion tattooed on it handed him and Hanrahan open bottles of beer.

Emiliano leaned toward the policemen, breathing fire, to whisper, "Like the ad says, it don't get no better than this. Now," El Perro whispered, "why you here?"

"Resnick's hardware," Lieberman said.

"Resnick's hardware," Emiliano repeated around a mouthful of food.

"You ran up a bill with Resnick," Lieberman explained. "You owe two hundred dollars and forty cents."

"Interesting," said Emiliano looking around at his fellow Tentaculos, who didn't seem to find it very interesting. "What if I say I ain't paying no two hundred dollars and forty cents?"

"Then we can negotiate," Lieberman said.

"Negotiate what?"

"We can forget the forty cents," Lieberman said.

"That's generous," El Perro said seriously, nodding his head. "Very generous."

"Two hundred bucks is toilet paper to wipe my *nalgas*," El Perro whispered, with his face now only inches from Lieberman's. He reached down, miming a wipe.

Someone laughed, but it was the wrong reaction. El Perro

squinted into the dark corner from which the laughter had come. Then someone stirred at the table behind Lieberman and he could hear whoever it was get up and move toward them. A large figure leaned down, whispered into Emiliano's ear, and then backed off.

"Piedras says we should cut off your *cajones* and throw both of you in the Garfield Park Lagoon," El Perro confided, sitting back. "Piedras is a good warrior but he is a little crazy. We wouldn't have to cut off your balls. We could just throw you in. So much shit in the lagoon, you'd choke on an old rubber before you came up for air." He turned to Piedras, who sat behind the policemen, and shouted, "You hear what I just said, Carlos? I said you can fight. You got more balls than an umpire but you crazy nuts, right? You don't kill cops if you don't have to. Besides, the Rabbi is special. He was the first cop to arrest me. I was a little shit, maybe ten, right, Rabbi?"

"A little shit," Lieberman agreed.

"Say you're crazy, Carlos," El Perro said softly.

"I'm crazy," Piedras admitted soberly.

"It's bad for the reputation of the Tentaculos to run up bills and not pay them," Lieberman said. "You pay your debts, you pay my good friend Resnick, word goes through the neighborhood, your neighborhood, that Emiliano Del Sol is a *patron*."

El Perro guzzled a bottle of beer and looked around the room.

"There are no women in here," he said. "How come there are no women in here?"

"Las mujeres estan a la casa donde usted dija . . ." someone began.

"I know that. I know that," El Perro said in exasperation. "It was just a . . . a . . ." He looked at Lieberman for help.

"A figure of speech," Lieberman supplied, though that wasn't quite what he needed.

"A figure of speech," El Perro repeated. "Carlos, pay *viejo*. You got balls, old man. Every grifter, drifter, *ladrone*, and *ramera* in the neighborhood from the old days respects you Rabbi, because you don't give a shit. Hey," El Perro went on, turning to the Tentaculos. "This old cop here with the sad face, one day he walked into the Mazatlan Bar couple years back and shot a hole in Pedro "The Train" Ramirez's hand. My brother was there. Ramirez had tore the place apart for the second time that month, and was coming at this old cop here with a broken tequila bottle. I wasn't there but my kid brother, who shouldn't have been there either, told me about it. *Viejo* here walked over the tub of guts on the floor, took the broken bottle from his fingers, all covered with blood, patted Ramirez's cheek, pulled Ramirez's wallet out of his pocket, took all the money, and handed it to Manuel Ortega, the Mazatlan bartender. My brother saw Ortega put the bills in his pocket instead of dropping them in the till. You didn't know that, did you Lieberman?"

"I didn't know that," Lieberman acknowledged, pretending to drink from his bottle of beer.

"But the *viejo* didn't arrest Pedro Ramirez," El Perro went on. "How you like this story?"

"Bueno," came a chorus from the dark and El Perro grinned with satisfaction and went on.

"Months later, even before his bandages were off, dead drunk, Ramirez stabbed a mailman named Perez. He took him for Manuel Ortega. So what's the moral, here?"

"Nail 'em when you get the chance," Hanrahan said.

"I'm gonna forget you said that," said El Perro. "You're lucky you caught me on a good day."

"Lucky we did," Hanrahan agreed.

A hand came over Lieberman's shoulder with two hundred-dollar bills in it.

"I got no change," came Piedras's voice.

"Someone come up with forty cents," El Perro said.

Hands came from all directions plunking coins on the table.

El Perro laughed. Everyone in the place laughed. Lieberman picked out four dimes and put them in his pocket.

"You like to know what we did with that stuff we bought from your amigo Resnick?" asked El Perro.

"No," said Lieberman, getting up.

El Perro shrugged and, as Hanrahan finished his beer and rose, asked, "Cubs gonna win it this year?"

"They're gonna win it every year," Lieberman said. "Only way to think."

"They need pitching," he said. "They need that little fat guy."

"Valenzuela," Lieberman said. "He's not what he used to be."

"Too bad," said El Perro.

Two minutes later Hanrahan and Lieberman were back on the street.

"I seriously considered shooting the little bastard," Hanrahan said when they were back on the street.

"No you didn't," Lieberman said.

"Hard to shoot a man who hands you a cold beer on a hot day," Hanrahan said. "Never heard that story before, about you shooting the Mex in the bar."

"Never happened," Lieberman said as they headed down the sidewalk.

The street smelled of bodies, gasoline, and Mexican food. If your nose was good you could also smell the blood of Polish sausages and frying kielbasa. The scent was mixed, like the people on the street, mostly dark-skinned and Latino but with a few older, round pink-white faces and heavy bodies that didn't want to or couldn't move from the neighborhood that used to be theirs.

"I used to live a few blocks from here," Hanrahan said as they walked down the street. "Went to St. Leonard's right across the park. When my mother shamed me into going to mass at St. Leonard's, these silent, old round-faced Irish were there, bunched together to the right of the altar in the first five or six rows. When I was a kid, the whole right half of St. Leonard's was filled with those pink faces. Every year there were fewer of them and every year they were older. Father Conlon, whose Irish accent was as much a mystery to the Poles as it was to my mother and the other Irish, seemed to address these faces more than ours but I was convinced it wasn't out of preference or prejudice to his own. He just found them harder to get through to."

They passed Slovotny's Meat Shop with the white sign in crayon saying that blood soup was on sale today, and went into Resnick's Hardware Store.

Lieberman did something with his mouth that resembled a smile or a stifled burp. His hand went into his jacket pocket and came out with a small bottle of Tums.

"Here," he said, dropping the money El Perro had given him onto the counter in front of Resnick. One of the bills floated into the little clear plastic display barrel of assorted key chains.

Resnick beamed and pulled in the bills, looking at Hanrahan and Lieberman with joy. The lids of Lieberman's hooded eyes drooped even further as he chewed on a Tums.

"How did you do it?" Resnick asked.

"We just asked him for it politely," Hanrahan said. "Abe and El Perro are buddies from way back."

"And to know him is to love him," said Lieberman.

"Who cares?" Resnick chimed in, opening the cash register and hiding the bills under the false bottom of the drawer next to the .32 Lieberman knew was there.

"What can I say?" Resnick asked, beaming at Lieberman, who scratched his hairy ear and glanced around at a display of colorful ceramic cups. "How about taking a wrench or something you can use around the house?"

"Make it a couple of cheeseburgers from Solly's next time we come by," Lieberman said.

When they were back in the car heading toward the lake, Lieberman popped a few more Tums and said, "Valdez."

"You want me to take her?" Hanrahan said.

"It's Friday," Lieberman reminded him.

Hanrahan nodded and said, "Got nothing better to do, Abraham."

"I'll take the next one," Lieberman said.

"We'll take 'em as they come," said Hanrahan. "We'll just take 'em as they come."

2

It was clear from the moment Abe stepped through the front door that Bess had a "topic." A "topic" was more important than "something to discuss." Hours before a "topic" was about to be laid out on the kitchen table, Bess's lips went tight and she smiled at everything Lieberman said whether it was about the day's mayhem or a bit of comedy overheard at Maish's. He also knew the "topic" would bubble near the surface of their Shabbat conversation till the blessings were finished and Lieberman had his glass of wine.

Other signs were evident, especially to a detective with thirty years' experience. His wife's dark hair cut short, her gray suit neatly pressed, her smile a little too sweet, and her conversation a little too mundane, were dead give-aways.

Above the flame of the two candles at the dinner table set with their best linen tablecloth, Bess had given him a look that said, "Prepare."

Bess was five years younger than Abe Lieberman. On a bad day she looked fifteen years younger. On a good day, she looked like his daughter. She was her husband's height, dark and slender. While she was not a beauty, she was a fine-looking woman, Lieberman thought, and a Lady with a capital "L." Her father had been a butcher on the South Side, but she carried herself as if he had been a banker, and she had a voice that telephone operators dream of.

After he had said the prayer over wine and shared a drink with her from her father's Kiddush cup, Bess served him a generous piece of pot roast and said, "I have something to say, a topic to discuss."

"I'm attentive," he said, eating a small, dark, tender slice of roast.

"Lisa and Todd aren't getting along."

Lieberman nodded and poured himself a more than generous glass of wine.

"I said," Bess repeated, "Lisa and Todd are not getting along."

"I heard," said Lieberman. "It's natural."

"It's serious," said Bess.

From the day she was born, the Lieberman's only daughter had been, in her father's opinion, "serious." She had been a beautiful child who took in everything and seldom laughed aloud. She had been a wonder student at Mather High, only one B among the As and that B had caused nights of anguish, heartache, tears, and eventual determination to prove to Miss Landis in Science 7 that she had made a grievous error. Lisa had gone to the University of Chicago on a scholarship to study biochemistry. She had met a serious young classics professor named Todd Croswell, had married and had two children, Barry, who was approaching his bar mitzvah, and Melisa, who was approaching her eighth birthday. Barry and Melisa, thank God, were neither serious nor wonder students.

"What's the discrepancy?" Lieberman said, finishing his first glass of wine.

"Don't say that," Bess said, closing her eyes.

"It was an attempt to lighten the tone before we plunged into the depths of despond," he said. He toasted his wife with wine.

Bess allowed herself a small, pained smile of amusement.

"I'm sorry," said Lieberman. "What's the trouble?"

"The usual," answered Bess with a shrug. "You're not eating lima beans. Lima beans are your favorite."

"I'll eat lima beans," he said, spooning buttered beans on his plate. "See, I'm eating. What's 'the usual'? He's going with other women? He takes drugs? He beats her?"

"You've been a policeman too long," Bess said.

Lieberman seriously considered her statement and started on his second glass of wine.

"No," Bess went on. "He doesn't make enough. She wants to go back to work. And other things."

"Other things," Lieberman repeated. He tore off a piece of challah.

"Abe, are you an echo or a father?"

"I'm listening," he said. "I'm listening and I'm dipping my challah into a delicious gravy. See, look, I'm dipping. I'm eating and I'm drinking a good wine. I'm looking forward to a peaceful evening with my wife. And I'm waiting to hear what you want me to do."

"Talk to her," said Bess. "She listens to you."

"She doesn't listen to me, Bess," he said. "She lets me talk. She looks serious. Then she does what she is going to do. That's the way she was when she was six. It's the way she is at thirty-six."

"Then let her talk to you," Bess said.

"That she can always do," he said.

"Call her," Bess said.

"Tomorrow," he said with a smile, holding up his glass to toast his wife.

"Tomorrow may be too late," said Bess. "But, if it has to be tomorrow, it has to be. If you're too tired . . ."

"It has to be," said Lieberman.

"You want rice pudding or carrot cake for dessert?"

"I want you for dessert," he said, feeling the wine.

"We'll see how you feel about that later," she said, shaking her head.

"In that case," replied Lieberman, "I'll have both the pudding and the cake."

There was no more said about Lisa and Todd. But Lieberman knew that if he didn't call his daughter the next day, he would pay for it with hurt rebuke the next night. The "topic" would linger between them like a grinning gnome.

They did the dishes together and Bess went on to a different topic, one that Lieberman found even more uncomfortable than the prospect of talking to their daughter about her marital problems.

"Have you thought about it?" Bess said as she dried the dishes.

"It? Which it?" he asked though he knew.

"Moving," she said. "To Skokie. A nice one-bedroom condominium apartment."

"I'm a policeman, Bess. I have to live in the city."

"You can retire. You're eligible. Do this one again. Look, right here. That's grease."

He took the dish back and plunged it into the soapy water in the sink.

"Three years," he said. "Then we'll talk about retiring."

"The neighborhood's changing," she said.

"They all change. Skokie's changing," he answered. "I like this neighborhood, the house. And where would we put Barry and Melisa when they came to stay? Sleeping bags on a living room floor?"

Bess and Abe had lived in the two-bedroom house on Jarvis for almost thirty years. They both knew that they could sell it for eight times what they paid for it and move into a safe, new one-bedroom in Skokie with plenty of money left over for the long-discussed trip to Israel which Lieberman had no interest in making. Lieberman felt reasonably sure that if he took a chance and told his wife he was ready to consider the move she would have second thoughts about it. Most of their friends had moved out of the neighborhood, but many still remained. The Liebermans knew where things were. When he gave in, she would back down . . . maybe.

"Change would do us good," she said.

"I get change all day," he said. He finished the last pot and reached for a towel to help her dry what remained in the drainer. "Criminals are in the business of making changes. I like to come home and know things are where they've always been, that nothing changes."

"We'll talk about this again," she said. She touched his cheek. He could smell something sweet on her fingers and knew that if she kept at him eventually she would win. His best bet was a delaying game.

They arrived at Temple Mir Shavot on California Avenue, just four blocks from their house, at seven, early enough to have good seats for the Shabbat services. Before they entered the synagogue, Bess adjusted the yarmulke that bobbed on top of Abe's curly hair. She greeted the Rosens, who had come up the stairs behind them.

"He tell you about his girlfriend?" Herschel Rosen said to Bess as they went through the double doors.

Herschel was twinkling. Herschel was a little raisin. Herschel, Lieberman decided, needed a rap on top of his freckled head.

"Which one?" Bess asked.

"The Latin from Manhattan," said Herschel, whose wife was giving Bess apologetic looks. "A real Mexican spitfire. Came into Maish's this morning looking for Abe."

The walls of the corridor leading to the sanctuary were covered with crayon drawings from the Bible done by the Hebrew School students. Lisa had gone to Hebrew School here. Her drawings, precise, neat, had once hung in the corridor. Lieberman wondered what happened to all those drawings.

"She's an informant," Lieberman said. He nodded at people as they passed, recognizing most of them in the dwindling congregation. Resnick of hardware store notoriety moved past with his wife and mother and gave Lieberman a wave.

"I'm not the jealous kind," said Bess, hugging her husband's arm. "Sarah, your husband has a dirty mind."

"You're telling me," said Sarah. She shook her head and dragged Herschel into the sanctuary.

"Abe," Bess said with a smile. "You fooling around?"

"If I was fooling around, would I have her meet me at Maish's in the afternoon in front of the Alter Cockers?"

Bess smiled and kissed him on the mouth as two couples moved past.

The services were, as always, the major meditation of Abe Lieberman's week. He had, in his life, gone through the usual range of emotions about religious services. For ten years, through his twenties, he had been a silent atheist, boycotting the services his father had made him attend as a boy. For another ten years, after he was married, he had toyed with becoming a Buddhist, a secret Buddhist but a Buddhist nonetheless. When Bess insisted that Lisa have religious training and tradition, Lieberman had gone to services when he couldn't avoid it. The constant thanks to God were at first an irritant. Then, one Yom Kippur, he had had an insight. The services, he discovered, were a meditation, something he could get lost in, not greatly different from Buddhist meditation. The Hebrew words of praise, said by the congregation and Rabbi Wass and sung by Cantor Fried, were a mantra.

Having made this discovery at the age of fifty, Lieberman had stopped fighting his tradition, though he was still not sure about what he made of the universe. But he was not only comfortable with services, he looked forward to them, to being lost in prayer, to sharing the ritual with others. He wasn't sure whether he attributed this to his age or wisdom. He did not choose or need to explore the question. That it was comforting was sufficient.

Rabbi Wass was the son of the original Rabbi Wass, who was himself the son of Rabbi Wass of the town of Kliesmer north of Kiev. He had been head of the congregation for nine years and was, in Lieberman's opinion, a definite improvement over his father, though some thought the reverse. The old Rabbi Wass, who still appeared a few times a year from Florida to lead the congregation, was a constantly smiling man whose sermons almost always dealt with his infancy in Poland and childhood in New York City. He had endless stories about his mother's compassion and his father's wisdom. The stories never seemed to have a point and Lieberman had found himself at times wondering what it would be like to get the old Rabbi Wass into an interrogation room and work him into a confession, to break the spell of clichés and smiles. Shortly before old Rabbi Wass retired, Lieberman finally acknowledged to himself that the old Rabbi was not now and had never been particularly bright.

Upon old Wass's retirement, Lieberman and Bess had considered moving to Temple Beth Israel, whose rabbi was young, smart, and progressive and whose congregation included many families with small children, but loyalty prevailed, and even when the new Rabbi Wass revealed himself to be no brighter than his father, they stayed because it was familiar, because it was convenient, because they didn't want to abandon their friends and they didn't want to hurt the new rabbi.

Rabbi Wass did have one saving grace. He was relevant. Israeli politics, Arab terrorism, racial relations, Jewish politicians at the local, state, and federal level were all material for Rabbi Wass's sermons, and he always concluded them with a sincere call for the comments of his congregation. It was at this point that Abe Lieberman usually left the sanctuary and headed for the lobby to wait for Bess. To listen to the meanderings was more than he could bear.

But tonight's sermon was of special interest to Lieberman.

"The issue," said the young Rabbi Wass, who was forty-eight years old, "is one our building committee has been exploring. The young have moved and are moving from our community. Can we continue to survive without new blood? Do we move where the Jewish families are moving or do we slowly fade and watch our numbers drop till we are in danger of losing even a morning *minyan*? More questions upon questions. Can we afford to maintain this building with fewer and fewer members? Your annual dues go up each year and the number of events we have has dwindled."

Rabbi Wass was obviously engaged in a conspiracy with Bess, a conspiracy which might well require that Lieberman sit through the discussions to respond to and defend against it or at least slow it down. Maybe it wouldn't be so bad. After all it would take time, possibly years and years, to find a new location, raise money, start building.

Ancient Ida Katzman, eighty-five, in her usual seat in the front row, put her hand on her cane and turned to examine the congregation. Her eyes met Lieberman's. Ida Katzman, whose husband Mort had died almost twenty years earlier leaving her ten jewelry stores, was the congregation's principle benefactor. Talk of fund raising was always, ultimately, directed at her, but Ida invariably looked around to see who might reasonably join her in her philanthropy. Lieberman was decidedly uncomfortable.

"The building committee has only this week reported to me," said Rabbi Wass with a knowing smile, "that the Fourth Federal Savings Building on Dempster Street is available for purchase at a very reasonable figure, that it could be quickly and beautifully redesigned, and that a generous offer for the building in which we now sit has been made by the Korean Baptist Church Foundation. The money we could make on the sale of this building would more than cover the cost of purchase of the Fourth Federal Savings Building and most of the needed renovations."

There was a stir of conversation around the room. Most, but not all, sounded to Lieberman like approval.

"Assuming we are to pursue this momentous change," Rabbi Wass continued, "and I am well aware that it will take extensive discussion, though I remind you that the offer from the Korean Baptist Church and the price on the Fourth Federal Savings Building are subject to change if we do not move quickly, then we will need a fund-raising committee to deal with renovations to our new Dempster location. We will need a chair and . . ."

Lieberman had had enough. In thirty years he had never said a word during or following a sermon, but Rabbi Wass was trying to railroad this thing through.

Lieberman raised his hand, caught Wass's eye, and began to rise. Ida Katzman strained to see what was going on.

Before Lieberman could say anything, he felt a tug at his sleeve. He was certain it was Bess trying to get him to sit down and shut up. But this was the moment to act. He was Mr. Smith and Congress would listen. Rabbi Wass, who looked vaguely like a pudgy Claude Rains, would listen. The tug came again and Lieberman turned his head slightly.

"Mr. Lieberman, telephone," said an old black man, who had been pulling his sleeve. Whitlock normally came into the sanctuary only to clean up. He seemed decidedly uncomfortable in front of the congregation, all of whom were looking directly at him.

"Man says it's emergency," Whitlock repeated.

"Lisa," said Bess. "Something's happened to . . ."

Lieberman and Bess followed Whitlock to the door and Lieberman was vaguely aware of Rabbi Wass saying. "Thank you. We have a renovation committee chair."

The congregation applauded.

"Mr. Lieberman," Rabbi Wass said, "please feel free to call upon me or any member of the building committee to assist you."

Lieberman paused for an instant at the door of the sanctuary, turned to protest, and was pulled outside by Bess.

The phone was in the rabbi's office, a small wood-paneled box lined with shelves filled with heavy books. One window looked out on the parking lot. Lieberman picked up the phone and touched Bess's hand.

"Lieberman," he said.

"She's dead, Abe," came Hanrahan's voice.

Lieberman looked at his wife.

"She?" he repeated.

"Estralda Valdez," said Hanrahan. He had trouble getting the name out clearly. Bill Hanrahan had been drinking. "I think you better get over here."

"It's Bill," Lieberman said covering the mouthpiece. "The woman Herschel mentioned. She's dead."

"Thank God," said Bess, sinking into the rabbi's swivel chair. And then she realized what she had said.

"I don't mean," she went on. "I'm just glad Lisa and the children aren't . . ."

Lieberman patted her shoulder.

"Where are you, Bill?" Lieberman asked.

"Where? Oh, at her apartment."

Lieberman hung up and put both hands on Bess's shoulders.

"I've got to go," he said. "The Rosens will walk you home."

Bess looked up at him with a smile and still moist eyes.

"You'll talk to Lisa tomorrow?"

"I'll talk to Lisa tomorrow," he said. "Why don't you sit here for a minute or two before you go back in?"

"I'll do that," Bess said.

The night air was still hot. The smell of curry from the Bombay Restaurant across California Avenue hit Lieberman as he headed back toward home and his car. Maybe it was time to think about moving, but he didn't want to think about it. He didn't want to think about his daughter's troubles. He didn't want to think about being chair of the temple's renovation committee, but all of these were preferable to thinking that Estralda Valdez was dead. He remembered Estralda the last time he saw her, beautiful, joking, planning, that morning. Next to him in the booth. He had smelled her. He remembered her the first time he had seen her, beautiful, defiant, speaking broken English. He wasn't looking forward to the next time he would see her.

Exactly four minutes before Bill Hanrahan entered Estralda Valdez's sixth floor apartment, Jules Van Beeber had lain drunk and apparently asleep a few feet from Estralda's body. Someone, he knew, had given him a drink, had led him to this place on the floor. That someone had not reckoned with Jules Van Beeber's needs. Jules had risen, oblivious to his surroundings, made his way to the kitchen, and downed the good part of a bottle of Scotch he found on the floor. Then, feeling more than a bit disoriented by the intake of something of reasonable quality, Jules had stumbled back through the living room to Estralda's balcony, clutching a small blue table lamp he planned to take with him when he left. The night air and the breeze coming off the lake lured Jules to the railing.

Jules had leaned over the railing and fallen just as Hanrahan had come through the door. Jules had spun three times in the air, cord of the lamp trailing behind him like a kite tail, and landed in a pile of Glad bags filled with grass.

Cushioned and blanketed by green plastic shining in the moonlight, Jules looked up at the stars in the August sky over Lake Michigan, smiled, and passed out.

At the same moment that Hanrahan entered the apartment and Jules Van Beeber went over the railing, not five blocks

away, Ernest Ryan, a bartender known as Irish Ernie, fell
down two steps after locking his tavern on Clark Street.
Cold sober, Irish Ernie hit his head on the sidewalk and
died. God makes some strange choices.

Jules, clutching the lamp to his chest like a protective
teddy bear, slept through the police cars and sirens, the
television crews and small crowds. He dreamed of a line
of amber bottles, an angry man, a soft bed, a beautiful
woman who spoke to him in a strange language. He saw the
woman lying naked before him and he felt himself walking
to a door, feeling the night wind, smelling dead fish on the
shore, and flying.

The garbage bags Jules Van Beeber had fallen on were in
the back of Sol Worth's truck. Worth's landscaping business
had, after eight years, just started to turn a profit, partly
because he had stopped using his wife's brothers as lawn
workers and partly because he had paid off a Democratic
alderman to put pressure on certain lakefront high-rises to
use Sol's service.

It was just before ten when Jules took his night flight.
No one had witnessed the miracle. When the drunk babbled
his tale and dream the next morning, Sol had no reason
to believe him. The police cars were gone. The television
crews were taking pictures of a giant salmon washed up
near Navy Pier. Sol had no reason to believe anything had
happened the night before. He pulled the drunk from the
back of his truck.

"Maybe the lamp is magic," muttered Van Beeber, looking at the lamp he still held.

"Maybe I'll break both your arms I catch you sleeping
in my truck again," replied Worth. He resolved never again
to leave his truck on the street overnight in front of a job
again.

Sol had his two Korean workers to pick up, seven high-
rise lawns to do. When he pulled away, Sol could see the
drunk in his rearview mirror sitting on the curb and looking
at his lamp.

When Sol was gone, Jules Van Beeber, who had once
owned a greeting card shop in Holland, Michigan, where

something had happened that he did not wish to remember, got up and wandered in the general direction of Lawrence Avenue. He remembered, or thought he remembered, a pawn shop there. He had a magic lamp to sell and a wondrous tale to tell if anyone would listen to him.

Sol didn't put the whole thing together till he got back home that night with an empty truck, an aching back, and a sore throat from yelling at his brother-in-law Bradley who, though safely off the lawns, was supposed to be answering phones in the office. Only when he was drifting off to sleep while his wife was reading her weekly pile of supermarket tabloids and listening to the ten o'clock news did Sol make a connection. Sol was only half-awake when the story came on the television and he realized that the woman the blonde anchorwoman was talking about had been murdered two blocks away from where he now lay almost but not quite asleep. She had been murdered in the building he parked his truck next to the night before. The truck in which he had found a drunk telling a crazy nuts story.

Sol sat up in bed, sending *Inquirers* and *Stars* flying. His wife hit him on the shoulder with her fist, but Sol didn't feel it.

"I think some drunk told me he killed that woman," he said.

"Yeah?" said his wife.

"Right next to the building. Told me just like that and I let him walk," said Sol Worth.

"So?" she asked.

"So, I'm calling the cops."

Two hours before Jules Van Beeber went over the railing on the balcony of Estralda Valdez's apartment, William Hanrahan had called Estralda to be sure she was there and all right. He called from the Chinese restaurant in the Lakefront Motor Inn across the street from the Michigan Towers highrise. The restaurant, the Black Moon, was the only commercial property on the block and Estralda had been right; there was a good view of the entrance to the high-rise from the window.

Estralda had told him she was fine. Hanrahan had said he would be watching all night but that there had to be at least two other entrances to the building, a service entrance and an entrance through the building's underground garage. He asked her to go to her window and pull the shade up and down. He found the window and when she got back on the phone he told her to leave the shade down but pull it up if she needed his help.

After that he had shown his badge to the pretty Chinese woman of no particular age who served him pork-fried rice and a double bourbon on the rocks. He had told her he would be sitting at that table till closing time.

The double bourbon was followed by a second and an order of egg foo yung. Customers came and went. People went in and out of the high-rise. Hanrahan watched the black doorman greet them, nod. No one suspicious. He watched Estralda's shade. It was still down.

When the last customer had left the Black Moon, Hanrahan motioned to the Chinese woman.

"You Irish?" he asked.

"Yes," said the woman, confused.

"You're Irish?" Hanrahan said again, taking a serious look at the woman.

"Iris," she said. "My name is Iris."

"Didn't think you were Irish," he said, relieved. "Irish and Chinese have a lot in common," he said, looking at his empty glass. The woman said nothing. She was not just pretty, she was delicately pretty and, he decided, she was about Maureen's age. He was wrong. She was ten years older than his wife. "Want to know what they have in common, the Irish and Chinese?"

"Yes," said Iris. She smiled at the policeman, who was definitely drunk.

"Children," he said. "Family loyalty. We marry late and stay together. Like the Chinese."

A couple went into the lobby of the Michigan Towers across the street. Hanrahan glanced at them. A taxi pulled up in front of the lobby a few seconds later. The cabby got out and went into the building.

42

"But never," he said, "marry an Irishman. Are you married?"

"No," said the woman.

"Ever go out with an Irishman?" he asked.

The thought had never occurred to her.

"No," she said. She smiled a nervous smile.

"Would you like to?" Hanrahan said. "I've never been out with a Chinese woman. I mean I've been with a . . . Never been out with a Chinese woman. Did go out once with a Siamese lady, I must admit. Couldn't take the curry."

She reached over and began to clear his plates. She called out something in Chinese to the kitchen and an old man's voice answered in Chinese.

"Calling for help?" asked Hanrahan, glancing out the window.

The cabby who had gone into the high-rise came out carrying two suitcases. He opened his trunk, put them in, and got into the driver's seat. The doorman opened the door and let out a woman. She was dressed in the same clothes Estralda was wearing that morning. She was also wearing a floppy wide-brimmed Annie Hall hat. She got into the waiting cab and waved to Hanrahan who lifted a hand in acknowledgment.

"Can't figure it," he said. "She asks for help and then packs her bags and goes out."

"Asking for help?" the Chinese woman said.

"Asking for . . ." Hanrahan repeated, and looked up at the window of Estralda Valdez's apartment. The shade was up. Hanrahan looked for the cab, remembered it had headed south on Sheridan. It was blocks away by then, or on Lake Shore Drive. He got up only slightly dizzy.

"I talked to my father," Iris said with a blush Hanrahan did not catch.

"Got to go," said Hanrahan. "I'll take your card. Call you."

"My name is Iris," she said, watching the policeman hurry to the door, drop a twenty-dollar bill on the counter, and take a restaurant card.

"And mine is William," he said. "And I think I'm in deep shit."

Iris watched him amble across the street and into the lobby of the apartment building. She wondered if he would call and if she really wanted him to and then she heard her father's voice scolding her from the kitchen and she knew she and her father would be getting into their car after they cleaned up and closed the restaurant and that they would drive to the apartment they shared and that he would burn incense and complain about the poor day they had had. And then if he was not too tired, her father would watch one of his Charles Bronson videotapes.

Iris decided that she wanted the Irishman to call.

Hanrahan had hurried across the street, but hurrying did not come easily to him, especially with two double bourbons. Once Bill Hanrahan had been the fastest lineman on the Chicago Vocational High School football team. Dick Butkus, who had graduated from CVS a few years after Hardrock Hanrahan, had told Hanrahan at a reunion that he had been an inspiration. In his senior year, Hanrahan had twisted his knee in a practice. The speed was gone. Just like that. He had still gone on to a football scholarship at Southern Illinois. He'd been hoping for Notre Dame or Illinois but even with a good knee that had only been an outside hope. He had lasted two years at Southern, a journeyman lineman who had lost his nickname and drive. Twenty-five years and three months ago, Bill Hanrahan had left Carbondale and come back to Chicago. He joined his father as a cop as his father had joined his father before him.

But those were the good old days and these were the bad new ones. Hanrahan had burst through the door to the outer lobby and pulled out his wallet and badge before the young black man in a doorman's uniform could speak. The young man, whose gold-plated name tag said he was Billy Tarton, wanted no problems.

"Valdez," said Hanrahan.

"Six-ten," answered the doorman. He pressed the button to open the inner door.

"You want me to announce—" Billy Tarton began but

the look from the burly policeman shut his mouth.

Hanrahan managed to keep from bowling over a trio of women who looked like bowling pins as they came out of the elevator. He entered the elevator, pushed the button to close the doors, and put his wallet away with his left hand while he pulled his Colt .38 Cobra out of the holster at his waist with his right.

The elevator stopped at five. An old man started to get in. Hanrahan hid his Colt at his side and motioned the man back. The man looked as if he were about to protest and then noticed that the drunk in the elevator had his hand behind his back. The old man backed out and let the door close. Before the doors were fully open on six, Hanrahan was out, gun at the ready, looking both ways.

No one in sight. At the end of the corridor to his left a door was open, letting out loud Latin music and light. The elevator pinged and closed its doors behind him.

Hanrahan moved down the corridor, back against the wall, weapon pointed at the open door.

At the door he went down low, gun leveled. The trick knee and the double bourbons almost did him in. He felt as if he were about to fall backward.

"Not now," he told himself. "Jesus, not now."

The music blared. From the doorway Hanrahan could see enough to make his already queasy stomach go sour. It was a one-bedroom with a kitchen alcove just inside the door. The refrigerator in the alcove was wide open. Broken bottles, a jar of Hellman's low-cal mayonnaise, slices of still-frozen Steak'ems and rapidly melting ice cubes littered the floor. It was a hot night. Hanrahan was sweating. The cabinets over the sink were open and boxes were torn apart. Michael Jordan smiled up at Hanrahan from a ripped-open Wheaties carton.

Hanrahan's hands were sweating. He alternated drying each one on his already sweat-soaked shirt and then he moved past the open bathroom, glancing in to see the medicine cabinets open, capsules and bottles on the floor and in the tub. The top of the toilet basin was off and its two cracked pieces were on the floor near the wall. The closet door next to the bathroom was open. The rod and shelf were empty. Clothes were on the floor in a pile, hangers sticking out like dark bones.

The voice of the man on the radio or phonograph repeated, *"Todos Vuelven,"* over and over again, pounding inside Hanrahan's head like a migraine.

And then he stepped into the living room and found what he had expected and feared. Lamps were turned over, the carpeting torn up. The dresser in the corner yawned with missing drawers which were roughly stacked upside-down, their contents thrown around the room. A red bra hung from a small fixture in the center of the ceiling and the man kept singing in Spanish as Hanrahan saw the overturned bed and the torn mattress heaped in a corner of the room. He moved around the bed and stood in front of the mattress.

"Oh Mother," he muttered, crossing himself. With his free hand he threw back the mattress and found himself looking down at the naked body of Estralda Valdez.

Hanrahan had seen many a body in his twenty-four years as a cop. His reaction had always been the same. Something in him denied what he was seeing. It was there, but for an instant the dead body had no meaning. But that moment always passed and Hanrahan felt an enormous pain in his gut. He wanted to moan, but if others were around, he had to pretend that death had no meaning to him. His father had taught him a trick to deal with those first moments.

"Don't think of them as people," Liam Hanrahan had advised. "Think of them as exact replicas, down to the tiniest detail. God's taken the real ones away and given instead these amazingly precise replacements. What you see is the evidence God left for the police to bring the killers to justice in our courts before they face his. That way, Billy, you stay sane and righteous."

And, more or less, it had worked. When Hanrahan saw a body, he always dutifully crossed himself. He had seen a family, including a baby, cut into large parts in the crossfire of a gang battle. He had seen a man who had abused his wife for years ripped by the woman's teeth and nails when after ten years she could take no more. He had seen . . . but, he suddenly realized, this woman before him was still alive. God had not replaced her. The illusion would not hold even for the needed instant. Blood pulsed in her wounds and her wounds were many and deep.

Hanrahan put his gun away and knelt at her side.

"I'll get you help," he said over the voice of the man singing in Spanish as he reached for a blanket to cover her.

Her head was at an angle but she turned her eyes in his direction and Hanrahan imagined that she said, "Where were you?"

He had no answer.

"I'll get help," he repeated.

Her mouth moved, perhaps a breath, perhaps the attempt at a word, but nothing came out.

"The phone," Hanrahan said, searching for it. "The phone."

He found it on the floor next to the bed. The music suddenly stopped. Behind him he heard a sound from Estralda Valdez and he knew it was death. He crossed himself but didn't look back. He made the call, reported the location, and nature of the wounds and the fact that it was an assault. He knew it was now also a homicide but he'd let them send the paramedics. He'd made enough mistakes for one night.

After he'd called in, he started looking for Lieberman. He found him at the synagogue on the second call. When he hung up, Hanrahan moved to the sink in the kitchen alcove, used the side of a spoon to turn on the cold water so he wouldn't disturb any prints, and filled his cupped hands. He plunged his face into his hands and felt the water curl down his neck and chin. It wasn't enough. He grabbed some melting ice on the counter and rubbed his face. He considered, but only for an instant, finding a bottle, a bottle of anything, taking a drink to straighten himself out so he could deal with what was coming. And, in fact, he did see an open bottle of Scotch on its side on the floor, the top off, the amber liquid dribbling over the lip of the bottle. Something told him that a drink now wouldn't be a grand idea and he listened to the something that spoke.

He turned off the water and stepped over debris as he moved out onto the small balcony. The moon was full, a white glowing ball casting a path on the rippling lake. It was beautiful but Hanrahan was in no mood for beauty. He leaned over the railing and looked down at the traffic. Across the way in an adjacent high-rise an early weekend party was in full swing. People were laughing. Directly below him Hanrahan saw a truck filled with something shiny and green. He couldn't see Jules Van Beeber who was passed out under three of the garbage bags clutching his lamp, dreaming of the naked woman who had spoken to him and handed him a present.

Something moved behind Hanrahan. His gun was out and leveled at the door when the one person he least wanted to see at that moment walked in.

Captain Dale Hughes looked at the scene, looked at Hanrahan, and muttered, "What the fuck's going on here?"

3

Lieberman pulled into the Michigan Tower's driveway between the ambulance whose lights were flashing and a blue-and-white Chicago police car. He got out, locked his car, and moved to the outer lobby where a uniformed cop he recognized as Clevenger was talking to the young doorman, who was trying to look cool but looked anything but.

"Six-ten," said Clevenger when he saw Lieberman.

"I know," said Lieberman as he moved through the now open inner door. Lieberman had never been to Estralda Valdez's apartment. She had not been there very long, but he did know the address, did have the phone number in his book, and did know the number of her apartment. He was also sure that he would never forget any of these numbers.

Lieberman hurried across the carpeted lobby to the elevator, which opened before he could push the button. Two men in their twenties in short-sleeved blue uniforms pushed a wheeled stretcher out. They were in no great hurry. The elevator door closed behind them and Lieberman stepped in front of them, his hand out.

"You her rabbi?" the first young man said, looking at Lieberman's head.

"Her . . ." Lieberman said reaching up and finding that his yarmulke from the evening Shabbat service was still atop his head. He took it off and put it into his pocket. "No."

He pulled out his wallet, flopped it open, and showed his badge. The paramedics eased off and Lieberman moved to the side of the stretcher and unzipped the plastic body bag to reveal Estralda Valdez's white face.

49

A middle-aged couple dressed for the evening came through the garage door next to the elevator. The woman said something about Genevieve and the man laughed. The laugh stopped suddenly when first he and then the woman saw the scene before them. Lieberman paused while the couple chose to go up the stairs instead of waiting for an elevator, and then he unzipped the bag the rest of the way. He looked at her wounds for a few seconds and the words of the Kaddish, the prayer for the dead, began to come to him. He closed his eyes for an instant, opened them, and motioned with his head for the paramedics to take her away.

Before they were out of the front door, the elevator was back. Lieberman stepped in, pressed six, and went up.

" . . . forty new cops, all grades," Lieberman heard as he walked down the corridor on the sixth floor to the open door of Estralda Valdez's apartment.

The speaker was a young uniformed cop who, according to the name plate on his shirt, was named Witten. Witten was standing just inside the doorway, his arms folded. He wore no hat. The man he was talking to was a lab tech who Lieberman recognized but whose name escaped him. The lab tech was in the kitchen alcove dusting the counter top.

"And," Witten went on, "not only in Tampa, but Orlando, Florida is booming, paying top dollar, good pension plan."

Witten looked up at Lieberman, recognized him, and backed out of his way. Beyond Witten and through the living room Lieberman could see the back of Hanrahan and the front of Captain Hughes on the balcony. Their heads were close together. Hanrahan's shoulders were down.

"Hughes's reaming your partner," the lab tech whispered without looking up. "Watch where you're walking. All kinds of shit on the floor."

Lieberman moved into the mess of a living room and walked carefully over the debris toward the balcony. Behind him Officer Witten went on, "So, I was saying, what's the point in going another winter. A man has to take a chance and what've I got to lose by taking a few vacation days in Florida, applying."

In front of him, Lieberman heard the voice of Captain Dale Hughes saying, "You sober enough now to get something done on this?"

"I wasn't drunk," Hanrahan said quietly.

"You weren't . . . " Hughes said and stopped to laugh and look away into the night.

Hughes was a big black man, bigger than Hanrahan, but without the growing gut. Lieberman had known Hughes for almost thirty years. They'd started even but Hughes was more ambitious and the better politician. He was also, Lieberman admitted, a good cop. Hughes was reported to work out for an hour with weights every morning before seven. Lieberman wasn't sure where he had heard this, but he believed it was true. Hughes never looked as if he needed a shave and he always wore a neatly pressed jacket and clean tie. Dale Hughes was ready for any superior, politician, or channels 2 through 32.

"Lieberman," Hughes barked out. "What the fuck is going on here?"

Hanrahan turned to Lieberman and held up his hands out of Hughes's line of vision.

"Woman's dead," said Lieberman stepping out on the balcony.

"That I know," said Hughes. "Tell me something I don't know. Tell me why I didn't know you two were staking out this building. Tell me who gave you an OK to give protection to a known prostitute. Tell me how she could get killed and the murderer walk away in front of your partner's face. Tell me how I answer Golluber and the TV people's questions on this one? I don't know what's going on and my men fucked up."

"It's a great load to bear," Lieberman said seriously.

"What's that? Hassidic humor?" Hughes said, straightening his tie. "Don't play games with me, Abe. You know who lives in this goddamn building?"

"One less person than an hour ago," said Lieberman looking back into the room where Estralda Valdez had died.

"I live in this building," said Hughes. "My wife and I live here. Two of my men are carrying on a surveillance in the building where I live and I don't even know about it."

He took two paces, shook his head, and glared at Lieberman.

"We were doing it off duty," Lieberman said. "On our own time. Estralda Valdez was an informant. She was leaving town tomorrow, wanted us to keep an eye on her in case a violent customer gave her a hard time."

"Ah," said Hughes looking at both of his men, "now I get it. We're providing off-duty free protection for prostitutes. You know what the papers are going to say? You know what that little landsman of yours, Rosenberg on channel two, is going to say? He's going to say he wonders if Estralda Valdez was paying you off for protection."

"No, he won't," said Lieberman. He moved next to Hanrahan on the balcony and looked down. He saw Sol Worth's parked lawn truck among the cars below and thought the green tarp was moving.

"He won't," Hughes repeated.

"I've known Walter Rosenberg's family since he was six," said Lieberman. "We went to his bar mitzvah. My daughter Lisa dated him for a while. He won't think I took money. He's a good kid. Now Allen at channel seven. Him I'm not sure of."

Larry Allen, who was black, was editorial director at channel 7. Larry Allen did not like the mayor, the fire chief, the chief of police, any alderman or women, and, most especially, Captain Dale Hughes, who had once mistakenly arrested Allen's brother as a rape suspect.

"We can count on what Allen will do," Hughes said. "Now, what do we do?"

"I told the captain a woman in Valdez's clothes got in a Green and White cab just before I went up," Hanrahan said. "Cabby went in and got her bags."

Lieberman's partner did not look good. Hughes was wrong. Bill Hanrahan wasn't drunk any longer and he wasn't hung over. He was feeling sorry for himself and guilty. Lieberman had seen it before.

"I had Witten call the cab company," said Hughes. "Dispatcher's checking. It's a busy night. You and Hanrahan can check the neighbors on this floor. Clevenger's talking to the doorman. What else do we know?"

"She lived here about three months," Lieberman said, turning his head to look around the room. It was a disaster.

"She didn't live here," Hughes said, pointing his right hand at the torn bed. "She worked here. Everything's new. Looks like she spent nights here working, but probably called someplace else home. Look around and tell me you don't read it the same?"

"I read it the same," Lieberman had to admit.

"And someone was looking for something in here," Hughes went on, now moving from the balcony and wandering about the room. "They didn't find it. Lieberman?"

"They didn't find it," Lieberman agreed.

If the killer had found what he or she was looking for, the place would probably not have been in this shape. It looked as if some of the damage had been done in a frenzy, and Estralda's body looked as if someone had tried to get her to say something. In addition, the killer had taken some big chances staying so long, making so much noise. No, whoever did this probably hadn't found what he was looking for. Hughes was right.

"What were they looking for, Abe?" Hughes said. "Drugs? She tell you?"

"A book," said Hanrahan.

"List of clients," said Lieberman.

Hughes turned on them both.

"Bullshit," he said. "Nobody does this because a hooker has his name in a book."

Hughes glared at the two detectives and watched Lieberman's impassive face.

"Well," Hughes finally grudgingly admitted, "maybe they do. Hanrahan, you in shape to go knocking on doors?"

"He's in shape," said Lieberman.

"Abe, I asked your partner," Hughes said. "The only thing saving his ass is that he was off duty."

"I can knock on doors," said Hanrahan. He pushed himself away from the railing on the balcony and stepped into the room.

"Then do it," said Hughes. "Maybe we got a chance of keeping this small. Papers, TV might not pick up on it, at least not big. Whore gets murdered. Nothing special."

"Nothing special," Lieberman said softly.

Hughes prodded a pair of pink silk underpants on the floor.

"Saw her around the building a couple of times," he said. "Good-looking woman. Not enough good-looking women around, whores or not, to have someone going around wasting them. The case is yours, Lieberman. Comes down to it and you want to lie to the press, you do it. You just let me know what's going on. Do it fast. Do it quiet and get it over with. I'm sending all the media shit, if there is any, to you and your partner. You earned it."

"We appreciate your confidence," said Lieberman.

"I'm going home," Hughes said. "I'm on the third floor, three-oh-eight. Don't come to my door. Don't tell me your problems. Be in my office tomorrow at ten with a progress report."

"I've got my annual department physical tomorrow morning at nine," said Lieberman. "I don't know if I'll be done in time to get—"

"Then come when you're done, as soon as you're done. Shit, wife and I were thinking of selling the apartment. This gets out and no one's going to want to buy toilet rights in here."

Hughes went past Witten and the lab tech and out the door.

"The man has charm," said Lieberman. "Got to give him that."

"I fucked it up, Rabbi," Hanrahan said. "She gave me the signal and I was four sheets to the wind and making a play for a Chinese waitress."

Lieberman found a clear spot to sit on the mattress and reached for the nearby telephone.

"You're right, Father Murphy," Lieberman said. "You screwed it up. We'll add it to your list of screw-ups, throw mine in including the Mideano case last year, remember? Then we'll divide by my granddaughter's age and add in the miles to Kankakee and what do we have?"

"A dead woman," said Hanrahan.

"And what do we do?"

"We find the perp," said Hanrahan as Lieberman dialed.

"Bess, it's me," he said when his wife answered. "I'll be home late if I'm home. You want to call Kitty and see if she'll come over for the night?"

"I got plenty of company," Bess said. "Lisa was here with the kids when I got home. She left Todd. She wants to talk to you."

"It's not a good time, Bess," Lieberman said.

"Are there good times for things like this?" she said sadly. "It's your daughter."

"Put her on."

"Dad?" said Lisa when she came on a few seconds later.

"Remember when your friend Mary moved out of town?" he asked.

"My friend Ma . . . you mean Miriam," Lisa said. "I was nine or ten. What's this got to . . . ?"

"I don't know," said Lieberman. "It just came to me. You want advice you won't listen to or you want to talk and I'll listen?"

"I guess I want to talk," she said.

"Can it wait till I get home? I'm sitting in the torn-up apartment of a woman who was murdered about an hour ago. I'd like to go out and try to catch the killer before I come home and try to save my daughter's marriage."

"You can't save this marriage, Dad," Lisa said emphatically.

"Sorry, before I come home and listen to my daughter's very good reasons why she is leaving her husband after more than thirteen years of marriage," he said.

"Fourteen years on our next anniversary," Lisa said.

"September sixth," said Lieberman.

"May sixteenth, Dad," Lisa said with a sigh. "We were married in the spring. You paid for it. You should remember. September sixth is Melisa's birthday."

"Right, I remember," said Lieberman. "The proximity of violent death sometimes affects my memory."

"Don't be funny, Dad," Lisa said.

"I won't be funny," Lieberman agreed. "I'll talk to you when I get home. Don't wait up. The kids OK?"

"No," said Lisa. "How can they be OK?"

"I'll talk to you later," Lieberman said and hung up the phone. He looked at Hanrahan but his partner showed not the slightest interest in the call.

"Lisa left Todd," Lieberman said.

"My sons could be divorced and remarried five times and I wouldn't know it," Hanrahan said. "You're lucky you got a daughter, grandchildren in the same town."

"I'm lucky," said Lieberman. "What kind of cab did the woman in Estralda's clothes take off in?"

"Green and White," said Hanrahan. He was looking at the spot on the floor where the body had been.

Lieberman got a small red notebook out of his jacket pocket and dialed a number.

"Hello, give me Leo Gedvilas," Lieberman said into the phone. "Leo? Abe Lieberman . . . What five bucks? I'm not calling about five bucks. I don't remember any five bucks you owe me. One of your cabs picked up a woman fare in front of four four four five Lake Shore tonight at . . ." Lieberman looked at Hanrahan whose eyes were fixed on the spot where he had found Estralda Valdez's body.

"Eleven fifteen," said Hanrahan.

"Eleven fifteen," Lieberman repeated into the phone. "Now. . . . He's checking."

Hanrahan grunted and turned to Lieberman with the first sign of interest. Over in the alcove, the lab tech said "Don't touch that" and Officer Witten responded, "OK, OK."

Leo Gedvilas came back on the line in two minutes.

"Abe? Driver was a Cajun named Francis Dupree. Just talked to him on the radio. Remembers the fare. Woman with red hair. Didn't say anything except to tell him to take her to Lawrence and Broadway. She paid him, got out, walked away."

"Ask him if he'd recognize her again," Lieberman said.

"I asked," Gedvilas said. "What'ya think I am here? He doesn't think so. Big floppy hat, sunglasses. Eleven at night. He figured she was floating on something. You ask me, off the record, Francis Dupree is floating on something tonight."

"How'd he get the call, Leo?" Lieberman asked, looking up at Hanrahan.

"Been looking for that while we been talking," said Gedvilas. "Pulled it up on the computer. Here it is. Call came from four nine two, oh nine nine nine. Customer's name was Valdez. Dupree had just dropped off a fare a few blocks away on Foster."

Lieberman looked down at the phone in his hand. The number was 492-0999.

"Any way of telling if the caller was a man or woman?" he asked.

"If the dispatcher remembers," said Gedvilas. "But with fifty calls an hour, who remembers."

"Thanks, Leo. We'll want to talk to Francis Dupree so don't fire him for a few days."

"We don't fire anybody," said Gedvilas. "We need the drivers. New subject. I helped you. You help me. You want to contribute to the St. Anthony Needy Children Fund this year, Abe?"

"Yeah, Leo. Put me down for five bucks. Then take the five bucks out of one pocket, put it in the right envelope, and give me credit."

"You got a sense of humor, Abe," Gedvilas said chuckling. "Dupree lives at four eight five one North Kedzie."

"Say hello to your charming wife," Lieberman said. He wrote Dupree's address in his notebook.

"You got it," said Gedvilas and Lieberman hung up.

"Call came from this room," Lieberman said as he got up. "Driver took her to Lawrence and Broadway. Ten blocks away, middle of Uptown."

Hanrahan looked at a cracked painting against the wall, its wooden frame trailing along the rug like a snake with rigor mortis.

"This don't look like a woman's touch to me," Hanrahan said.

"You want me to tell my daughter you said that?" Lieberman said with a deep sigh. "Sexist comments again. A woman isn't as capable as a man of wanton destruction and violent murder."

"Abe," said Hanrahan. "A man did this. You know it. I know it. Hughes knows it."

"Well," said Lieberman moving toward the front door. "Let's knock on some doors."

Witten was still talking about his dreams of Florida gold when Hanrahan and Lieberman stepped into the hall.

Lieberman took the even numbers and Hanrahan the odd numbers on the sixth floor. It was almost midnight when they knocked at the first door.

"Who's there?" came a frightened woman's voice.

"Police," said Lieberman.

"Who?" the woman repeated.

"Police. The police. I'm Inspector Lieberman of the Chicago Police. I'd like to ask you a few questions."

"I'm alone," the woman said.

"I'm sorry to hear that," said Lieberman.

"Nobody's in here with me," she said.

"I appreciate that," said Lieberman.

"But I have a very big dog," she said.

"That's a good idea," he said. "Can we talk for just a moment."

The door opened slightly to reveal chain and a very short woman. Lieberman could see that the woman was wearing a blue robe and a look of total panic.

"That's all I'm opening," she said. "My dog is right here."

"That must be reassuring," said Lieberman. "I'm sorry to tell you this, but there's been an accident next door. Miss Valdez. Did you hear anything Miss . . . ?"

"Mrs. Warnake," the woman said. "I heard plenty. Noise, throwing things. Woke my cat."

"You mean your dog."

"My dog," she corrected.

"You hear any voices, words?" he asked.

"Music, noise," she said. "I'm sorry if she's had an accident but I think I'll complain to Mr. Silver in the morning."

"She's dead," said Lieberman.

"Oh," said Mrs. Warnake.

"You ever see people coming to visit her?" Lieberman asked.

"I go to bed at ten," said Mrs. Warnake. "Go to bed, watch Johnny, and Caroline and I go to sleep and mind our business."

"Caroline?"

"My cat . . . dog."

"Deceptive name for a large dog," said Lieberman.

"It's meant to be," said Mrs. Warnake. "Was she murdered?"

"Yes," said Lieberman.

"You said it was an accident. Murdering someone is not an accident."

"You're safe," said Lieberman. "We'll have a policeman standing guard all night, but we're pretty sure this was something personal and the killer is long gone."

"That's reassuring," said Mrs. Warnake. "I'm not staying in this building."

And with that she shut the door.

The rest of Lieberman's journey down the even numbers yielded the following information, which he shared at a quarter to one with Hanrahan in the building lobby. Five people were either not home or would not answer their doors. One man named Martin Franklin with a pinched face and receding hairline knew Estralda by sight though not by name and was sure she deserved whatever she got for dressing that way. His wife agreed. Mrs. Yavonovitch in 620 was somewhere in her late fifties, very lonely, and had a batch of cookies she wanted to share with Lieberman. Mrs. Yavonovitch did not remember seeing Estralda Valdez but Mrs. Yavonovitch was very grateful to Lieberman and the police force in general.

Hanrahan's information was a bit better. He checked his notes and passed his information on to Lieberman: an identical five unanswered doors, a man named Culp who did have a dog and said he wanted nothing to do with the police, a trio of women in their sixties who spoke a language Hanrahan knew was Scandinavian. None of the women acknowledged that she spoke English. The gem came from apartment 619.

"Couple who live there came home from dinner and a show about nine-thirty," Hanrahan said rubbing his chin. Hanrahan's face was rapidly growing stubbly and he looked like Edward G. Robinson at the end of *Little Caesar* after he's spent weeks in a flophouse, Lieberman thought, but there was a touch of excitement in his partner's voice.

"Couple both saw a scruff of a character in a long coat," he said. "A wino they've seen in the neighborhood. Saw him on the stairwell when the husband and wife went to throw out the garbage. Wife says she called down to the doorman when they got back into their apartment. I checked with Clevenger and the doorman, Billy Tarton."

Hanrahan paused and looked at Lieberman. A good sign. Father Murphy was playing his audience.

"And you wrapped up the case," said Lieberman.

"Not exactly, but I got a name. Jules the Walker. Hangs around the high-rises on the block, goes in when someone lets the door open, finds a place to curl up, usually a car parked in a garage. Guy's been picked up dozens of times. Doorman sent a night maintenance man named Olson up to look. Couldn't find our Jules."

"Let's go back and write a report," said Lieberman.

"How about you going back and writing it, Abe?" said Hanrahan. "I'd like to spend a while looking for Jules. Leave it on my desk. I'll sign it by morning and have it on Hughes's desk before he gets there."

"You're all right?" asked Lieberman.

"No," said Hanrahan. "You?"

"We owe her one, Father Murphy," he said.

"We owe her one," Hanrahan agreed.

The two men walked to the door of the outer lobby of the Michigan Towers. A new doorman was on duty and Officer

Clevenger was gone. The ambulance with Estralda's body was probably standing in front of the coroner's lab on Polk Street by now. They may have owed her one, but Estralda Valdez was beyond caring about vengeance. No, Lieberman thought as he moved toward his car and watched Hanrahan walk to the corner, we'll do it for ourselves. We'll do it and try to convince ourselves that when we find whoever did this everything will be even, the books will be balanced. We'll try to convince ourselves.

It was almost one-thirty and Lieberman had a report to write and a daughter to talk to if she was still up when he got home.

Hanrahan moved around the corner and got into his car. He sat for about three minutes wondering which way to drive. He sat looking at the truck in front of him filled with green garbage bags and remembered that from the sixth floor it had looked like a beautiful blanket of silk.

He reached into his shirt pocket and fished out the card for the Black Moon Restaurant. Her name, he thought. She gave me her name. What was . . . ? Iris. Like Irish. Nice-looking woman, he thought. And then he remembered another nice-looking woman whose body was . . . He started the car and pulled into the street to start his search for Jules Van Beeber, Jules the Walker, who at that moment, hearing a car pull away, turned in his sleep and reached up to pull a vinyl bag of leaves over him like a blanket.

4

Lieberman pulled up in front of his house just before three in the morning and parked in front of a fireplug, the only space left on the block. One of the advantages of being a cop. He had a garage in back but it was filled with junk, junk he planned to throw away, give to Goodwill, or move in the corner before winter came.

He tiptoed up the three outside stairs, touched the *mezuzah* on the door, inserted his key, and turned it as quietly as he could. The report had taken him longer than he had anticipated. Covering himself and Hanrahan took everything short of a complete lie. There were a few places Hughes could nail them if he wanted to, but the report had been as good as he could make it. He had written it extra long, six pages, in the hope that Hughes would skim it instead of reading it carefully. It wasn't much of a hope but it was a possibility and Lieberman didn't want to miss any possibility.

He closed the door gently. Barry and Melisa were sleeping in the living room. Melisa was in the hide-a-bed and Barry was in a red sleeping bag on the floor. It was Saturday. No summer school in the morning for Barry. No day camp for Melisa. Lisa, always the scientist, had picked the perfect day of the week to leave her husband.

Lieberman took off his shoes, tucked them under his arm, and headed past the dining room toward the bedroom. He wouldn't even brush his teeth and shave. He'd lay his clothes out in the dark and . . .

"Dad?"

Lisa was sitting in the kitchen at the table. She had whispered to him as he moved past. Lieberman stopped. The only light on in the kitchen was the night light on the oven. He stepped into the room, closed the door, turned on the light, and looked at his daughter.

She was wearing a pink robe with a frilly collar. Her dark hair was tied back. In front of her was a glass of milk and a plate with Oreo and chocolate chip cookies. She was dunking a chocolate chip the way she always did when she was a kid.

Lieberman put his shoes down on the floor near the door, went to the refrigerator, pulled out his special carton of artificial dairy creamer, grabbed a glass, moved to the table across from his daughter, and reached for an Oreo.

"Mom's asleep," she said.

"I would hope so," he answered around the soggy piece of cookie he had just dunked and put into his mouth.

"You had a homicide?"

"Yes," he said.

"Want to talk about it?"

"No," he said. "Let's talk about you."

And for the next hour they whispered about Lisa's failed dreams, broken illusions, disappointments, memories, and fears for the future. Lieberman ate cookies, said practically nothing, nodded in appropriate places, and paid close attention. There were inconsistencies in her monologue. Lieberman had learned to pick up inconsistencies in people's statements. There were protestations, sincere protestations that were a bit too sincere, a bit too emphatic. Lieberman had learned partly from instinct, mostly from experience, that it usually did no good to point out the flaws in a suspect's statement unless you wanted to risk alienating her. There often came a point when alienation was the right step, but it would not come with his daughter, so he listened, made mental notes, attempted to remain awake, tried to keep the memory of Estralda in the zipper bag from haunting him, and found solace in the domestic tangle of his daughter's life. He knew why. What had happened to Estralda Valdez was chaos. Murder was chaos.

63

Family fights, even divorce, were part of the normal world Lisa's words became a pattern like the praises to God on Friday night.

When she was sufficiently exhausted at 4:00 A.M., he said they would talk again later, not tomorrow. It was already tomorrow and had been for four hours. He kissed her forehead and let her clean up the glasses and remains of the cookies while he went to bed.

Bess stirred when he took off his holster and gun, draped the holster over the nearby night light she had left on for him, and put the gun in the drawer near his bed. He locked the drawer with the key and then hung the key on the little hook at the head of the bed before getting undressed and putting on the pajamas she had laid out for him. He got into bed. The air conditioning was humming soothingly. It had recently been repaired, though the air conditioning man made no promises for next year.

Lieberman turned off the night light and lay in bed. He squinted at the illuminated red numbers on the digital clock on the dresser. He had about three hours to sleep and was sure that sleep would not come. But it did.

Lieberman had a dream. He didn't remember it when his eyes opened automatically at seven in the morning as they always did. He didn't remember it but he knew he had dreamed and that the dream had been a bad one.

He got out of bed, kissed Bess, who stirred slightly, and went into the bathroom off their room where he showered and shaved, put on a clean shirt and tie, and settled for his blue slacks and favorite gray jacket. He looked at himself in the mirror and saw a very weary-looking man who should have been greeting mourners at Piser's Funeral Chapel.

Lisa was sleeping in her old room. The door was closed. Lieberman moved to the front door, shoes in hand. He put them on.

"Grandpa," came Barry's voice.

"How you doing, Pirate?" Lieberman whispered.

"You don't have to whisper," Barry said. "Melisa's only pretending to be asleep."

"I'm not," Melisa said, her eyes closed tightly.

"You going to work?" Barry said.

"Annual physical and then to work," said Lieberman, looking at the boy who was sitting up on the floor. Barry looked exactly like his father, which means he didn't look in the least Jewish. His hair was corn yellow and straight. He was tall, taller than Lieberman, almost as tall as his father. He looked, Lieberman thought, like a young Spencer Tracy.

"You know what happened?" Barry said. "Between Mom and Dad?"

"Some," said Lieberman.

"They're talking about a divorce," Melisa said, her eyes still closed. Melisa looked exactly, heart-tuggingly like Lisa.

"We'll see," said Lieberman.

"We still going to the game Monday?" Barry asked.

"Still going," agreed Lieberman.

"Am I going?" Melisa asked.

"You don't like baseball, come on," Barry groaned.

"I like baseball," said Melisa. "Michael Jordan."

"He's basketball, nitwit," said Barry.

"If your mother says you can come, you can come," said Lieberman.

Barry groaned again.

"She'll be asking to come home in the third inning," sighed Barry.

"I won't," said Melisa. "I promise. They have hot dogs."

"What are you working on, Grandpa?" Barry asked. He had had enough of his sister.

"Murder," said Lieberman.

"Tell me about it later?" asked Barry.

"Me too," said Melisa, eyes still closed. "Can you bring us bagels and cream cheese from Uncle Maish's when you come back?"

"That's Sunday food, stupid." said Barry.

"I'm not stupid," said Melisa. "I'm going to sleep. Wake me when PeeWee's on."

"I'll see you later," said Lieberman. "I'll bring bagels and cream cheese."

The morning was sunny and already warm, promising a muggy Chicago August day.

Lieberman checked his watch. No hurry. Instead of heading east on Peterson toward Uptown, he went south on California for twenty blocks to Foster, then turned west and went to Kedzie. There he turned south, looking for 4851, where he hoped to find Francis Dupree at home. Dupree, the hackie who had picked up the woman who pretended to be Estralda Valdez, lived in Lieberman's old neighborhood in Albany Park. Maish had owned his first deli, a ten-seater with two tables, a few blocks from here. Their father before them had owned a small tailor shop on Lawrence, also in the neighborhood. Temple Mir Shavot had originally been four blocks from where Lieberman now parked in front of an upholstery shop.

The neighborhood was mostly East Indian now with a few really poor Russian Jews and a smattering of Haitians, Jamaicans, and even Cajuns like Dupree. The alderman in Albany Park was an independent named Lester Sax who had been reelected four times by substantial margins in a neighborhood with one of the lowest voter turnouts in the city. No administration had found it worthwhile to negotiate with Sax, who had no real power base, which was why Kedzie Avenue was one of the last streets swept in the summer and one of the last plowed in the winter. Forget about the side streets.

Lieberman found 4851 wedged between a hot dog shop which smelled of yesterday's onions and a used book store featuring books in foreign languages. Dupree's name was marked in pencil on the mailboxes just inside the door. The five others who had apartments over the stores had written their names in everything from crude capitals in crayon to flowing Arabic script.

Lieberman rang the bell. He thought he heard the distant sound of ringing. Nothing. He rang again and then heard a door open and someone pad out of an apartment and down the stairs. Lieberman walked to the inner door and looked through the dirty glass. A lean man in a gray and black robe and bare feet appeared on the steps and said, "What?"

"Francis Dupree?"

"So?"

Lieberman showed his badge.

"Come in," said Dupree. "The damn door doesn't lock."

Lieberman went in and followed Dupree back up the stairs. Dupree moved slowly, coughing once, and entered the open door of an apartment on the first floor. Lieberman followed him. Dupree closed the door behind them, bolted and chained it.

"What you think?" asked Dupree, looking around his room.

Lieberman looked at Dupree, figured him for about fifty, maybe younger. Life had kicked him in the face with golf shoes. His skin was bad, his eyes were bleary, his hair a gray-yellow that suggested he had once dyed it but had long since given up the pretense. The room was reasonably neat, the furniture furnished-apartment unmatched, cheap, built so that if some tenant walked with it it could be replaced for a few bucks.

There was a small television on a table, an unmade bed in the corner, and one surprising item, a neatly polished violin on a small chrome-legged table with a cracked white Formica top.

"You play?" asked Lieberman.

"Used to play with Louisiana Fonso's Band," said Dupree, running a hand through his hair and accomplishing nothing. "Never made no money, but had fun, you know? Then I got this."

He held up his left hand. The small finger and the one next to it were missing.

"Can't play good stuff no more," said Dupree. "Jus' play for myself. I'm talkin' too much. You got questions. You wanna know about that fare las' night, right? Dispatch called. He said somethin' funny goin' on. You wanna sit down? Drink a beer?"

"No thanks. Woman was killed last night," said Lieberman.

"That got somethin' to do with my fare?" asked Dupree, touching the fiddle and sitting down at one of his two kitchen tables. His knees were knobby and there were marks

67

around his ankles. Lieberman had seen flea bites before.

"Where did you pick up her bags?" asked Lieberman. "What floor?"

"Don't remember for sure," he said, looking down at his feet and wiggling his toes. "Think it was sixth floor. She was out there with them before I got to the door. Told me she was in a hurry. I took her to the corner over on Broadway and Lawrence. She gave me fare, a tip, never another word."

"She have an accent?" Lieberman asked.

"No, she talked . . . you know. Like you maybe," he said. "Sometimes I think I'm getting the arthritis of the toes from cabbing, you know? Step on the pedals, feet sweating."

"I don't think you get arthritis from sweating," Lieberman said. "But you may be right. I've got it in the knees from walking."

"That a true fact?" asked Dupree, looking up as if he were receiving confirmation from a specialist.

"A true fact," said Lieberman. "Think you could recognize this woman if you saw her again?"

"Don't know, maybe," Dupree said with a shrug. "She had a big chapeau like this." He demonstrated the size of the brim. "And dark glasses. I think she was a good looker though. Smelled *tres bon*. Think I would recognize that par-fume."

"Thanks," said Lieberman. "We may get back to you."

Dupree was fingering the fiddle again.

"I'll be here or in the cab," said Dupree. "No place much else to go."

Lieberman put his notebook away and went back out onto Kedzie. He checked his watch and got into his car.

Dr. Ernest Hartman's office was in Uptown on Bryn Mawr right next to the el stop. Dr. Hartman's patients could, while they were waiting or having their fluids drained or taken, indulge in neighborhood bird watching. The trains came rumbling in front of his window and a sharp-eyed woman with the flu or man with a murmur would occasionally spot a Black-Jacketed Daytime Mugger on the platform, though you were more likely to catch sight of a Fleet-Footed Purse Snatcher.

Dr. Hartman's office was small and ancient and smelled like decaying wood. Parking was difficult, even for a cop, and the waiting room had only four chairs. Hartman's other offices were in the Fullbright Building downtown on Wacker Drive across from Marshall Field's and in the Carlson Building in Evanston across from the library. The Edgewater office was primarily for the cops and to satisfy Hartman's belief that he should be doing charity work. Lieberman had arrived five minutes late, taken the tests, which lasted fifteen minutes, and was asked by Hartman to have a seat.

"Results," Hartman said, coming into the small office next to his examining room where Lieberman sat flipping through an old *People* article on Princess Di.

An el rumbled into the station and Lieberman looked across the desk at Hartman, who was, at forty, decidedly overweight. Other than his weight, Hartman, his sparse hair brushed forward like a cartoon Napoleon, carried a cheery smile even when announcing inoperable tumors and terminal diseases. Hartman was wearing a blue lab coat over his suit. He looked less like a doctor than an actor about to do a commercial for Maalox.

Behind Hartman's desk was a light box to which he was now clipping x-rays of Lieberman's innermost parts and processes. Hartman, when he had finished clipping the x-rays, sat in his swivel chair and examined them.

"Yep," he said. "See, right there."

Lieberman looked in the general direction he was pointing.

"What?" he asked.

"The knees, both of them," he said. "Arthritic joints. Padding, that white stuff between the bones. Right there. Worn down."

"I know," said Lieberman. "You told me last year."

"A little worse this year," said Hartman. "Not a lot but a little. Knees ache, tender?"

"When I walk a lot," said Lieberman.

"You walk a lot?"

"I walk," said Lieberman.

"Impact's no good for knees like that," said Hartman, looking at Lieberman. "You don't play volleyball, jog, basketball, things like that?"

"No."

"Good, but you'll probably need an operation," said Hartman, swiveling again to examine the x-rays.

"When?"

"Who knows," said the doctor. "When it starts hurting, interfering with your walking. Ten years, possibly twenty. Maybe never if it doesn't get bad enough and you don't do a lot of impact."

"What else?"

"Blood pressure is under control," Hartman said, looking at the check list in front of him. "You take the Tenormin every morning, right?"

"Every morning," agreed Lieberman.

"Liver enzyme is still up there," said Hartman. "You still come out positive for hepatitis. Liver's a little large."

"I've had that for thirty years," said Lieberman.

"Have it till you die probably," said Hartman. "You can't give blood."

"Can I take it?" asked Lieberman.

"Do you need it?" asked Hartman.

"What else?"

"Let's see," the doctor continued. "Bone spur in the little finger of the left hand. There on the next x-ray. Should have been taken care of when it happened."

"That was 1969," said Lieberman. "Broke it chasing a woman named—"

"I'd leave it alone since you don't seem to mind that you can't bend the finger," Hartman said, looking at the x-ray.

"Go on," said Lieberman.

"Heart's OK. Lungs OK. You do anything for exercise?"

"Nothing," said Lieberman.

"I don't either," Hartman confided. "Probably should. I mean I probably should. Metabolism. You've got a little belly starting but your weight is fine. Upper back still giving you trouble?"

"When it gets cold," said Lieberman.

"Allergies are the same," Hartman said, looking at the bottom of his list. "Milk intolerance."

"I don't drink it anymore," Lieberman lied.

"Then," said Hartman standing, "that's it. Considering the climate, your age, and your profession, you're a healthy man. I'd suggest when you hit that pension age you sell everything you've got and move to Florida. I hear Fort Myers is still cheap. That's what I'm going to do."

"I'll think about it," said Lieberman, also standing. "Can I ask you a question?"

"Ask me a question," said Hartman. "I've only got a few charity cases waiting."

"Hanrahan come in for his physical yet?" said Lieberman. Hartman removed the x-rays from the light box and turned it off.

"Hanrahan," said Hartman, turning to face his patient. "Hanrahan. Yes."

"He's my partner," said Lieberman.

"Right, I remember," said Hartman. "I told him to watch his liver, his weight, and his mental attitude. I encouraged him to go on a diet, stop drinking, and make an appointment with the police psychology office. I told him it was up to him this year but if he didn't, and he survived till next year, I'd put in a recommendation. That what you want to know?"

"It's what I want to know," said Lieberman.

The visit to Hartman had taken less time than Lieberman had thought. Since it was more or less on the way back to the station, and since he had the time, Lieberman drove south about ten blocks to Wilson and then away from the lake to the dead-end street in Ravenswood where Hanrahan's house stood. Kids were playing in the street when Lieberman went up the steps and knocked on the door. Every third word the kids said was something that would have gotten them drop-kicked by Lieberman's mother half a century ago. None of them could have been more than ten.

Hanrahan answered by the second knock. He was dressed in a clean shirt and tie and had obviously recently shaved and showered. Only his pink face and bloodshot eyes betrayed him.

"Come in," he said, backing away from the door. "I'll get you a coffee."

Lieberman went in. It had been at least five years, when Maureen was still living in the house, since he had been inside. The house, like Hanrahan, surprised him. It was neat, uncluttered, clean. They moved to the kitchen, where a pot of fresh coffee was brewing.

"Place looks nice," said Lieberman. He accepted a hot cup and noticed that the dish drainer was empty.

"Abraham," said Hanrahan. "I can see beyond those drooping eyes. You expected me to be hung over. You expected this place to smell and look like the inside of a dumpster, like Strewbecki's apartment or something out of a TV cop show."

"Good coffee," said Lieberman, sitting at the kitchen table. The top of the wooden table was spotless.

"I keep it like this," said Hanrahan, looking around and taking a sip. "I do the laundry, put it away, vacuum the rugs, have Mrs. Boyer come in every two weeks. It's my therapy, Rabbi. I keep thinking maybe Maureen will knock at the door some night and I'll be sitting in here with a pot of stew I made . . . I've turned into a good cook . . . and . . . you get the picture."

"Yeah," said Lieberman.

"I let this place fall apart and I'm that much closer to falling apart," said Hanrahan. He finished his coffee and moved to the sink, where he washed the cup with liquid Palmolive, rinsed it, and put it in the dishwasher.

"Just came from Doc Hartman," said Lieberman finishing his coffee. "Says aside from my bad knees, blood pressure, screwed-up back, trick finger, and weak stomach, I'll be good for another year."

"Never doubted it," said Hanrahan with a smile, taking Lieberman's now empty cup.

"He says you should see the shrink," Lieberman said.

"Don't believe in them," said Hanrahan. "Believe in them less than I believe in the God of my fathers. Let's change the subject."

"New subject is last night," said Lieberman. "How are you feeling?"

"Responsible," said Hanrahan. "And I don't want to lose that feeling. I didn't find our friend Jules the Walker. Kept at it till about three. Came home and went to bed sober. I'm tired but I'm ready."

"My daughter talked to me till after four," said Lieberman. "I'm tired and I don't know how ready I am but I'm walking. Let's go."

They took separate cars and arrived at the Clark Street Station just before ten. It was a busy Saturday. People were lined up to fill out complaints. The squad room was filled, mostly with Hispanics from the immediate neighborhood, sitting stone silent and frightened or angry.

Mel Hobson looked as if his temper was about to go. The last time it went was in the winter, when he almost ripped the ear off of a mugger named Jonas who wouldn't answer questions for his rap sheet. Allen Bootes and Joanna Mishkowski were in the corner talking to a frightened little black girl who kept looking up at an equally frightened black man handcuffed to a bench across the room.

"Calls," said Connie Parish, covering the phone with her hand. "On your desk. And a prelim on the P.M. corpus."

"I like the hairdo," Lieberman said. "Very chic."

Connie, whose uniform was perfectly tailored and whose skin had been badly dealt with by heredity, smiled, touched her tinted straw hair, and went back to the phones. Lieberman was on the phone at his desk making a call and reading the preliminary autopsy report on Estralda Valdez when Hanrahan came in. Lieberman waved to him.

"Right," Hanrahan heard as he approached Lieberman's desk. "I hear you, Sol. You're right . . . I don't know . . . Who knows? You have any idea where he might be? . . . I'll try it. I may need a statement from you . . . Maish's fine. His son, my nephew Joe, remember? The lawyer, running for alderman. Why would I kid? You stay in touch and you'll know . . . Bess'd like that . . . I might not be home but you can look at the lawn. You can knock. You can hope. Keep your brother-in-law out of trouble."

Lieberman hung up and looked at the notes he had written. Some of it didn't make much sense. He told Hanrahan what he had, handed him the autopsy report, and the two of them moved through the squad room to the hallway and up the stairs to Hughes's office. Hanrahan did the knocking. Lieberman opened the door and Hughes looked up at them from the report he was reading. The office looked more like that of an accountant or a ward committeeman than a police captain. The furniture, donated by various grateful businesses in the area, was somber, dark, serious wood. The bookcases were filled with books on the law and weapons, and department regulations, along with a thesaurus, dictionary, and assorted reference books. One wall was a picture window looking out into the parking lot so Hughes could see his men coming and going. The other three white walls each held a single photograph. The one behind Hughes was of the captain shaking hands with the late Mayor Washington, who had his left arm around Hughes's shoulder and his right hand clutching Hughes's hand. The photograph on the wall to the corridor was of Hughes, Senator Ted Kennedy, and Adlai Stevenson III in black tie at a Democratic fund raiser.

The photograph directly across from Hughes's desk was a reduction of the front page of the Chicago *Sun-Times*, March 16, 1969. Patrolman Hughes's photograph was on the front page and the headline blared, LONE POLICEMAN WINS GUN BATTLE WITH GANG MEMBERS, TWO DEAD, SIX INJURED.

It was impressive. It was supposed to be. Lieberman and Hanrahan sat in the two chairs opposite Hughes's desk.

"I've read it," Hughes said putting the report on his clean desk and tapping it with his finger. "There's nothing in it. Where's this Jules Van Beeber you mention? You got him yet?"

"No," said Lieberman. "But we just got a report from a lawn service man who says he found someone fitting Van Beeber's description in his truck outside the victim's

74

window this morning. The man in his truck was holding a lamp and claimed to have flown over a balcony. He told the lawn service man, Solomon Worth, a strange story."

"You telling me this Van Beeber fell off of the Valdez woman's balcony and walked away from it?" said Hughes.

"Fell or jumped," said Lieberman. "Landed in bags full of grass and leaves."

"I've heard stranger," Hughes said, looking at Hanrahan, who shifted uncomfortably. "Go nail him. Wrap it up. A homeless nut shouldn't be hard to pick up."

"How's your wife taking it, Captain?" Hanrahan said.

"My wife is fine. My wife still wants to move. You get this guy and fast and we might still be able to sell," Hughes said. "Get him fast with a solid confession and this piece of shit report gets my blessing and no recommendation for investigation for discipline. Fast means today. We understand each other?"

"We do," said Lieberman. "We've got the prelim on the autopsy. Eight penetrating wounds to the abdomen. Blade was thin, about six inches long. Lab reports the murder weapon wasn't on the premises. Tony V and the evidence boys say there was no money in the apartment, no bank book, no address book."

"I've seen the reports," said Hughes. "Remember what I said last night? The case is yours. Go find this Van Beeber, ask him what he did with the knife or whatever it was, and nail him shut. Do it. I've got some work to get done." Hughes picked up the phone and looked at the two detectives, who got up and went out the door.

"I don't think he likes us, Abraham," said Hanrahan.

"I think he's that way to the just and unjust alike," Lieberman said. "I got a call to make, then let's go find Jules the Walker."

Lieberman called Maish and asked him to put together a dozen fresh bagels, some nova lox, and a tub of cream cheese with chives.

"Lisa and the kids are staying with us a while," Lieberman said.

"Like that, huh?" said Maish.

"Who knows?" said Lieberman.

"I like Toddy," said Maish. "I don't always know what that Greek stuff is he talks, but he's a good kid. I like him."

"I do too," said Lieberman. "Maybe all is not lost."

"I don't know if I could take little kids anymore," said Maish.

"I got a choice?" asked Lieberman.

"Rosen wants to talk," said Maish.

"I've got no . . ." Lieberman began, but Herschel was on the phone.

"A bunch of Alter Cockers here want to know when you're bringing your girlfriend back for a visit," he said, a wave of ancient chortles behind him. "She picked up some limp spirits."

"She's not coming back," Lieberman said. "You'll have to settle for Gert Bloombach."

"You're going to keep the cutie all to yourself," said Herschel, obviously playing to the chorus behind him.

"She's dead, Hershy," Lieberman said.

"You're kidding," Rosen said, suddenly sober.

"Would that I were. Put Maish back on," Lieberman said and Maish's voice came back.

"What'd you tell him?"

"Give the Cockers a piece of chocolate cheesecake on me," said Lieberman. "I'll be by later to pay you and pick up my order."

5

Since Jules the Walker had last been seen by Sol Worth clutching a lamp, Lieberman decided to check the pawnshops within easy walking distance, starting on Devon and working his way north to Howard. Hanrahan would try St. Bart's Church on Granville six blocks away. St. Bart's had a walk-in for the homeless and about a dozen beds. They might know Jules or where he hung out. The detectives would meet for lunch at McDonald's on Howard near Western at one. If they had nothing, they'd try to think of another angle.

St. Bart's was close enough to Broadway so the homeless could find it without getting lost and close enough to Little Saigon so that many of the parishioners were now Asian. An editorial writer for the *Sun-Times* had been the first to note the oddity of a congregation of Vietnamese supporting an assortment of black and white homeless men and women.

Hanrahan parked in the small parking lot of the church and walked in. The door was open but the church seemed deserted. At the sight of the crucifix inside the door, Hanrahan crossed himself. His eyes found a stained-glass window above the door that let in blue-red light and cast a dancing image on the wooden floor in the open lobby. Hanrahan looked back and up at the vision of Jesus in glass being taken from the cross. His eyes followed the outline of dark lead that formed the crown of thorns on the head of Jesus. One of the four women in the glass looked vaguely like his wife Maureen.

"Can I help you?" came a man's voice and Hanrahan turned to see a young black man about thirty in a perspiration-stained grey University of Illinois sweatsuit.

"I'm looking for a priest," Hanrahan said.

"You found one," said the man, stepping up and holding out his right hand. "Sam Parker."

"Father Parker," Hanrahan said taking the offered hand. "I'm Detective Hanrahan."

Hanrahan showed his badge. Parker looked at it carefully.

"Want to come in my office?" said Parker, pointing back the way he had entered. "I just got back from running. I don't dress like this for work, at least not usually."

"None of my business, Father," Hanrahan said. "I don't think we need your office. I just have a question or two."

Parker wiped his moist brow with his sleeve and said, "Go ahead."

"Man, homeless man named Jules Van Beeber, known as Jules the Walker," said Hanrahan. "You know him?"

"Yes," said Parker.

There was a slight echo in the hallway. Hanrahan knew that just beyond the wooden doors would be an aisle and down the aisle, a high ceiling overhead, would be an altar, and over that altar would be a crucifixion and . . .

"Officer?" Father Parker said.

"Sorry," said Hanrahan, "I'm just . . . I didn't get much sleep last night. A woman was murdered not far from here."

"Estralda Valdez," said Parker. "Word travels fast. You think Jules had something to do with it?"

"We'd like to talk to him," said Hanrahan.

"Haven't seen him for a while," said Parker. "When it gets cold, he spends some time with us, shares a meal."

"You know where I could find him?" asked Hanrahan.

"Let's ask Waco Johnny," said Parker. "He was here last night. Still is, I think. Come on."

Parker led the way down the corridor into darkness and down a short flight of stairs to a narrow basement. He stopped at a door at the left and pushed it open. A tired brown Salvation Army Store sofa sat in one corner facing two unmatched sagging chairs, one a blue vinyl, the other an orange tweed. Six beds lined the walls. Two battered Formica-top tables, one blue, one white, stood in the middle of the room with chrome chairs around them. At one of the tables, a man thin as a broom and wearing baggy denim overalls sat looking at a cup of what must have been coffee. The man was worn and wrinkled, his face a creviced series of canyons. His mouth was toothless, but his eyes were the brightest blue Hanrahan had ever seen.

"Waco Johnny," said Father Parker. "This is Detective Hanrahan. He's looking for Jules. Can you give him a hand?"

Waco Johnny looked up from his coffee cup at the policeman.

"What's the Walker done?" asked Waco Johnny.

"Don't know that he's done anything," said Hanrahan. "We need his help."

Hanrahan considered a lie that would get Waco Johnny talking, but remembering he was in a church he couldn't bring it to his lips.

"You got a buck you can lend me?" asked Waco Johnny

"Hey," said Father Parker. "Tell the man or don't tell the man, but don't put a price on it here."

"I got thirty pennies," said Hanrahan. "Thirty pieces of copper. You want 'em."

Waco Johnny flashed his blue eyes.

"I ain't no fool, Mr. Cop," he said. "I'm not selling the Walker out. And what the hell kind of cop are you anyway? You want something from me and you insult me royal."

"A tired cop," Hanrahan said. "Why do they call you Waco Johnny?"

"Don't remember," he said. "Something to do with something I used to do. Circus maybe. I think I rode a horse or shot a gun at something."

"Jules," Father Parker reminded him.

"Jules hangs out near the beach on Chase, under the breaker near the rocks, when the weather lets him," said

Waco Johnny. "You know where the playground is? Nights sometimes he sleeps inside the pipe thing in the playground looks like a truck. Cops can't see him and boot his ass. That's all I know."

"Thanks," said Hanrahan. "I'm giving Father Parker five bucks in your name for coffee or whatever."

"Good enough," said Waco Johnny. "I'll put it down on my income tax as a charitable donation."

Father Parker laughed and Waco Johnny grinned tooth-lessly, his blue eyes dancing bright. Hanrahan didn't feel like smiling. He turned and went out the door and up the stairs with Father Parker behind him.

"Can I ask you something?" the priest said when they got back to the church lobby.

"I gotta get going, Father," Hanrahan said, uncomfortably checking his watch. It wasn't too early for a beer.

"You're Bill Hanrahan, right?" said the priest.

"Right," Hanrahan said.

"Come with me," the priest said. He turned and opened the double doors.

Hanrahan hesitated and then followed. Father Parker genu-flected and crossed himself. Hanrahan did the same, though an abbreviated version. They walked down the aisle and turned right at the altar. Jesus looked down. Jesus wept.

There was a door to the right of the altar. Parker went through, holding it open for Hanrahan.

"My office," said the priest.

The office was large, cluttered. Hanrahan thought it looked more like what Lieberman probably had expected Hanrahan's house to look like that morning.

"Over here," the priest went on.

The walls were filled with photographs, mostly football players. Most of the photographs were signed. Hanrahan looked at the photos while Father Parker found the one he was looking for.

"Here," Parker said and Hanrahan looked. It was a shot of four men, three white, one black. Hanrahan recognized himself. He didn't recognize the others.

"That's you," Hanrahan said. "You're Whiz Parker?"

"I was Whiz Parker," the priest said. "Bad knee like yours. You told me about it the day that picture was taken. Homecoming 1978."

"I don't even recognize those other guys," said Hanrahan looking closely at the picture.

"I don't either," said Parker, "but I remember you."

"Long time ago," said Hanrahan.

"Not so long," said Parker. "You're a Catholic, aren't you?"

"I dropped enough clues," Hanrahan said with a smile. "My name for instance. I gotta go, Father. Maybe I'll drop by we can talk football again some time."

"You look tired, Hanrahan," said Parker.

"Things on my mind," Hanrahan said "Gotta go I can find my way out."

He turned, opened the door, and went out into the hallway, closing the door behind him. He stood there for a few seconds, sighed, turned, and knocked on the door.

"Come in," said Parker.

Parker was sitting at the desk in front of the cluttered table, wiping his face with a crumpled towel.

"Father," said Hanrahan, "I want to confess."

"Give me a few minutes to shower and change and I'll meet you upstairs," said the priest.

Hanrahan nodded and went back through the door and through another door into the church. It was still empty. He walked up the aisle. He almost kept walking. His knees were shaking the way they'd shake when he was a kid and his mother told him to confess. He sat in the back row and tried to put his thoughts in order, but images, names, anger, sorrow came in waves. The dead woman, Maureen, his sons, Lieberman, even the Chinese woman last night, who had, he was sure, seen through his blustering and looked at him with understanding.

William Edward Hanrahan had not been to confession in almost twenty years. He looked at his watch, the watch Maureen had given him for his birthday six years ago. He had had it repaired beyond the point where it made sense to repair it. This was taking too long. Hanrahan didn't have the time. Jules the Walker might be moving now. He was just getting to his feet when Father Parker appeared near the altar wearing a cassock and collar. He came up the aisle, ran his right hand down from collar to sash, and said, "You get the whole show."

Hanrahan hesitated.

"God's waiting," said Parker.

Lieberman started with the Golden Earring Pawn Shop on Devon. The owner, a Korean named Park, which was the last name of ninety percent of the Koreans Lieberman had encountered in his life, said that he had never seen Jules or that he had seen so many people like Jules that he couldn't tell the difference. In any case, no one like him had been in today to try to pawn a lamp.

"Don't need lamps," said Park. "Even good lamps. No room for them. Need anything with gold, silver, or electric stuff that works, radios, watches, razors. No more guitars. Got a CD player? I'll take it off your hands, even it don't work good."

Lieberman made his way down the street finding nothing and saving Raw Izzy for last.

Raw Izzy was in the shop sitting in an overstuffed chair in front of his cage reading a book. Raw Izzy was pale, as pale as Estralda Valdez in death. He was white and short and fat. A tuft of brown hair stood up on his otherwise bald head and with glasses perched on his nose he looked like an intellectual Muppet.

"Izzy," said Lieberman, stepping into the shop to the sound of the little bell on the door. "How you doing?"

Izzy looked up over his glasses and book.

"Since last you saw me, I got a pacemaker. You know about this book?" asked Izzy, holding up the book. "The H.L. Mencken book?"

"Heard he was an anti-Semite and a bigot," said Lieberman.

"This news surprised you?" said Izzy, who had a Ph.D. in philosophy and another in theology from the University of Chicago.

"I don't know much about Mencken," said Lieberman.

"Overrated," said Izzy. "Could turn a phrase but he rode the liberal tides. I wasn't surprised. Actually, I was pleased. If Mencken could be one of them, anyone could be. You can't trust. That's also the motto of my business, which, as you can see, is why I have been so enormously successful. You know the last time you came to see me, Lieberman?"

"Hansford case," Lieberman guessed.

"Case . . . case. You were looking for a trumpet for your grandson," said Izzy, still sitting. "You ever find one?"

"No, but he switched to the drums. Then the piano."

Lieberman found himself looking at a shelf of harmonicas safely locked behind a thick glass panel. When he was a kid Lieberman had a harmonica. He'd learned to play "Tara" from *Gone With the Wind*, an accomplishment that earned him half a buck from his emotional mother who loved Abraham and MGM as much as Abe loved the Cubs. He had gone on to a chromatic harmonica in his twenties when he was working nights in the patrol car with Tuna Kingsford and learned to play "Cherry Pink," "River of No Return," and the song from *Shane*. Tuna had been tolerant and Lieberman had improved, but one night after a domestic violence call in Uptown, the harmonica was missing when they got back to the car.

"You're not looking for a piano today," said Izzy. "What are you looking for besides memories?"

"Wanderer known as Jules the Walker," said Lieberman.

"Lamp," said Izzy.

"That's him," said Lieberman.

"Over there," said Izzy, pointing behind a carefully enclosed three-level case of watches.

Lieberman moved behind the watch case to an almost black-stained end table. On the table was a lamp, the exact duplicate of one he had seen broken on the floor of Estralda Valdez's apartment.

"This is it," said Lieberman. "Talk to me."

"Not much to say," said Izzy removing his glasses. "Man wanders in holding the lamp like a sick baby. He tells me it's a magic lamp. I consider his condition, offer him two bucks, which, apparently, is two bucks more than anyone else on the mile offers him."

"He say anything else?" Lieberman said.

"That he was going to tell his tale to the Wonder Man," said Raw Izzy.

"The bartender at Blarney Inn?"

"One might think so, but your man was not focused on this planet or dimension when he entered or left," said Izzy.

"I'll give you three bucks for the lamp," said Lieberman.

"Five," said Izzy.

"I could take it as evidence for nothing," said Lieberman. "It's stolen property."

"I could call my lawyer," said Izzy, pointing his glasses at the policeman.

"For a two-buck lamp?" Lieberman said.

"For a principle," said Izzy.

"Four," said Lieberman.

"Compromise is moral defeat," said Raw Izzy.

"All right, five," agreed Lieberman, pulling out his wallet.

Izzy remained in his chair to receive the five singles and then handed Lieberman a key.

"The case you were looking at, the harmonicas. Take one, a premium. Goes with the lamp. Special today."

Lieberman opened the case, removed a Hohner, key of C, put it in his pocket, locked the case, and returned the key to Raw Izzy.

"Life," said Izzy, "is a series of strange and seemingly pointless stories. Meaning is derived from a relationship of story, storyteller, and listener, but by far the hardest task is that of the listener."

Lieberman picked up the lamp and went to the door.

"I'll be in touch," he said.

"Come back when you can play 'Smoke Gets in Your Eyes,'" said Izzy, returning to his Mencken book.

Jules the Walker had been at the Blarney Inn that morning, but he was long gone by the time Lieberman got there. It had taken him less than an hour to drink his two bucks and be on his way. Wonder Man, the diminutive bartender, did remember that Jules had headed east down Chase. Lieberman thanked him, went out the door, and moved as quickly as his tender knees would let him to his car.

Five minutes earlier, Hanrahan had arrived at the Chase Street beach. Jules the Walker was not in the truck and he wasn't under or near the rocks. Hanrahan decided to walk west on Chase in the vague hope of spotting Jules or someone who looked as if he or she might be acquainted with someone like Jules.

Hanrahan had gone only half a block when he saw Jules Van Beeber heading toward him. Jules Van Beeber also saw Hanrahan and knew instantly that the big Irishman was a cop. Jules, who normally walked, turned and ran. He ran right into the arms of Abraham Lieberman, who had also seen the Walker as Lieberman drove down Chase toward the lake. Lieberman had seen him, parked, and stepped out to approach him when Hanrahan had appeared.

"I did nothing," Jules whispered in Lieberman's arms.

Van Beeber and Lieberman lay on the sidewalk, suspect on top, cop on the bottom.

Hanrahan hurried over and lifted the man off of his partner.

Jules repeated to the big cop, "I did nothing."

"You hungry?" Lieberman asked getting up.

"I could use something," Jules conceded.

"Good, let's get a Big Mac," said Lieberman.

Less than ten minutes later, they were sitting in a booth in the McDonald's on Howard Street. The place was nearly empty. A fat woman with three kids sat at a table nearby. No matter what the kids said, the fat woman replied, "Just eat your fries."

"That's not good for you," Jules the Walker said as Lieberman took a bite out of his Big Mac.

"I'm celebrating," said Lieberman. "Wipe your mouth when you eat."

Jules took a big, messy bite and wiped his mouth.

"Celebrating?" said Jules.

Jules was wedged into the booth next to Hanrahan. Lieberman sat across from them. Jules had ordered a Coke, a cheeseburger without mustard, and a large fries.

Hanrahan settled for a coffee and Lieberman went for the Big Mac and Diet Coke. Jules's burger had taken an extra five minutes because it was a special order.

"I'm celebrating two things," Lieberman explained, helping himself to Jules's fries. "Passed my annual physical and we caught you."

"I flew," said Jules pausing in midbite, mouth full. "I gotta tell you. I flew. That's the God's truth."

"Chew your food and swallow it," said Hanrahan. "You're disgusting."

"I'se regusted," said Jules. "That's what Andy used to say on *Amos and Andy* when I had a TV."

"Mouth shut when you eat, Jules," said Hanrahan.

"OK," Jules agreed and continued eating, a task made difficult by his lack of teeth. "Easier to eat the burgers without false teeth."

"That's good to know," said Lieberman. "Can I ask you a question?"

"I don't know," said Jules, looking at Hanrahan.

"Why did you kill Estralda Valdez?"

"I killed—" Jules said in midbite again.

"Chew," said Hanrahan.

Jules resumed chewing.

"You were in her apartment last night," said Lieberman. "She was there. You went in, killed her, took the lamp, and—"

"Flew the coop," said Jules.

"You got a knife?" asked Hanrahan.

"No," said Jules. "Used to have one. No. Don't think I killed anyone last night."

"When did you kill someone?" Hanrahan asked.

"War," said Jules between bites.

"Which war?" asked Lieberman.

"Don't remem . . . Yeah, there were guys. Australians we were shooting at," said Jules. "Yes, Australians."

"We've never been at war with Australia," said Lieberman.

"Then I don't know what war," said Jules. "Can I have a drink?"

"Coke," said Hanrahan.

"A drink," said Jules. "Then I'll talk."

"Just eat your fries," the fat woman with all the kids screamed.

"What'll you say?" asked Lieberman.

"Anything. You tell me."

"You killed her," said Hanrahan.

"I . . . no, I don't think so," Jules repeated. "Not this time."

"Not this time?" Lieberman said.

Jules's eyes suddenly focused on another universe. His mouth dropped open. Bits of cheese dripped out.

Hanrahan reached over with one hand and pushed Jules the Walker's right shoulder gently to bring him back to Chicago. Jules jerked back and hit his head on the wall. The fat woman with the three kids stopped chewing in midbite and looked at the three men.

"I hardly touched him," Hanrahan told the woman with the kids and his partner who shrugged and kept on chewing.

"I'm here," said Van Beeber.

"That's good to know," said Lieberman, handing him a napkin. "Wipe your mouth."

"I know where I am," said Van Beeber, focusing on Lieberman. "I just don't know for sure when I am."

"Valdez'd never let him in," said Hanrahan, examining the creature at his side. "And if she did, she could take him with one hand."

"Maybe I didn't kill her," said Jules, rubbing his head where it had hit the wall.

"Who did?" asked Hanrahan.

"Just tell us what you remember about last night," said Lieberman.

Jules rubbed his hands on his filthy shin and dug his dirt-caked nails into the fries.

"Last night," he said around a mouthful. "It's hard to . . . Which one was last night."

"You were in the Michigan Towers, sixth floor," Lieberman tried, deciding not to finish his fries. Watching Jules eat had taken his appetite.

"The guy who told me about the bottle," said Jules, spitting pieces of fried potato.

"Don't talk with food in your mouth, I told you," Hanrahan said.

"Who was this guy who told you about a bottle?" asked Lieberman.

"A guy. I don't remember. All messed up in my head, you know what I'm saying? Wait, I got some of it now. I heard them. The door was open. Open." The fat woman with the kids opened her mouth but before she could speak, Jules screamed, "Just eat your fries."

The woman looked at Jules and shouted, "Fucking creeps."

"Where was I?" Jules asked, digging in for more fries.

"Open door," said Hanrahan.

"Yeah," said Jules, closing his eyes and nodding as if he were a particularly bright student who had given the professor a particularly bright answer to a very tough question. "I went in. Mess. Mess. Bottle on the floor wasn't broken. Then I heard . . . She was doing like this." Jules the Walker then proceeded to gag and cough.

"Beautiful," said Lieberman.

"I talked to her," said Jules. "I said to her, 'What?' I'm not feeling so good. Can I get to the john?"

"You asked her if you could use the john?" asked Hanrahan.

"No," answered Jules. "I mean now. I need the john."

"What'd she say to you, Jules?" Lieberman asked.

"'Under the house at my mother's,'" said the Walker proudly. "That's all."

"'Under the house at her mother's'?" Lieberman repeated.

"Can I go to the . . . I gotta piss."

"What else did she say?" asked Lieberman.

"Nothing," said Jules. "I got the lamp and flew out the window. Hey, I gotta . . ."

Hanrahan moved into the aisle and stood up. Jules scooted out holding his crotch. The fat woman gathered her brood and went for the exit, pulling one of the kids, who didn't want to go, behind her. Jules went into the toilet.

Both cops knew there were no windows in the restroom and no way Jules could hurt himself unless he tried to drown in a toilet or basin or bash his head against the walls.

"What do we do?" asked Hanrahan. He sipped his coffee and then looked deeply into the dark liquid.

"Book him, hold him," said Lieberman. "Tell Hughes we found him and keep looking. You know who Jules looks like? Remember Dustin Hoffman in *Midnight Cowboy*? Ratso Rizzo."

"Yeah. You know what I did today?" asked Hanrahan.

"Voted early in the Bud Bowl?" Lieberman tried. "It's Bud Light's turn, but my grandson figures they'll pull a fast one and go with . . ."

"Abe, I'm serious here. I went to confession," said Hanrahan, still looking at his coffee.

"Mazel tov," said Lieberman. "Feel better?"

"A little," said Hanrahan. "What you think about Chinese women?"

"Don't think I've ever considered them as a category," said Lieberman, reaching up to touch his mustache. "You want me to?"

"No, where the hell . . . ?" Hanrahan began, but Jules came out of the restroom and silenced him.

"No towels," said Jules, dripping dirty water on the floor.

"Use napkins," Lieberman said, handing a stack to the Walker.

Jules took the stack of napkins, wiped his hands, and looked for someplace to deposit the sopping mess. He settled on the bag in which their sandwiches had come.

"You're not an appetizing sight, Jules," said Hanrahan.

"I used to have a card shop in Holland," said Jules, standing next to the table and glancing at a trio of teenage girls who giggled through the door. "Kids, a wife. Something happened."

Jules began to cry. The teenage girls looked at him and giggled.

"We're going to jail, Jules," Lieberman said.

"What happened?" asked Jules, wiping tears on his ragged sleeve. "I was selling cards one minute. Next thing I know it's where and when. What the goddamn hell happened?"

"You learned how to fly," said Hanrahan.

"No," said Jules, shaking his head. "I was lying to you. I was lying to me. I fell. You guys getting me a drink?"

Lieberman and Hanrahan were up now. The teenagers with their sandwiches were looking for a place to sit far enough to be safe from these weird men yet close enough to watch them.

"'Under the house at her mother's house'?" Lieberman said.

Jules nodded. His energy was draining off somewhere and his eyes were losing focus again.

"Under the house at my mother's house, she said," Jules agreed. "Her name is Maureen. Wife."

Hanrahan's knees almost buckled. Lieberman touched his partner's arm.

"Whose wife?" asked Lieberman.

"Mine," said Jules. "My wife's name is Maureen."

"So's mine," said Hanrahan.

"Haven't seen mine in years," said Jules, looking at the big policeman. "I think she was good in bed. Don't remember what she looked like."

Lieberman stepped between the two men before Hanrahan did something new to bring to confession.

"Let's go for a ride to the station," he said.

As they walked back to the car with Jules Van Beeber between them, Hanrahan said, "Rabbi, if I believed in the devil, I'd think he had a hand in giving me the screws."

"Not the devil, Father Murphy," said Lieberman. "God's got a sense of humor. It's one of the things I like about him."

"Amen," muttered Jules Van Beeber, his eyes fixed on the driveway. "Amen."

6

Captain Hughes sat in the interrogation room listening to the tape and drinking coffee from a white cup with Beethoven's picture on it. His pink and blue tie was just slightly loose to make room for the open top button. His dark brow was furrowed in concentration. The door was closed and Hughes had informed Feitler, the morning clerk with the overbite that earned him the nickname Bugs, that no one was to bother him. No one. Period. No one, Feitler knew, meant no one but the mayor, chief of police, and Hughes's wife. Lieberman sat at the end of the table taking notes on the back of a Northern Illinois Gas Company receipt. Hanrahan operated the tape recorder.

The tape recorder was a small cassette player confiscated from the apartment of a drug dealer named Murrayhoff. It should have been in the evidence room, but the squad's two recorders were unavailable. One was being repaired. The other one had been stolen.

LIEBERMAN

. . . last night.

JULES VAN BEEBER

Last night?

HANRAHAN

The lady and the lamp.

JULES

Oh, life's like that.

HANRAHAN

Like what?

JULES

Hard to remember. There was a guy, I think.

A guy?

JULES

I think a guy. Gave me bottle. No, he told me where to find a bottle. Don't know what.

HANRAHAN

Could you identify this guy if you saw him again, heard him?

JULES

Looked like him.

LIEBERMAN

He looked like Captain Hughes? He was black?

JULES

Big. He was big. (Long pause) She told me. She told me that it was under the house in her mother's house. She told me. Nice-looking lady. Seen her before on the street. Didn't look good on the floor.

LIEBERMAN

Did you kill her, Jules?

JULES

Maureen?

HANRAHAN

The nice-looking lady.

JULES

Kill her? I don't think so. Maybe. I took a drink and the lamp and I told you. I flew. No, fell. You're not going to tell my wife?

LIEBERMAN

Maureen. She's . . .

JULES

. . . in Michigan. Got two bucks for the lamp from the Raw Izzy.

"Turn it off," said Hughes with a sigh. He examined his Beethoven cup. Beethoven was frowning.

Hanrahan turned off the tape recorder.

"We book him?" asked Lieberman.

Hughes looked at the detective and shook his head.

"That's shit and you know it," sighed Hughes. "You can

92

maybe drop it on him if we get Judge Dreuth or Shoenberg on the prelim and your Jules pleads guilty. Who's the PD?"

"Public defender on this one is Sheridan," Lieberman said.

"He'll go along with this?" asked Hughes, standing and looking at Hanrahan who rewound the tape.

Lieberman shrugged and said, "He owes us. We owe him. Who knows?"

"I know," said Hughes. "It's shit. That sorry bag of scum isn't competent to plead anything. Even Dreuth wouldn't go for it. It'd come back and haunt him. The Valdez woman could have beat the crap out of him. Son of a bitch doesn't have the strength or the balls to stab someone once, let alone eight times. What about the weapon? What about . . . shit."

Hughes shook his head.

"I've got three homicides going today," he went on. "My wife's got a theory. You want to hear my wife's theory on this one?"

"Sure," said Hanrahan.

"The fuck you do," said Hughes, "but you're going to hear it anyway. She thinks some pimp did her in or some guy she brought up there who went nuts."

"I think your wife's right," said Lieberman, putting his pen and envelope into his pocket.

"You want to know what else my wife thinks?" said Hughes getting angrier. "She thinks she wants to get out of that building. She's got another theory. There might be a lady-killer living there. She's off staying with her mother till I prove we've got our killer. She thinks the pimp or the john might live . . . You think she's got something?"

"Maybe," said Lieberman. "Doorman couldn't identify anyone who might have . . ."

"You think she's got anything?" Hughes repeated.

"Not that hard to get into the building," said Lieberman. "Someone got our Jules in. You know what we say in Yiddish?"

"No," said Hughes. "How the hell would I know? What's more, I don't want to know. You see the papers? The *Sun-Times*? Page eight. Nothing much, but they've got it. No television. Least none I saw or heard about. You?"

Hanrahan and Lieberman both shook their heads no.

"Bring the bum in here," said Hughes.

Hanrahan got up and left the interrogation room.

"Place smells like piss," said Hughes.

"It is piss," said Lieberman. "Novotny had a guy in here—"

"Abe," said Hughes, looking at the door and then across at Lieberman. "Your partner fucked up. He's on the bottle hard. Don't answer. I been there and back with a whole string, Dysan. You remember Dysan?"

"I remember Dysan?" Lieberman said.

"Got his partner killed," Hughes whispered. "You know what it takes to get a cop booted? Shit, you know. But I'm thinking about it, Abe. I'm thinking serious. You going to back me if it comes down?"

Lieberman was saved from answering by the opening of the door.

Jules Van Beeber came in with Hanrahan behind. Jules had been cleaned up, not much, but washed, shaved, and given clean clothes from the barrel in the closet. Nestor Briggs, whose father was a barber, had even cut his hair. Jules looked like a new person, but the new person wasn't much of an improvement over the old one.

"Van Beeber," Hughes said.

"Schubert," said Jules.

"Your name is Schubert?" asked Hughes.

"No, on your cup, Franz Schubert," said Jules the Walker, pointing at Hughes's coffee cup.

Hughes looked disgusted.

"He does that a lot," said Lieberman.

Jules looked at the captain, eyes trying to focus.

"You hear me, Van Beeber?" Hughes asked.

"I hear you," said Van Beeber, leaning against the wall and closing his eyes. "It's day. I don't do day very long."

"I've seen you around the streets near my place," Hughes said. "Look at me, man."

Van Beeber opened his eyes and looked at Hughes.

"You kill her, Jules?" Hughes asked, moving around the

94

table toward Jules, who would have slumped to the floor if Hanrahan hadn't reached over and pulled him up by the collar.

"Yes," said Van Beeber. "My wife. She irked me. I hit her. Back of the card shop. I don't know when. Elsie was her name or Kate. No, Maureen. Kate's my sister. Elsie's the Borden cow."

"You killed your wife?" asked Lieberman.

Van Beeber shook his head.

"You said you didn't want us to tell your wife?" said Hanrahan.

"I'm a little confused by life," said Van Beeber, trying to shake his head.

"We all are," said Lieberman, "but we don't all kill our wives. Jules, think. Did you really kill your wife?"

Jules the Walker laughed. "That's why you arrested me," he said. "Don't you know . . . Where's my lamp? No, I remember, Izzy, two bucks."

"Get him out of here," said Hughes.

Hanrahan opened the door with his left hand and kept a firm grip on Jules's collar with his right. When Jules and Hanrahan were gone, Hughes said, "You think maybe the son of a bitch really killed his wife?"

"Who knows?" said Lieberman. "I'll run a check."

Hughes smiled, clenched his fist, and shook it.

"All right," he said. "If he did it once, we got him on this one if we want him."

"I don't—" Lieberman began.

"Lieberman," Hughes warned, "I'm in a good mood now. It won't last but you don't want to cut it short. I checked your sheet this morning when you were sleeping in. You two have an outstanding seven-eleven robbery, a home invasion, an assault with intent, and two other murders, one gang related, the other domestic. You don't have enough work I've got a long list for you and some of them you wouldn't like at all."

"I'll check the story," said Lieberman, and Hughes went through the door.

Lieberman went to the barred window and looked out

on Clark Street. There was a concrete playground across the street beyond the scrawny trees in little patches of soil embedded in stone in front of the station. Four kids were playing basketball. Their shirts were off. Lieberman watched. When he was a kid, his high school team, the Marshall Commandos, had set a record, won a hundred straight games, a record never equaled. A team of Jewish kids, mostly short Jewish kids, and they still held the record. Maish Lieberman was on that team. Maish Lieberman hardly ever got in a game, but he was on that team and his picture, along with the ten others, hung on the wall of Maish's deli. Abe had gone to every game his older brother had played in.

The door opened behind him but Lieberman didn't turn.

"I told Nestor to book him material witness and possible suspect," said Hanrahan. "Sheridan's off for the weekend."

Hanrahan moved next to Lieberman at the window and looked out at the kids playing basketball.

"You wanna check with Michigan? Holland police," Lieberman said.

"Skinny kid's not bad," said Hanrahan.

"Team game's gone," sighed Lieberman turning from the window. "Everything's one on one. Let's call Michigan before our Jules confesses to every open murder from Cal City to Prague."

The squad room was empty when Lieberman went to his desk, empty and hot. There was a message taped to the telephone from Nestor Briggs. A man had called four times. Left no name. No number. The man had said it was about what happened yesterday. The man had said he would see Lieberman about what happened to "her." Two workmen were taking apart the air conditioning vent and talking about the pennant race and the Cubs's chances at the play-offs. Lieberman had some thoughts on the subject but he called home instead.

"It's not fun here, Lieberman," Bess said. "I'm schlepping kids, listening to Lisa complain, canceling, calling, hauling."

"You love it," said Lieberman. "You're needed."

"Don't psychoanalyze," said Bess.

"Part of the job," he said. "I'm picking up from Maish's for breakfast tomorrow so don't stop at the Bagel Boys or the Kosher."

"What time you coming home?" Bess said.

"When I can," he said. "How's Lisa?"

"Kvetching, brooding, drinking coffee," said Bess. "You know."

"Keep pouring and listening. I'll relieve you when I've rid the city of crime. Should have that done by seven. Kids?"

"Dropped them at the library. They're showing *Roger Rabbit* again," said Bess. "Kids don't read at libraries anymore, Lieberman. They watch movies."

"Could be worse," he said.

"Could be worse," she agreed. "Rabbi Wass called. Renovation committee meeting tonight at eight."

"He's a rabbi," said Lieberman with a sigh, watching the air conditioning men argue. "He's not supposed to be making calls on Shabbas."

"Levan called for him," said Bess. "What's the difference?"

"God's watching," said Lieberman. "God has a sense of humor."

"Get home when you can," said Bess. "I'm making leftover brisket."

Lieberman hung up and looked at the air conditioning men and over at Hanrahan, who was on the phone at his desk across the room. They were partners. They should have been together, but shift changes had messed up the beautiful floor plan laid out by Central when the building opened. Central never talked to any working cops when they designed a new space. They designed from memory and the imaginations of kid architects who grew up on reruns of *Baretta*.

"We got a bingo," called Hanrahan across the room.

Lieberman and the air conditioning men looked at him.

"Damned if there isn't an outstanding on Van Beeber," said Hanrahan. "Wife was a murder victim, blunt instrument, nineteen seventy-nine. Our Jules was nowhere to be found. Prime suspect. Michigan'll want him."

The air conditioning men listened attentively and whispered to each other.

"Why aren't you smiling, Father Murphy?" called Lieberman. "We can tell Hughes the case is a wrap. We can tie Jules the Walker up in a bow."

"He didn't kill Valdez, Rabbi," said Hanrahan.

"He didn't do it, Murph," agreed Lieberman.

"I'll go back to her building," said Hanrahan.

"I'll find the boxer," said Lieberman.

Before he left for the afternoon, Lieberman told Sergeant Nestor Briggs that if the man who called saying he wanted to talk about what happened to the woman yesterday, he should try to get the man's name or a phone number.

"Got it," said Briggs.

Briggs was about Lieberman's age, a sack of a man who had once been chest heavy, but the weight had dropped to his middle. Briggs had an unfortunate purple birthmark on his forehead, not the big Gorbachev kind, a little one shaped uncannily like the head of Bob Hope in profile. Nestor's nickname was, in fact, "Bob." Briggs lived alone in an apartment two blocks from the station. He put in double hours and never asked for overtime. Nestor didn't like being alone in his apartment. Because Nestor was a bore, he had no friends, but Nestor was a prime resource, for Nestor Briggs remembered everything and everyone.

The Empire Athletic Club was on Chicago Avenue just far enough west to be out of the Rush Street cheap glitter aura and just far enough east to be out of the area where none but the down-and-out would wander after dark. Lieberman had been here before. He had been through the double wooden doors before with the painting of two boxing-gloved hands shaking just above them. There was enough wrist in the picture to show that one hand was black and the other white.

Lieberman had been through these doors when his old man had taken him there to watch Henry Armstrong work out.

"That," Harry Lieberman had whispered to his son, "is the best fighter pound for pound that ever lived." Of course,

Harry Lieberman said this in Yiddish, which embarrassed his son. Harry could speak a bit of English, enough to get by when the sight-seeing goyim in Jew Town wandered into the store for a hot dog, a chocolate phosphate, some fries, and a good gawk. Abe had hated working Sundays in the place. He liked weeknights and the regular customers, the locals, liked the smell of onions, steamed rolls, and grilled or boiling dogs, but he didn't like being looked at by the customers, didn't like having them point to the yarmulke perched on his father's head when his father worked the grill on Sundays.

Abe Lieberman had developed his dryness early. Abe had frequently glanced at himself in the mirror as he washed his hands behind the curtain that separated himself, Maish, and his old man from the customers who bought a ringside ticket for thirty cents to Jew Town with a hot dog, fries, and a drink thrown in. In the mirror Abe had practiced his look of amused boredom. He had perfected that look, worn it, and made it his own.

Now, as he glanced at himself in the full-length mirror at the top of the landing outside the main door, he saw the face of a far-from-young man who appeared to know a hell of a lot more of life than Abe Lieberman.

Lieberman opened the door and was greeted by the smell of sweat and the sounds of a heavy bag being pummeled and a light bag being rata-tat-tated. A big sign on the wall, red letters on white, shouted NO SMOKING but Lieberman knew that in this business, kings and one-eyed jacks could smoke big cigars wherever they went.

In ring two in the dark corner of the Empire a big black heavyweight, in shorts and a T-shirt, was doing some serious shadow boxing. In ring one, where it had always been, near the bank of floor-to-ceiling windows, a white-haired old man in a gray sweat suit was jabbing a broom handle at a young man in a red sweat suit wearing boxing gloves and head gear. The young man's job was to use his hands to keep from getting wood in the face. He was doing fine.

"Seen *Karate Kid* too many times, Old MacConnell," came a voice at Lieberman's elbow.

Lieberman turned and found himself looking at Whitey. Almost every boxing club and gym has a Whitey, someone who's been around since Mayor Cermak took a bullet in the thirties. Whitey is supposed to have a flat nose, slurred speech, and a rotten memory. People are supposed to humor Whitey, but this was no common Whitey. This one had never been in the ring except to tell an old guy named Sturges how to mop it up. This Whitey was a philosopher who had been profiled in the Chicago *Tribune* magazine a dozen years ago, an ex-lawyer who loved boxing and when his wife died had sold his house and bought the Empire. Whitey knew everything about boxing. He knew all the middleweight lefties since Irish Jimmy Morgan. He knew *Ring Magazine*'s end-of-the-year top ten in every weight division going back to 1934, the year of his birth. And he knew from just watching a fighter spar if he was a winner or loser. But most important, Whitey, who probably gave himself the nickname, kept the place clean.

"Lieberman the cop," Whitey said, looking him over. "Last time I saw you was . . . ?"

"Bad apple heroin drop part-time trainer, Sonny Warsham," said Lieberman.

"Drug store cruiserweight," said Whitey. "Lousy trainer. Sparred with Leon Spinks way back when. Now he's doing three to five in Joliet."

Whitey was wearing jeans, a white shirt, a silk tie, and a serious grin. Lieberman took Whitey's extended hand.

"Good to see you again," said Whitey. "Picked a bad day. No talent around."

"Silk," said Lieberman. "I called about an hour ago and someone said he was here."

"Dressing room," said Whitey. "But even if you'd made it earlier, you wouldn't have seen much. Escamillo saves it for the crowds."

The Empire had both a locker room and a dressing room. They were exactly the same but the dressing room was reserved for those who were now ranked, had once been ranked, or stood a reasonably good shot at being ranked by anybody anywhere.

"How's he look?" asked Lieberman.

Whitey shrugged. "Too smart," he said as the guy in ring one let out a groan from a broom jab to the midsection. "Too sane. Good looks. Knows it won't last and looking for ways he can make a living outside. No desperation. All the talent you could ask for. Trains fine, but . . . what're you gonna do?"

"He's scheduled for . . . ?" Lieberman asked, watching a tiny Latino kid with a little mustache pound the heavy bag.

"Stickney Welles, the man with the bells, three weeks from today on *Top Rank Boxing*, main event," said Whitey. "Welles will be ringing out the month on his back. Our Escamillo will be hot stuff for a while, but the long haul . . . forget it."

"Thanks, Whitey," said Lieberman, heading toward the dressing room.

"We do have a bantam worth watching," Whitey called after him. "Jewish kid, would you believe it? Russian. Name's Yakov Bitt. Bantams don't draw but this kid— eight and the big zero with six KOs and only one bum in the lot. He'll be on the undercard for the Silk-Welles match."

Lieberman waved to Whitey and went through the dressing room door where he found Escamillo Silk fully dressed in neatly pressed slacks, a wrinkleless short-sleeved yellow button-down shirt, and a yellow, taupe, and gray paisley tie. Silk was brushing his hair in a mirror above a basin against the wall. The floor had been carpeted since Lieberman had last been here. Lieberman didn't like it. The Empire was turning into one of those places Cher advertises on television.

"Real silk," said Escamillo Silk, looking at Lieberman in the mirror. "Nothing gaudy."

He put the comb in his pocket and turned to face Lieberman with a perfect white-toothed smile. Silk was about Lieberman's height and weight but the distribution of that weight made the difference. Escamillo Silk was taut and muscular.

"Silk," said Silk, running his thumb down his tie. "Trademark. You know?"

"I saw the first four rounds of your fight with Ty Turner," said Lieberman.

"Yeah?" said Silk, adjusting his shirt sleeves and checking the creases in his pants. "Four rounds?"

"I was with a fella who left," said Lieberman, looking around the room.

"Why'd he leave?" asked Silk. "Round five I—"

"I don't know," said Lieberman. "He didn't tell me. I was following him on a drug setup."

The smile did not leave Escamillo Silk's face but it dimmed from 250 to 50 watts.

"I thought you were the promoter from ESPN," said Silk. "I'm waiting for a promoter. I don't use shit in my nose, arms, ears, eyes, mouth, or anywhere. Anyone tells you I do is a liar. Test me."

"Estralda Valdez is dead," said Lieberman.

"I know," said Silk. "Whitey told me. He read it in the papers."

"When did you see her last?" asked Lieberman.

"When did I . . . ? Wait. I need a lawyer or something? You plannin' to jerk me around?"

"Yeah," said Lieberman. "I'm going to lock the door and beat a confession out of you. When did you see her last?"

"What's today?"

"Saturday."

"Last Monday," said Silk. "You wanna sit?"

"No, I wanna listen."

"Last Monday," Silk repeated. "Took her to dinner at Escargot. You know Escargot?"

"Heard about it," said Lieberman.

"Dinner with Oprah's people," he said. "Talk about putting me on a show about handsome athletes and women. Thought Estralda would look good at dinner. Put them in the mood."

Silk laughed.

"Maybe we should continue this some other time," said Lieberman. "I can see you're really broken up by Estralda's death."

"Hey, my man," said Silk, putting up his right hand, palm

102

up, as if he wanted to touch gloves with Lieberman before the battle really began. "I'm sorry someone did her. All right? She was a smart lady. Good skin. Liked her work. She looked good places I go. But we weren't talkin' two bedrooms in Oak Park and kids named Carlos junior."

"Carlos junior?" Lieberman asked.

"My real name," said Silk, hooking his thumbs in his belt. Lieberman had it now. Escamillo, or Carlos, was posing. He was trying to look like an ad in *Gentlemen's Quarterly*.

"Escamillo's the bullfighter in *Carmen*," Silk explained. "All the papers know my real name's Carlos Mendenarez."

"Choice inside information," said Lieberman. "Estralda tell you she was worried about anything? Some customer?"

"No," said Silk. "She talked about moving back to Texas, talked about . . . Called her sister and said something about Frank something. I got a good memory. I work on it. Read that book by what's his name and—"

"Where is this sister?"

"Who knows?" said Silk with a handsome grin. "She didn't say."

"Where does Estralda's mother live?"

"Mother? Who knows she got a mother?" said Silk, moving close to Lieberman and whispering, "and who really cares?"

"I do," said Lieberman.

"Lupe," said Silk. "Wait. She said her sister's name was Guadalupe and the guy who wrote the memory book was Lorraine Lucas, something like that. Can I go now?"

"No," said Lieberman. "Where were you Friday night? Say ten to after midnight?"

"I knew it," said Silk, putting his hands behind his head as if he were about to go down on the floor for therapeutic sit-ups. "You're looking for pasty."

"Patsy," Lieberman corrected.

Silk pulled a small white notebook from his pocket and a little click pen. He wrote quickly and he silently mouthed "patsy" as he wrote.

"Thanks," said Silk, putting the pen and notebook away. "I was born in Juarez. You hear a accent?"

"No," said Lieberman. "You are eloquent."

"Eloquent?"

"You talk good," said Lieberman. "Talk, and don't write 'eloquent' in your notebook till you're alone. Friday night. Ten to midnight."

"Home, with the wife and kids," said Silk. "Ask them. Ask my mother-in-law and her boyfriend. They were there. We watched a tape. Woody Allen."

"Too bad Estralda couldn't make it," said Lieberman.

Silk shook his head.

"You mean a crack there?" he asked. "It's not like that. I got an image. You know what I'm saying? I can't be the guy with the kids who goes home and watches Clint Eastwood on the tube with the little lady. Notoriety gets you noticed."

"My son-in-law calls that a tautology," said Lieberman. "I'll spell it for you. Look it up. And the other word was 'eloquent.' You can go now."

"It's that I'm late," said Silk, walking to the dressing room door.

"We'll talk again," said Lieberman with a very small smile.

"How'd you like the four rounds you saw, me and Turner?"

"You were lyrical," said Lieberman.

"Thanks," said Silk, looking around for a mirror and finding it on the wall near the door. "I hope you find the guy who punctured Estralda. She was a class broad, you know?"

With that eulogy Silk went through the door. He didn't hear Lieberman answer "I know."

Lieberman was at the T & L by four. It was Saturday. The sky was dark and smelling of rain but none had fallen. The Ancient Atheist contingent of the Alter Cockers was in session in the booth where Lieberman, Hanrahan, and Estralda Valdez had sat. Most of the Alter Cockers had to stay home or go to services till sundown. Al Bloombach, Gert's brother, held atheist court with Morrie Stoltzer and

Howie Chen. Howie, strictly speaking, wasn't an atheist, but whatever he practiced wasn't in session on Saturdays.

Two men and a woman sat at another booth. They were talking Russian. Russians were taking over the neighborhood, which was all right, but they fooled the old timers. Because of their accents, old timers thought the Russians could speak Yiddish. None of them could. Because they were Jews, old timers thought they would be religious. Few of them were. The influx had begun about eight years ago, but the old timers had never adjusted. As far as Lieberman was concerned, the Russians were good for the neighborhood. Most of them were well educated. Few of them committed crimes. Most of them wanted to be accepted and to get rich or at least have a house in Glenview.

Maish was talking to Manuel the cook, a grizzled little man who had learned the art of Jewish cooking as an observant bus boy at the Bagel Restaurant. Maish saw his brother and turned to nod.

"Coffee?" called Maish.

"Why not?" said Lieberman, nodding at Al Bloombach in the booth and sitting at the end of the counter near the cash register away from the Russians. Thunder rolled. Lieberman turned to see if the rain had started. It hadn't but it looked more like midnight than afternoon.

Maish brought the coffee and a large brown paper bag, which he placed on the counter next to the cup.

"Corned beef, lox, cream cheese, bagels—garlic, onion, sesame—and three smoked fish," said Maish.

"How much?" said Lieberman.

"You won fiftieth prize in the Publisher's Clearing House," said Maish, wiping his hands on his apron. "Carry-out from the T & L. Tell Lisa it's from Uncle Maish. Make me a big man for a few bucks."

"You got it," said Lieberman, drinking his coffee.

"Want the radio? Wanna hear the game? We're playin' the Giants. Sutcliffe started," Maish said. "Game might still be on."

"Yeah," said Lieberman. "But I gotta get home."

Last year Lieberman had taken his grandson, Barry, to a

Cub game. Free passes from an old friend of Lieberman's who worked in the Cub front office. Rick Sutcliffe had started that game against the Mets. Barry and Lieberman had been sitting in the front row on the third-base side where Sutcliffe was warming up. Barry was wearing his Cubs cap and infielder's glove. Sutcliffe had walked over to Barry and thrown him the warm-up ball. From that moment on, Rick Sutcliffe, who by the way went the distance and won the game three to two, could do no wrong.

The Russians in the booth started to laugh at something. Lieberman sipped his coffee and looked at them. The brown bag on the counter smelled of memories.

"Sorry about the woman," said Maish. "Notice I said woman. I'm getting modern, not like the Cockers. I didn't say 'girl.' Not too old to learn at sixty-six. Yetta tells me that all the time."

"You're not sixty-six, Maish," said Lieberman, finishing his coffee. "You're sixteen and I'm ten and Willie Brochesceu is about to beat the shit out of me on the way home from school behind Kuppenheimer's factory. And you come rolling behind him sweating from basketball practice and land on his back. Knock the wind out of him, hit him in the face with your math book."

"Science book," Maish said, looking into space.

"Like yesterday," said Lieberman. "Broke his nose and arm. Kicked you out of school for a month."

"That was a great month," said Maish. "You going good-old-days on me, Avrum? They weren't that goddamn good. Little apartment full of people, rats. Polish kids across nineteenth like Willie waiting for you. Negro—black—kids across Crawford giving you looks if you crossed. Had to almost use a map to get safely to the Jewish People's Institute on Douglas. Good old days are, thank God, gone."

"Maish," Al Bloombach called. "Refills."

Maish nodded. The clouds outside rumbled and crashed.

"How's Yetta's kidney?" said Lieberman.

"Still pumping," said Maish, moving for the coffee pot.

"I'll stop by tomorrow," Lieberman said. He stood up and took his package.

Maish nodded and moved with his coffee toward the booth of the atheists.

The rain had started to fall when Lieberman stepped into the street. Canopies were coming down in front of Kim the Korean's Devon Television/VCR Repair Shop, and the Dollar Store, also owned by Kim. The Pistoki brothers were hauling in their fruit displays, and someone in one of the doorways was watching Abe Lieberman walk slowly to his Buick and get in. Lieberman adjusted the mirror to see the person in the doorway between Discount Toys and Devon Animal World, but whoever it was was well back, hidden by a display of Nintendo games and a dirty window. Whoever it was had also been outside the Clark Street Station when Lieberman came out earlier.

Lieberman turned on his windshield wipers and pulled out into traffic as the clouds exploded like a water balloon. Whoever was in the doorway, a man, ran for a nearby car. Lieberman could have taken a quick left and another left into the alley next to the barber shop to get rid of the tail, but it would have been pointless. The man knew where Lieberman worked and where he hung out. The man might also be the one who had called four times about "what happened to her yesterday." It could have been many other things. It could have been any of six dozen people Lieberman had put away or been on top of for a quarter of a century.

Lieberman pushed the button on the radio and caught Harry Caray saying that the game was tied in the twelfth and delayed because of rain.

Instead of turning right and heading home Lieberman turned left and drove slowly down a side street. The man followed half a block back. The rain was coming harder now. Lieberman knew where he was going. He pulled next to a fire hydrant between a pickup truck and an old Datsun. He got out slowly, giving his pursuer time to find a parking space. Lieberman looked neither right or left as he locked the car. The rain was coming in warm sheets now.

Soaked through, Lieberman walked slowly to the passageway between two twelve-flat apartment buildings, went down the stairs into darkness, and walked to the end of the cool cement corridor where there was a doorway to the furnace room. Six years earlier Abe and Hanrahan had nailed the building janitor in this room with a stack of stereos he had stolen from apartments in the neighborhood. Lieberman fished out his semidry handkerchief, wiped his nose, took out his gun, and waited, listening to the rain and thunder. Lieberman had always loved the rain, felt protected by it, excused by it. He had never loved the outdoors. The rain gave him reason to remain inside, blanketed by shower.

The footsteps were quick. They came down the three cement stairs and started down the cement passageway. Lieberman stepped out, gun leveled at the dark figure dripping in front of him.

"Hold it there," he said. "Hands behind your head."

"I've got to talk to you," said the man, his voice trembling. "I've got to talk about what happened between her and me. I . . . I did it."

Lieberman put his gun away and stepped toward the figure.

"I didn't have the nerve to face her, you," the man went on.

"Whose car are you driving?" Lieberman asked.

"Rental. Mine's in the shop."

"I've got a dry sweat suit in the trunk," Lieberman said to his son-in-law. "Let's go someplace for a cup of coffee and dry out."

7

Hanrahan felt better. He didn't feel good but he did feel better as he sat parked in front of the Black Moon Restaurant on Sheridan Road watching the rain waterfall down his front window.

Confessing to the Whiz had helped. Now he was doing something that might help even more. He looked over at the high-rise. A cab pulled up to the door and two people, a man and a woman, ducked under the concrete canopy of the Michigan Towers as the doorman rose inside. They went through the revolving door and laughed. Hanrahan let out a chuckle. He didn't know why.

The Black Moon Restaurant was open for dinner. It was still early. No customers inside, but he could see Iris. He was in a no parking zone so it had been no problem getting directly in front of the restaurant. Hanrahan, fifty-two years old and a grandfather, was nervous. His first plan had been to go into the Black Moon and talk to Iris. Now he decided to work first. When a break in the traffic came, Hanrahan took it and pulled into the driveway of the high-rise. He parked as close to the door as he could and ran in.

"Can't leave your car there," said the fully uniformed doorman, the same black man who had been on duty the night before.

"Police," said Hanrahan, showing his badge. "Saw you last night."

The doorman, Billy Tarton, nodded. "I got no more answers man," he said.

"Woman who got in the cab last night before I came running over," Hanrahan said. "Tell me about her."

"I told the other guy," said Tarton with a sigh. "I didn't see her good. Hat over her eyes. Sunglasses, went right out. Cab was waiting. Cabby right with her with her bags. She didn't say nothing, do nothing."

"She white or black?" said Hanrahan.

"White," he said. "Couldn't tell her age but she wasn't old. Young mostly. If I remember anything else, I'll call you, but there's nothin' more to remember. Zip. Nada. Nothing. You made a trip for nothing."

"I didn't come here to talk to you," Hanrahan said.

A bolt of lightning cracked the sky.

"Does like that in Florida almost every day in the summer," said the doorman. "Used to live in Lakeland. Thinking of going back."

Hanrahan grunted and pointed to the door. Billy Tarton pressed the button to open it and Hanrahan went in. Behind him a soaked woman jogger pushed through the revolving door panting, her dark hair plastered down over her forehead and across her face. Hanrahan moved toward the elevators.

He had a simple plan. He would knock on every door in the building and ask everyone they hadn't already talked to and some that they had what he, she, or they knew about Estralda Valdez or Jules Van Beeber or the fall of the Berlin Wall. He would ask until he was sure no one had anything to tell him. He would ask because in spite of the absolution given him in confession Bill Hanrahan still believed that he was responsible for the death of Estralda Valdez.

In the front seat of his car while the rain thump-thudded on the roof, Lieberman took off his sopping jacket, shirt, and tie and put on a blue sweat shirt with CHICAGO POLICE DEPARTMENT printed on it in white block letters. In the back seat, Todd struggled into a plain gray sweat shirt half a size too small.

"You want a bagel?" Lieberman asked.

"I can't eat," said Todd, forcing his arm through a sleeve.

"Then let's talk while I eat one," said Lieberman.

"'Long am I silent. Struck down by disasters exceeding speech and question,'" said Todd, slumping back and running his hands over his wet hair. Todd was an associate professor of comparative literature at Northwestern University. Todd was a specialist in Greek tragedy.

"That's a line from . . . ?" Lieberman said, fishing a bagel from the bag and releasing the smell of corned beef.

"Aeschylus, *The Persians*," said Todd.

"Sure you won't have a bagel, half a bagel?"

"No," said Todd.

"'Better a bagel in the rain than a pain in the ass,'" said Lieberman. "Papodopolus said that. He's a Greek too. Ran a little diner near the train yards till he did in his girlfriend with a variety of kitchen utensils. Actually, he didn't say 'bagel.' He said 'bun,' but I'm allowed poetic license, right?"

Todd didn't answer. Lieberman examined his son-in-law in the rearview mirror. Todd was thirty-five, a little on the thin side for Lieberman's taste, sandy haired and long of face.

"'The load I bear can never be laid down,'" said Todd. "'And would you add to it by lightening yours?'"

"Sophocles?" tried Lieberman.

"Euripides. *Iphigenia in Tauris*," said Todd without enthusiasm.

"A joke," said Lieberman, turning in the seat to point half a bagel at Todd. "Papodopolus told it when we took him in. Use the word 'Euripides' in a sentence?"

"Abe—" Todd began.

"Euripides pants, I breaka you neck," said Lieberman straightfaced.

Todd looked at the serious sad face of his father-in-law and groaned. Then he let out a small laugh.

"That's terrible," he said.

"I'll make a deal," said Lieberman. "I stop telling Papodopolus stories and you stop quoting dead Greeks."

"Papodopolus is alive?"

"Doing life in Joliet," said Lieberman, shaking his head. "You want to talk now?"

"I didn't do it," said Todd. "I talked to Anastasia Holt, sure, even had lunch with her a couple of times. She's a Plato scholar, but I never touched her, never—"

"Lisa doesn't think you did," said Lieberman.

"She doesn't? I thought—"

"If you're thinking of quoting another dead Greek now, forget it or get the hell out of my car," said Lieberman. "She says you don't spend time with her. You think about your work. You look right through her. You make it clear you'd rather be at work. You never ask her what she thinks or feels. She's a professional without a profession. She feels like a nonperson, the days going by, the kids getting older and she getting no place. She had seven-ten Graduate Record Exam grades in both verbal and quantitative, which, she says, were higher than yours. You following this?"

"Yes," said Todd, brushing his wet hair back with one hand.

"Good, because I was up most of last night listening to it," said Lieberman. "And I'll probably be up half the night tonight hearing it again."

"She's right," said Todd. "It's all clichés but it's right. The maddening thing about clichés is that they're so often right. That's how they became clichés. Do you like me, Abe?"

"Have you been drinking?" asked Lieberman, wiping his hands on a tissue from the box in his glove compartment.

"Yes, a little. You think I normally follow policemen and cry in front of them? Do you like me, Abe?"

"Yes," said Lieberman.

"Bess is disappointed that I'm not Jewish," said Todd.

The rain had suddenly ceased its waterfall noise and turned into a strong patter, which gradually eased to a moist whisper as they spoke.

"She got over it," said Lieberman.

"What should I do?" whispered Todd. "I love Lisa, the kids."

"Go back home. Watch the fights on television. Read a science fiction novel. Take a long bath. Better yet, you ever see *The Man Who Could Work Miracles*? With Roland Young, the guy who played Topper?"

"Abe—"

"Let her think it over, Todd," said Lieberman. "Don't push it. Call our house and say you'd like to know how she is. Tell me or Bess to tell her you love her. Tell us to tell her you want to see a marriage counselor."

"I can't just—"

"I know a good one," said Lieberman. "Levan's daughter-in-law, Darla. In Evanston, not far from you."

"The kids," said Todd.

"The kids can go too. Talk to them. Tell them you love them. They can use a few days' vacation. Let me tell you a story. When I was kid, maybe eight, nine, my parents got in a fight. Maish went to my Aunt Sadie's for the night. My older cousin Lenore took me out to a movie. Never forget it, *Dr. Cyclops*, hell of a movie. Albert Dekker was bald, big thick glasses. He made people little in the jungle. After the movie Lenore took me home. My mother and father were still fighting. Lenore took me back to the movies, a double feature, *The Cat and the Canary* with Bob Hope and *Charlie Chan at the Opera*. When we got home just before midnight, my mother and father were having coffee and holding hands. I'll never forget that day."

"Is there a point to that story, Abe?"

"Hey, you came to me. One of the prices you pay is listening to me remember when I was a kid," said Lieberman. "There's a point. Let it alone. Lisa's like my mother. She wants to come to you she'll work it out and come to you."

"Your story didn't have anything to do with that," said Todd after a sigh.

"I forgot I was talking to a professor," said Lieberman. "The point of the story was you should postpone feeling guilty and go get a tape of something and relax and wait. Nobody waits anymore. I'll work on Lisa. You call later. I want to go home now, take a shower, eat some of this corned beef, and play Yahtzee with your kids."

"OK," said Todd, opening the door, his crumpled jacket in one hand.

"You want a corned beef sandwich for the road?" asked Lieberman.

Todd shrugged. Lieberman dug in the bag and put together a corned beef sandwich by tearing open a bagel and sticking in a stack of meat. Todd took the sandwich and closed the back door.

"Thanks," said Todd.

"You're welcome," answered Lieberman.

The rain had completely stopped.

"I love Lisa," said Todd, biting into the sandwich as a Toyota splashed by.

"So do I," said Lieberman. "Go home."

Lieberman left his son-in-law standing in the street, his wrists sticking out of the sleeves of the tight sweat shirt, his hands around a corned beef sandwich. Five minutes later Lieberman pulled up in front of his house, got out with his bag, went to his front door, opened it with a key, and stepped in to say, "I'm here."

"Grandpop the cop," said Melisa, looking up from the television set.

"Hi," said Barry, looking away from the television only long enough to smile.

"What're you watching?" asked Lieberman, kicking off his shoes.

"*Lifestyles of the Rich and Famous*," said Barry.

"They're doing the guy who plays the monster in those movies," said Melisa.

"Sounds very educational," said Lieberman. He moved into the kitchen where Bess and Lisa sat whispering.

"Lieberman," Bess said, looking up. "You been jogging in the rain?"

He put the bag on the table, kissed his wife and daughter, and sat down.

"I've been solving the problems of the world," said Lieberman, "and it has made me hungry."

"Eat fast," Bess said. "You've got fifteen minutes to get to the synagogue. There's a meeting of the Committee to form a Fund-Raising Committee."

Bill Hanrahan was tired. He had knocked on forty-three doors and received twenty answers, a damned good percentage, which he attributed to people staying home or coming home because of the storm. He took pages of notes and found probable cause for a narcotics arrest in three apartments. Eight people refused to let him in. He talked to five of them through closed doors and persuaded three of the refuseniks to let him in. A few he talked to remembered seeing Estralda Valdez, at least a few admitted it. He had the feeling that some of the married men had noticed her but didn't want to say so.

He struck silver twice. A pair of men in their forties, definitely gay, said that they had seen Estralda Valdez talking several times to a woman named Gwen who lived on the ninth floor. Hanrahan, who had been working his way down, went back up to the apartment of Gwen Dysan on nine. He had already talked to her, a quiet woman in her midtwenties with her hair combed straight back, her skin clear, her glasses too large for her face.

"Another few questions if you don't mind, Miss Dysan," Hanrahan said with his most winning smile as the woman opened her door.

"I told you I didn't know her," Gwen Dysan said nervously.

"You knew her, Miss Dysan," said Hanrahan gently.

"I didn't," she said.

"I can continue this with you down at the station if need be," he lied. "I don't want to."

"Come in," she said, stepping back.

The apartment was efficient, furniture modern, not comfortable looking, easy to move out of fast. Gwen Dysan left the door open and folded her arms, not defiantly but defensively.

"How well did you know her?" Hanrahan asked.

"Not well," she said.

"Why didn't you tell me you knew her?"

"She . . . I knew she was a prostitute," said Gwen Dysan. "She told me. I was embarrassed I guess. I didn't know her all that well."

"You liked her?" he asked.

"Yes," said Gwen, looking him in the eyes.

115

"She talk about men, people she knew?"

"No," said Gwen. "She talked about her family. I told her about mine."

"Her family?" Hanrahan asked, trying to keep from sounding particularly interested. "Father, mother . . . ?"

"Her father is dead," said Gwen. "Her mother and brother."

"They live in Chicago?"

"Yes," she said.

"You know where?"

"South Side somewhere. I think she said Ogden Avenue. I'm not sure."

"You think Mrs. Valdez knows what happened to her daughter? It didn't even make the ten o'clock news on television."

"Her name isn't Valdez," said Gwen Dysan. "It's Vegas. She wasn't what you think. I mean Estralda. She was—"

"I knew her," said Hanrahan.

"We talked," said Gwen Dysan softly.

"Talked, yes," said Hanrahan.

Gwen Dysan's sigh was enormous.

"I'm a Catholic," she said. "Your name is Irish. Are you a Catholic?"

"Yes," said Hanrahan.

"I work in a print shop," said the woman, looking out the open door into the empty corridor.

Hanrahan turned. There was no one there.

"I'm a secretary," she said. "My family is in North Dakota. I'll grow old and die a secretary in a print shop. Estralda said I was too pretty to do that."

Gwen Dysan looked at the policeman with wet eyes.

"You are," he said.

"She said I was pretty enough to do what she did, that I could make enough money in two years to buy a print shop or a beauty shop or a . . . I knew I couldn't do it."

"I know," said Hanrahan. "Anything else you can tell me? Anyone you know in the building who . . . ?"

"Nikki Morales," said Gwen Dysan softly. "Eighth floor. I don't know the apartment number. I've never gone down there. But Estralda talked about her. I know they were friends."

Jealousy echoed in her words.

"Did Estralda ever mention a sister, Lupe or Guadalupe?" Hanrahan began.

"No. Can you leave now?" asked Gwen Dysan.

Hanrahan considered pushing just a little, but the woman folded her arms and set her jaw in a way Hanrahan had encountered hundreds of times. He might have broken through it but it wasn't worth the effort, at least not now.

"Sure," he said, leaving the apartment.

The door didn't close behind him as he went for the elevator. He had a name, Vegas, and a neighborhood, and he remembered what Jules Van Beeber had said about Estralda saying something was under the house at her mother's house. He also had another tenant to check out, Nikki Morales on eight. He had rung every bell and knocked on every door on eight, but none of the people who had answered were Nikki Morales.

Hanrahan went back to the doorman, who was sitting at his desk and watching the video monitor that showed the garage entrance. Billy Tarton sat up when Hanrahan came through the door. Tarton didn't smile, but he did look up with an eager to please curiosity.

"Nikki Morales," said Hanrahan.

"Eight-ten," answered the doorman. "But she's not in. Went out early, carrying a couple of suitcases."

"Where was she going?" asked Hanrahan, glancing through the window toward the Black Moon Restaurant.

The doorman shrugged.

"Said she'd be away a while," Tarton said. "But she'd be back for more of her things before she left town."

"What does she look like?"

"Morales?" Tarton said getting up. A car was pulling into the driveway and making the turn to stop in front of the entrance. "Good-looking lady. Lives alone."

He moved toward the door and adjusted his hat.

"Friend of Estralda Valdez?" asked Hanrahan.

"Who knows? Could be. Never saw them together. Or

maybe I did and don't remember," the doorman said, going out the door to help an old woman out of the backseat of a black Pontiac. The woman beamed at the doorman and touched his cheek. Billy Tarton smiled. Hanrahan wanted a drink, needed a drink.

The old woman came in on the doorman's arm.

"Gotta help Mrs. Dinkst to her apartment," he said.

Hanrahan nodded.

"Nikki Morales, she look anything like Estralda Valdez?" he asked as the doorman pushed the button to the inner lobby and moved slowly with Mrs. Dinkst on his arm.

"Maybe," said Tarton over his shoulder. "About the same height, weight, build. Miss Morales is a little younger, darker hair, maybe lighter skin. Who knows? You know what I mean?"

"I know," said Hanrahan, following the doorman and the old woman through the inner lobby door.

Hanrahan could have called it a day and gone out looking but he wanted to check every door where someone was home. He took the elevator up to the third floor and got out, leaving the doorman and the old lady behind him. On the third floor, Hanrahan knocked at the first door and found himself facing Captain Dale Hughes in YMCA shorts and a white T-shirt. Captain Dale Hughes was sweating. Captain Dale Hughes was obviously also in good shape. A door was open behind Hughes to Hanrahan's left. Inside it was a Nautilus machine or something that looked like one.

"Hanrahan, what do you want?" he said panting.

"Nothing," said Hanrahan. "I've been knocking on doors. Forgot you were on this—"

"You mean you hoped I wouldn't be behind one of the doors," said Hughes. "You could have asked the doorman where I lived and walked on by. Come in."

Hanrahan came in and Hughes closed the door.

"You want a cold drink? Iced tea?" asked Hughes.

"No thanks, Captain," said Hanrahan.

"I'll finish mine." Hughes moved through a door to his right and Hanrahan knew from the layout of the apartments he had been in that beyond the door was the kitchen. Hughes came back with a towel around his nack and a glass of iced tea in his hand. "Sure you don't want one?"

There were wedding pictures in the hallway. Hughes smiling in a tux, arm around the bride, his family surrounding the couple. Hughes took a sip and watched Hanrahan's eyes.

"I just talked to her, my wife," Hughes said. "Told her about Van Beeber. She'll come back home from her mother's tomorrow. Don't come back and talk to her. She thinks we have our killer."

"I understand," said Hanrahan.

"You and I and Lieberman don't think we do," said Hughes after a big satisfying gulp. "But we'll just keep that to ourselves. You keep looking but officially we've got our prime suspect. Understood?"

"Understood," said Hanrahan.

"You turn up anything, let me know. I'll give you support," said Hughes. "You fucked up, my man, but maybe you don't have to go Ward Seven over it. Sure you don't want a drink?"

"No, Captain," said Hanrahan. "There's a woman lives on eight who Estralda Valdez knew, name's Nikki Morales. You ever see her, you remember?"

"I don't know names," Hughes said, brushing sweat from his nose. "A building like this isn't one big happy family."

"This Nikki Morales packed up and left this morning," said Hanrahan.

"Shit," said Hughes, shaking his head. "You want to go in and check the apartment?"

"Yes sir," said Hanrahan. Suddenly the image of his mother at the stove looking into a pot of boiling beef came to him. He could almost smell the beef.

"You all right, Hanrahan?" asked Hughes.

"Yeah," said Hanrahan. "I'd like to get in there."

"You figure the Morales woman might be the one you saw getting in the cab?" asked Hughes. "The one dressed in Estralda Valdez's clothes?"

"It's something to try," said Hanrahan.

"It's something to try," agreed Hughes. "I'll give Judge Handelman a call. Go for the warrant. Handy maybe owes us one or two more. Nikki Morales, eight-ten?"

"Yes sir," said Hanrahan.

After a brief report on what he had found, Hanrahan managed to make his escape from the captain. He went through the remaining apartments, made nine more contacts, none of them yielding information, and walked across the street to the Black Moon Restaurant. The night had cooled from the rain and a breeze coming off of the lake. Hanrahan thought he owed himself a drink, but decided not to pay the debt.

He had missed the Saturday dinner rush. A few people were still eating, two couples at a back table, a pair of young women at a table in the front. He sat at a table where he could watch the entrance to Michigan Towers, smoothed the white cloth with his big hands, and looked up as Iris came out of the kitchen and saw him. She smiled and he smiled back.

"You want to order?" she asked.

"No," he said, then, "I guess. What's good?"

"Moo shu pork," said Iris. "You look tired."

"Working," said Hanrahan. He ran his hand over his face. "I could use a bath and a shave."

"Last night," she said. "You were tired too?"

"I was drunk last night," he said. "Can you sit down?"

"No."

"I asked if you'd go out with me," he said. "I meant it. I'm sober now and I mean it."

"I said yes," she said. "I'll get your moo shu."

When she returned with his moo shu, Hanrahan said, "You know what I like about you?"

"No," Iris said, deftly laying out the thin pancake and spooning a line of shredded pork, bamboo shoots, and vegetables down its middle.

"You don't remind me of anyone," he said. "I mean that as a compliment."

"Then I feel complimented," she said. "I have never done this before."

She rolled the pancake up with two wooden spoons.

"You look as if you've been doing it all your life," he said.

"No," she said, laughing. "I don't mean moo shu. I mean, you know, going out with a man."

"You've never been out?" he said, looking down at the crepe-like creation in front of him. "Do I pick this up like a taco?"

"Yes," she said. "I was married. My husband died. My father picked him out. I'm a grandmother."

"I'm a grandfather. You got pictures of the kids?"

Hanrahan ate, drank tea, and exchanged compliments with Iris over their grandchildren. He was looking at a picture of her grandchildren, Walter and Mary Ho, when the woman got out of the cab across the street. She was dressed differently and wore no hat. Her hair was not the same color it was the night before and she was dressed in a lightweight suit. The doorman made no connection between this woman and the woman who had pretended to be Estralda Valdez. Hanrahan, had he been looking, would have known. He would have known by her walk, the way she held her shoulders, her height, her weight. He had been on hundreds of stakeouts, watched men, women, and those of androgynous bent through binoculars and with the naked eye at long distances. He would have known, but he was looking at a photograph of two young children and smiling, not the smile of a man seeing the folly of life in general and his own in particular, but the smile of a man who was enjoying the moment.

When he did look up and out the window, the woman was gone. He wrote down Iris's address and arranged to pick her up at six on Monday, the day the Black Moon was closed. And then Bill Hanrahan went home. In the morning he would call Abe. In the morning, they would track down Estralda Valdez's mother. But first in the morning, Sunday morning, he would go to Mass at St. Bart's church. Hanrahan also considered giving his son in Canada a call. It was a little late for that, though. He would, he decided, give him a call tomorrow afternoon.

8

Lieberman was sure that if the Committee to Select a Renovation Committee meeting went on for one more hour he would be calling Irving Hamel, Irwin Rommel. He would let it slip out accidentally once and apologize. Then it would happen again and he would apologize again. Then, if God were watching as was His sacred duty, He would inform Irving Hamel that he should be quiet.

Irving was not a bad man, but he was an irritating one. He was also young, not yet forty, and a lawyer. He had all his hair and it was black. He wore contact lenses. He stood tall and worked out every morning at the Jewish Community Center on Touhy. His wife was beautiful. His two kids, a boy and a girl, were beautiful. Irving Hamel would one day be king of Denmark or at least the first Jewish mayor of Chicago or a Supreme Court chief justice, but right now he was a pain in the ass.

"People will not give for renovation," he said. "They want their name on a rock wall, something."

"The building committee has the rooms and the walls," said Syd Levan.

The three men and a woman were seated in the little library and conference room around the oak table. Rabbi Wass smiled knowingly at everything that was said. Syd Levan was dedicated to proving that nothing was possible. Ida Katzman sat looking intently at whoever spoke. As the oldest person in the room and the wealthiest member of the congregation, which was why she was in the room in the first place, Ida had certain rights, among them the right to ignore the proceedings. Ancient Ida Katzman appeared to understand almost nothing of what was going on. Whenever young Rabbi Wass spoke, Ida looked at him through her thick glasses in the hope that divine guidance would come from his lips. She was always disappointed.

"The furniture!" Lieberman tried. "We can put plaques on the furniture. This table right here has a plaque." He pointed at a bronze plate at the head of the table where he, as acting chair of the committee, sat looking glumly but hopefully at Irving Hamel.

"The building committee has asked for dedication rights for the furniture," said Rabbi Wass.

"The toilets," Lieberman said, looking at his watch and seeing that it was after ten and nothing had been settled.

"That's in bad taste," said Syd Levan.

"The toilets also belong to the building committee," said Rabbi Wass.

"Las Vegas Night," said Lieberman, who dreaded all fund-raising events.

"Last one lost two hundred dollars," said Hamel. "I was treasurer."

"Auction," said Lieberman.

Syd Levan was shaking his head slowly. Ida Katzman's mouth had dropped open.

"Lost money," said Hamel.

"Show a movie," Lieberman tried. "*The Frisco Kid, Hester Street*, a *Friday the 13th* marathon."

"You know what it costs to rent a movie, get a projector, advertise?" said Hamel with a sigh. "And nobody comes. They have cable. Movies are a sure loser."

"Bingo," said Lieberman with little confidence.

"We're Jews," said Levan, shocked.

"I'm aware of that," said Lieberman. "But we have a building to renovate."

"No bingo," said Hamel.

"Why?" said Lieberman.

"Who would come?" said Hamel.

"Catholics," said Lieberman. "I know lots of Catholics. My partner's a Catholic."

"I don't like it," said Levan. "What do you say, Rabbi?"

"I don't think we should trivialize our endeavor," said Rabbi Wass.

Ida Katzman strained forward, tilting her head to one side like a little bird.

"On the other hand," the Rabbi went on, "pride has been the downfall of many a righteous man"—he looked at Ida Katzman and added with a knowing smile—"and woman."

Ida Katzman sat back satisfied.

"I suggest we have a committee and we let the committee figure out where to get the money," said Syd Levan.

"We are the committee," Lieberman said, looking at Hamel for support.

"Strictly speaking," said Hamel. "We are not. We are an ad hoc committee to make a recommendation possibly to appoint a committee."

"Rabbi," said Lieberman. "You want to call this the committee? If not, it's fine with me. I'd like to get home. My daughter and my grandchildren are staying with us. I'm working a homicide and I'm tired."

"It's a committee," said Rabbi Wass.

"It can't be," said Hamel. "We have made no recommendation and we've not followed any rules of order. This has been an informal discussion by an ad hoc committee."

"He's right," said Levan.

"We have renovations to fund," said Rabbi Wass. "Renovations that could come to fifty thousand dollars over building costs.

Ida Katzman reached into her cloth bag for something while Lieberman said, "Let's throw a polka party."

"Abe, is this the time for jokes? I ask you?" asked Syd Levan.

Ida Katzman was writing something behind her purse. Hamel glanced at her and prepared to call for a point of order. This, Lieberman decided, was the moment to blitzkrieg the king of Denmark who was about to be dubbed Irwin Rommel. But God and Ida Katzman intervened.

"Is this enough?" she said, tearing out and handing a check across the table to Rabbi Wass.

Wass looked at the check.

"Exactly enough," said the rabbi, passing the check made out to the synagogue around the table.

"Can we go home now?" she asked standing up. "I'm going to miss *Saturday Night Live*. Someone has to drive me or get me a cab."

"We can go home," said Lieberman. "Irving lives near you. He can give you a ride."

Hamel prepared to shoot a warning look at Lieberman but pulled it back before it showed to anyone but the detective.

"I'll be happy to drive Mrs. Katzman," said Hamel.

"I think we deserve some credit here," said Syd Levan, reaching into his pocket for a cigar and putting it in his mouth. Syd thought it was all right to do this as long as he didn't light up.

"You've all done well," said Rabbi Wass.

And everyone departed except for the rabbi and the policeman.

"Rabbi," Lieberman said. "I know a setup when I see one. You ever see *The Sting*?"

"Mrs. Katzman was invited to join the committee because I knew she wanted to help in some way," said the Rabbi.

"I thought she already pledged a hundred fifty grand for the new building," said Lieberman, standing and massaging his knees. "What does she get a plaque on?"

"Kitchen," said the Rabbi. "Abraham, Ida Katzman's husband and son are dead. She has no grandchildren. This congregation is her family. And God is watching her deeds and we will thank him and praise him and he will bless her if our congregation does his will."

"You got me, Rabbi," said Lieberman.

"I hope so, Abraham," said Rabbi Wass.

When he got back to the house, Barry was in the living room with the lights out. The pullout bed was open and he sat cross-legged, a pillow on his lap, playing something he had earlier identified as a Game Boy while at the same time watching television.

"Where's Melisa?" Lieberman asked.

"Sleeping in Mom's bed," Barry said.

Lieberman threw his grandson a wrapped mint and said, "I stole it from the temple. Brush your teeth when you're done."

"Come on," said Barry without looking up. "You didn't steal it."

"Alright, it was given to me as a reward for raising fifty thousand dollars. What're you watching?"

"*Saturday Night Live*," said Barry.

"So's Ida Katzman," said Lieberman. "I'm going to bed. I'll see you in the morning. Good night."

"Damn," said Barry whacking the pillow and glaring at the glowing game in his hand. "I almost had him. Sorry Grandpa. We still going to the Cub game Monday?"

"Still going," said Lieberman.

"Good night," Barry said without looking up.

"Good night," Lieberman answered.

The light was on in the kitchen. Lieberman prayed silently. God owed him one. He hadn't insulted Irving Hamel. He hadn't threatened Syd Levan. He had participated in a charade to lead Mrs. Katzman on the path to fiscal righteousness. God could at least let him make it to the bedroom, to the sink, to his pajamas, and to bed without another trial.

He made it past the kitchen. No one had been in there. He was sure of it. And he heard no voices. He was five feet from the closed door to his and Bess's bedroom when Lisa's door opened.

"Dad," she whispered. "Is that you?"

"It's me," said Lieberman.

"Dad, he called. Todd called. Can we talk a few minutes? I know you're tired."

She stepped out of her old room, her robe wrapped around her with a mismatched belt from one of Lieberman's old robes. Even in the flickering light from the television in the living room he could see that his daughter's face was scrubbed clean.

"The morning would be better," Lieberman said.

"The morning may be too late," said Lisa.

"Where's your mother?" asked Lieberman.

"In your room waiting for us."

"You want coffee or tea?" he asked.

"Tea," she said.

"I'll have tea also," said Bess through the bedroom door. Lieberman headed for the kitchen.

Hanrahan waited to call till seven on the dot. Lieberman reached for the bedside phone and got it before the second ring. Bess moaned, pulled the sheet over herself, and turned away from him.

"Yes?" said Lieberman.

"Rabbi, I've got a lead. Estralda's mother and her brother are living over in Mextown near Ogden. I think they're using the name Vegas. You got an idea?"

"You should be in church, William," whispered Lieberman. "Giving communion, eating crackers, drinking wine. It's Sunday morning. I pray on Friday night and Saturday morning. You pray on Sunday. Easy to remember."

"You take communion," Hanrahan explained. "You don't give it. Priests give it."

"I neither take it nor give it," said Lieberman.

"Do we have a point here, Abe?" Hanrahan asked.

"No," said Lieberman. "I'm just trying to wake up. I'll call Guttierez in Gangs at noon. Guttierez definitely goes to church on Sunday morning. What else did you find out?"

Hanrahan went over what he found behind the doors of Estralda Valdez's apartment building. He told about Hughes, Gwen Dysan, and Nikki Morales.

"Our Estralda was recruiting, Rabbi," Hanrahan said. "Not heavy and serious maybe but keeping her hand in."

"Father Murphy," Lieberman said, scratching the top of his head. "We're not trying to get her canonized. We're trying to find out who stuck a long blade in her eight times."

"Yeah," said Hanrahan without conviction.

"You slept?"

"Some," said Hanrahan.

There was a very long and pregnant pause before Hanrahan went on, "I haven't had a drink since this happened, Abraham."

127

"Get some sleep, William," said Lieberman with a sigh. "I'm going to call Guttierez and take a shower."

When he hung up, Bess mumbled something.

"What?" asked Lieberman.

"The kids are up," she said. "I can hear them. See if they're all right."

"They're big kids," said Lieberman, "and their mother's sleeping in the next room."

"They're in our house," Bess said without turning around.

Lieberman got out of bed. He was wearing one of his favorite T-shirts, an extra large blue with a picture of the Evanston lighthouse on the front. It looked like a night-shirt on Lieberman's frail body. He found his robe in the closet and walked out of the room, closing the door behind him.

The kids were sitting on the open bed watching television and eating bagels with globs of cream cheese and thin strips of nova lox.

"It's better with slices of onion," Lieberman told them.

"Don't like onions," said Melisa.

"The game?" Barry asked. He looked up, a dollop of cream cheese climbing to his already fuzzy upper lip.

"It's afoot," said Lieberman. "I've got a call to make, a shower to take, and a headache to shake."

Melisa laughed. Barry smiled.

"And I've got a beer to bake," said Melisa.

"That's not funny," sighed Barry. "You're so unfunny."

"It's a sincere attempt in the proper context and vernacular," said Lieberman.

"You sound like Dad with his dead Greeks," said Barry. "Only you're joking. My dad's always serious."

"Spread more cream cheese on the furniture and I'll be right back," said Lieberman. He went into the kitchen and closed the door behind him to drown out the voice of Alf and at least suggest to his family that he might want to be left alone a few minutes. He found Simon Guttierez's name and number in the address book in the kitchen. He dialed.

"Hello?" came a woman's voice.

"My little rose of the prairie," said Lieberman.

Estralita Guttierez chuckled.

"Lieberman," she said. "You're the only one who calls me that."

"I'm the only one who calls you who has a soul," said Lieberman. "Everyone else sold theirs for weight loss programs that don't work and seats at Bulls games. Simon there?"

"I'll get him. We were getting set to go to Mass," she said.

"I'll be fast," Lieberman assured her.

A few seconds later Simon Guttierez came on the line with a clipped, "Abe."

Lieberman had worked on and off for fifteen years with Simon till Simon got the transfer and promotion to Gangs. Simon was ambitious. If he'd had a college degree he might be giving Captain Hughes a run for chief of police in five years.

"Simon, I need something."

Lieberman went with the phone to the bag on the counter. As he talked, he pulled out a garlic bagel, tucked the phone under his chin, cut the bagel, and put it in the toaster.

"What?" asked Guttierez.

"Valdez killing. You up on it? I need a line on Estralda Valdez's mother and brother. Live down on or near Ogden." Lieberman was pulling the lox, onion, and cream cheese out of the refrigerator. The cream cheese—what remained of it—was a smarmy mess.

"Name?"

"No name but Valdez," said Lieberman. "And that's probably not it."

"Do I owe you one?" Guttierez asked.

Lieberman could hear Estralita Guttierez in the background urging her husband to get off the phone.

"No, I owe you one from the Bratcovkic case," Lieberman admitted.

"Now you're gonna owe me two," said Guttierez. "I'll make a couple calls and call you back after Mass. You home?"

"I'm home," said Lieberman.

Guttierez hung up. Lieberman finished making his sandwich, poured himself a glass of iced tea made the night before, and settled down at the table to eat, drink, and wait. He waited five whole minutes before Lisa came bursting through the door.

"Dad," she said. "The kids are in the living room getting cream cheese and crumbs over everything. You were out there. Why didn't you stop them?"

"I've got a confession," he said biting into his sandwich. "There's more of Peter Pan in me than Mary Poppins."

"You could give me a hand here a little," Lisa said.

"Take a shower. Wash your hair. Brush your teeth. Shave your legs and then come out and talk," he said. "You'll feel better."

"You're just trying to get me off your back," she said, brushing her hair back with her hands.

"Unfair," said Lieberman. "I'm trying to do a variety of things. Getting rid of you is just one of them. Come back with a smile and a song, preferably not a rap song, and we'll decide if we want to put cuffs on the kids or the refrigerator."

"You never change, do you?" Lisa asked, taking the last piece of bagel-lox-cream cheese-onion from his hand and gulping it down. "I try not to," he said. "But I fail most of the time."

The phone rang. Lieberman again picked it up after the first ring.

"What'd you learn, Abe?" Hanrahan asked.

"Patience," said Lieberman, pouring himself another iced tea.

"I got a feeling," said Hanrahan.

"Take a hot shower," said Lieberman. "I'll call you when I've got a reason to call you."

They hung up and Lieberman moved back to the bathroom for a hot shower. He sang his usual medley while the water steamed down on his back and legs. "The Love Bug Will Get You If You Don't Watch Out" was followed by "The Devil and the Deep Blue Sea" and "Just One More Chance." Lieberman continued singing—"Silver Dollar" and "Tangerine"—as he toweled off and dressed, and "Moon Over

Miami" as he stepped back into his and Bess's bedroom.

"You're in high spirits, Abraham," Bess said, sitting up.

"Trying to delude myself," he whispered. "It almost worked."

"It never works," said Bess.

The phone was ringing.

"You know what time it is?" Bess said, getting out of bed.

"I didn't know what time it was," Lieberman sang.

Bess shook her head and headed for the bathroom while Lieberman answered the phone.

"Abe."

"Simon."

"I got something, maybe," said Guttierez.

"I thought you were going to Mass?"

"I'll go late," said Guttierez. "You want to hear this or you want to make me feel guilty?"

"Talk," said Lieberman.

"We got a maybe," said Guttierez. "Brother may be José Madera, also known as José Vegas. Seventeen. Word's out Madera said his sister's been killed."

"Word's out, Simon?"

"One of our informants was in a bar with Madera last night. Madera said the dead prostitute was his sister."

"Where does Madera live?"

"Got me, Abe," said Guttierez. "Conlin's on in records. I checked with him. Madera has seven priors, no convictions. No known address. He used to run with Los Vampiros, El Perro's swarm. Deadheads. Now he's with Los Gatos. More ambitious. Crack farmers."

"Thanks, Simon," said Lieberman.

"You owe me two," said Guttierez, hanging up.

Lieberman dialed Hanrahan, who took five rings to pick it up.

"I was in the can," explained Hanrahan.

"I appreciate your candor," said Lieberman. "Meet me at the Chapultepec on North in half an hour. El Perro may know how we can find Estralda's brother."

Lieberman unlocked the night table drawer with the key

on his chain, removed his weapon, and put it in his holster under his jacket.

"Gotta go," said Lieberman, coming out of his room.

"Dad," Lisa said under her breath. "Todd is coming at noon, remember? You said you'd be here."

"I'll be back," Lieberman assured her.

"Lieberman," Bess said. She was still in her robe, pulling it around her. Lieberman had given her that robe for her birthday five years ago.

"She calls me Lieberman and I'll be in trouble," Lieberman confided to Barry and Melisa, who were listening.

"Very big trouble," Bess agreed. "You be back when Todd's here. Worry less about someone else's family and more about your own."

He moved to her and gave her a kiss.

"Take care," Bess said, as she had thousands of mornings. He headed out into the morning heat.

The morning proved to be a bust. Hanrahan and Lieberman went to the Chapultapec and found it empty except for a young couple and their baby. The old lady serving, who had been there when Lieberman and Hanrahan had confronted El Perro over Resnick's money, claimed that she knew no one named El Perro or Del Sol. She looked more than frightened. She was trembling as if it were January on the lake shore.

"Give him a note if he comes by," Lieberman said, pulling out his pad. "Tell him it's from Lieberman. He can reach me tomorrow morning or night. I'm going to the ball game in the afternoon."

The note was simple: "I want to talk to José Madera."

He signed it "Lieberman" and the two cops went back outside.

"Come on home with me," said Lieberman. "My son-in-law's coming over to fight with my daughter."

"Sounds like fun," said Hanrahan, "but I've got a date."

Lieberman looked at him as they approached Hanrahan's car. Four *Latino* teenagers, big, tattooed, wearing little black caps, were sitting on the hood looking mean.

"A date?" Lieberman said.

One of the kids got down from the hood and moved toward the cops.

"This your car?" asked the kid, who looked a little like Roberto Duran but had no accent.

"Yeah," said Hanrahan. "Be with you in a second." Then to Lieberman, "Nice woman. Name's Iris. Chinese. Family owns the Black Moon Restaurant."

"Hey," said the kid who looked like Roberto Duran, "I'm talking to you."

"Why not bring her over to the house later?" asked Lieberman.

"You fuckers want to get in this car, you gonna pay fifty bucks," said the angry kid. His buddies were off the hood now. One was standing in front of the door. The other two stood behind Roberto Duran.

"Don't think so Abe, but thanks," said Hanrahan. "Maybe next time. This is a kinda get acquainted . . . You know. I'm still . . ."

The kid with the Roberto Duran face was angry now.

"I'm talking to you," he shouted between gritted teeth.

"You got a weapon?" Lieberman asked wearily.

"What? I got a weapon," the kid said. He pulled out a folding knife with a five-inch blade.

"Your sisters have weapons?" asked Hanrahan, nodding at the three others.

Roberto Duran's face was red now.

"You two give me your wallets and watches," he said.

"Why?" asked Lieberman.

"Or we cut you, old man," said the boy.

"You got time to take them in, Father Murphy?" Lieberman asked.

Hanrahan looked at his watch.

"Plenty of time," he said, turning to the kid with the knife in his hand. "Son, you are one stupid asshole."

"He called you Father?" asked the kid, confused.

"I'm a cop," Hanrahan said. "You can't recognize a cop on the street with the sun up in the morning on a summer day. I'd call that stupid."

"You know," the kid said, afraid now that he would lose

face. "I don't give a shit on your Chinese girlfriend's face if you are a cop. Hand over your—"

Hanrahan's hand came up in a backhand slap that caught the kid on the nose and spun him around. The two nearby moved forward. One of them reached into his jacket pocket. It was too warm a day for a jacket unless, like the cops, you had a weapon to hide. Lieberman's gun was out and pointed at the two, who stopped dead.

Roberto turned, his nose a mess of blood, his knife up. Hanrahan kicked him solidly in the groin. The kid on the hood of the car was already halfway down the street.

Someone applauded from the house nearby but there was no one in any window. Cars had slowed down to watch the action and then shoot away.

"You change your mind about later, give me a call, you and . . . " Lieberman began turning the two kids around and pushing them into position against the car so he could cuff them.

" . . . Iris," said Hanrahan, helping the moaning Roberto up and turning him so he could be cuffed. "I'll think about it."

They hustled the trio into the rear of Hanrahan's car.

Half an hour later Abe Lieberman was at the kitchen table presiding over a meeting between his daughter and his son-in-law. Bess had taken the kids to Maish's for pop and knishes. A large pitcher of iced tea sat on the table for Lieberman. The coffee was dripping for Lisa.

"Ground rules," said Lieberman. "No quoting Greeks. No name calling. No comments about the Cubs. And I'm the only one who can say, 'shut up.'"

"This isn't funny, Dad," Lisa said, looking at Todd across the table.

Todd looked terrible, needed a shave, and hadn't combed his hair. His shirt was green and his pants brown corduroy.

"She's right, Abe," said Todd.

"We start with agreement between the warring parties," said Lieberman. "A good sign."

9

Bess had come back a little after four, as agreed by all parties. Todd was already gone.

"Can we see the new *Friday the 13th*?" Barry said before the door was even closed.

"I don't want to see *Friday the 13th*," Melisa complained.

"No one's seeing *Friday the 13th*," said Lisa from the dining room table, where she sat drinking her sixth cup of coffee. The last three had been decaffeinated, as was the one in front of her.

Bess looked at Lieberman, who closed his eyes lazily to convey his belief that he didn't know what, if anything, had been accomplished. Bess closed the front door and moved to the table with a bag.

"Halvah," she announced. "Marble. Want some?"

Lisa gave a half-hearted shrug and continued to sip her coffee, her eyes fixed on the table. Bess looked at Lieberman again but this time in addition to closing his eyes he shrugged almost imperceptibly. Bess moved into the kitchen for a knife and wooden board for the halvah.

"Who's pitching tomorrow?" Barry asked.

"Sutcliffe," said Lieberman. "Who else would I take you to see?"

Barry smiled knowingly.

"Am I going?" asked Melissa.

"You are going," said Lieberman.

"Is Grandma going?" asked Melisa.

"Grandma does not go to baseball games," said Bess, slicing the halvah. Lieberman snatched the first piece, offered it to the kids, who refused it, and downed it in two bites. "It's not that Grandma does not like baseball. It's that Grandma cannot sit on a hard bench or even a bench with a pillow for two or three hours."

"Let's play bounty hunter," Lieberman said. "Go out in the backyard and look for a snake. A buck for a snake. A penny a worm. Other noninsect creatures are negotiable."

"Don't bring them in the house," Bess said.

When the kids were gone, Lieberman took another piece of halvah and looked at his wife.

"Well?" asked Bess, sitting down and taking a sticky piece for herself.

"Nothing," said Lisa. "We got nowhere."

"We agreed to meet again," said Lieberman. "And there was progress. Lisa's 'no' was less emphatic after an hour. Todd's promises were more sincere."

"Dad, you are wrong," Lisa said looking at him. "You are wasting your time, my time, and making it harder, harder on me, on the children, on Mom, on Todd. It's over."

"Maybe," said Lieberman. "A definite maybe. Todd volunteered to convert to Judaism."

"I don't want him to convert," Lisa said. "I don't know where that came from. That's not part of the problem. He'd rather come up with some grand gesture than deal with the problem."

"What's the problem?" Bess said. "I mean, if it's not—"

"Mom, the problem sounds like a cliché," said Lisa, pushing her cup away. "I don't want to talk clichés about wanting some freedom, wanting to know I can go where I want to go, do what I want to do, say what I want to say without someone else's approval. Mom, Todd doesn't know it but he needs it too."

"And Barry and Melisa?"

"More clichés, Mom," sighed Lisa. "You want more clichés? They're better off with us apart and happy than together and miserable. And if they're not better, they'll survive. I'll do for them but I don't think I have to be miserable for them. I love them. I'll take care of them."

The back door opened with a bang and Melisa came in panting. "Grandpa, how much for a cat?"

"Alive? I only negotiate for live animals. Nothing for dead ones," said Lieberman with a yawn.

"Alive," said Melisa eagerly.

"Alive, one dollar, if you let him go in the alley," said Lieberman. "That's my best offer. If it's not good enough, you'll have to take me to court, but I warn you I know all the judges."

"It's enough," said Melisa happily, running back into the kitchen.

"Ladies," Lieberman said, standing. "This is a moment filled with melancholy. Bess, tell your daughter what I never do in the afternoon."

"You want me to . . . ?"

"Not that," said Lieberman, leaning over to kiss his wife. "I never take a nap. Never. But I'm going to do it now. I'm not sure if this desire for rest is a temporary lapse or a new phase. If it's a new phase caused by age, I promise you at least a week of depression and a demand for attention. My speech is over."

He moved around the table and kissed his daughter on the cheek. Lisa gave him a hug.

"Thanks for trying, Dad," she said.

"I'm not prepared to admit defeat," said Lieberman, who padded off in his stockinged feet to the bedroom.

Hanrahan changed his mind six times about what he would wear on his date with Iris. He had two suits, one in acceptable shape, the other a wrinkled mess. But a suit might be too formal for dinner and a movie. He tried on blue slacks and a blue blazer with a white turtleneck sweater. The mirror told him he was trying too hard to be sporty. Maybe Iris's father would think he wasn't serious. He took off the turtleneck and put on a blue shirt and conservative tie. No, still too . . . He changed to a white shirt, and lied to himself and the mirror by promising to take off twenty pounds. He was sorely tempted to take just one drink, a small one. Even people who didn't drink had one small one before dinner. But William Hanrahan couldn't fool himself. He remembered Estralda looking up at him before she died.

Hanrahan checked the locks and turned off the lights. He didn't bother to leave a light on. A good burglar wasn't fooled by a light being left on. A good burglar would get in no matter what Hanrahan did. A lousy burglar wouldn't catch the wires and would take off when the alarm went off.

Hanrahan checked his face once more to be sure it was reasonably smooth. It was. It was still light when he pulled away from the front of his house.

He drove slowly, running no yellows, thinking through how he should behave, wondering if this was a good idea. He got to Iris's apartment building on Hoyne just north of Granville as the sun was thinking seriously about going down.

A pair of kids about eight, one white, one Chinese, both boys, looked him over as Hanrahan went to the door, found the bell, and pushed it. The kids were looking at him through the windows of the small lobby. Hanrahan looked back at them and smiled. They didn't smile back. When the click of response came, Hanrahan reached for the inner door and went in.

Across the street, a blue Honda found a parking space. The Honda had followed Hanrahan from his house. The driver had been careful, not too close, not too far, always letting a car or two or three remain between his car and Hanrahan's. He was careful. There was a lot to be careful about.

Normally, even with a few drinks in him, or maybe, especially with a few drinks in him, Bill Hanrahan would have spotted that blue Honda. But this was not a normal night.

The man in the Honda looked over at the two kids in front of the apartment building. If they had looked back at him, he would have moved his car or gotten out and walked around the corner. But they went running down the street.

The man in the Honda leaned back, hoping the darkness would come before Hanrahan came out of the building. The man did not want to kill the policeman, and perhaps he wouldn't have to. Killing whores was one thing. That

138

would fade and die after a few days. But killing a cop, that was a very different tale.

The man leaned forward and opened the glove compartment. The gun was there, oiled, clean. He preferred, if it were necessary, to use the gun. But sometimes, like with the woman, you couldn't always do what you wanted to do. Sometimes you had to use whatever you had handy.

He sat back, resisted the temptation to turn on the radio, and to pass the time tried to remember the names of all of his cousins.

10

Wrigley Field is a solid, comforting, four-sided gently curved mass of concrete, girders, and white paint with a vine-walled park in its center surrounded by more than thirty thousand wooden seats in which adults can watch other adults playing ball. Other structures in which baseball is played can call themselves parks, but Wrigley truly is one. Its gates open like a metal smile on the morning of each game, letting in swarms of loyal fans from as close as the next block and as far as Sarasota, Florida. Wrigley Field smells like home, real grass, real vines, and bright sunshine, in spite of the lights installed two years ago.

Lieberman loved Wrigley Field as he loved the Cubs. He loved the smell of the freshly painted green seats on opening day. He loved the vendors who slopped beer down the aisles. He loved the bleacher bums waving flags, shouting for their favorites, trying to rattle the other team's outfielders.

Lieberman snuck away four or five times a summer, put his visor down to show his "police business" card to get a place to park, and found a single seat. You could almost always find a single even on crowded days, even at the last minute. Augie Slotsow, who worked security at Wrigley, could always get in an old friend. Lieberman had only one rule about Wrigley. He would not go to a night game. Period. Zero. Never. It didn't feel right. It didn't feel like the Cubs. At night the grass looked blue-green. The players looked like zombies. Ballplayers didn't look as happy at night. At night, baseball was a job. In the daytime, baseball was still a game even if you were making two or three million dollars a year.

Today, Lieberman had bought three seats. They were good seats, about ten rows up in the boxes right behind third base. Lieberman sat Melisa next to him and Barry next to her. He offered to buy them both Cub hats, but Barry said he was too old. Melisa accepted. Lieberman bought one for himself and one for Melisa.

They had gotten to the park early enough to watch Sutcliffe warm up but not early enough for batting practice. They got to the park early enough to finish hot dogs, peanuts, and Cokes before the game. They got there early enough to hear the four guys in front of them give their opinions to each other about the game, opinions which both Barry and Lieberman knew were wrong, a knowledge they shared with an arch look.

"I saw them all in this park," Lieberman told his grandchildren. "When I was still in diapers my mother took me here to see Babe Ruth play. He was with Boston. Legend has it a foul ball of his almost hit me in the head."

"Can we get more peanuts?" asked Melisa.

"Later," said Lieberman. "I promise to let you get sick if you wait till the late innings so we don't have to miss anything. Deal?"

"Drinks?" she asked.

"Drinks," he agreed. "Bill Nicholson," he went on. "Saw him hit one way out over Waveland. Right on the roof of that building. The one over there."

Barry looked where he was pointing and then back at Sutcliffe moving to the mound.

"Hank Sauer hit one almost that far," he said. "And Kiner at the end of his career hit—"

"Is that André Dawson?" shouted Melisa as the Cubs ran out on the field after the "Star Spangled Banner."

"Quiet," said Barry. "That's not Dawson. That's Dunston."

"One game," said Lieberman to Melisa, who clearly didn't know what he was talking about, "against Cincinnati. Fondy was on first. Terwiliger at second. Smalley was at short. I think Baumholtz was in right. Kluzewski, a giant, wore his shirts cut at the shoulder to show his muscles, hit one almost tore—"

"Who's playin'?" came a voice next to Lieberman.

Lieberman didn't even look at El Perro. A moment earlier a little man wearing a green eye-shade had been sitting in the seat.

"Cubs and Cincy," said Lieberman. "You want some peanuts?"

"No," said El Perro, looking around with a big smile. He looked out of place in the sunlight. "I should get out here more often. What you think, *viejo*?"

"You should get out here more often," Lieberman agreed.

Barry and Melisa looked at the man next to their grandfather. The man looked back at them and grinned. The man was wearing tight black leather pants and a vest over a short-sleeved Day-glo shirt. His hat was also black, leather and wide-brimmed.

"Are you the Joker?" asked Melisa.

"His left-hand man, *niña*," said El Perro. "They sell beer here or what?"

"Yeah," said Lieberman.

"Rabbi," said El Perro. "You know something? You look kinda cute in that baseball hat."

"I know," said Lieberman. "José Madera."

Sutcliffe had struck out the first batter. Lieberman considered this a bad sign. But the next batter grounded out and the one after him hit a long fly to center field for the out.

"Why you think El Perro is here, Rabbi?" asked El Perro. "You think I just dropped in for an inning to catch the sun and see an old friend?"

"Can I tell you something?" Lieberman said, leaning over to El Perro as Ryne Sandberg came out to lead off the bottom of the first inning. "You've seen *Treasure of the Sierra Madre* too many times."

"You think so? Thanks. I like that picture," said El Perro. "Now, can I tell you something?"

"Tell," said Lieberman as Sandberg led off with a first-pitch single to left.

"I'm a lovable person," El Perro whispered. "Just ask anybody. But I got a deal to make. Yesterday you pulled my cousin and my brother in. They in the can now. Assault with a deadly weapon. Assault on a police officer."

"Your brother look like Roberto Duran?"

"No, that's Ernesto, my cousin," said El Perro. "They're kids, you know. They don't mean nothing. Besides your buddy broke his balls. Drop charges. I give you José Madera."

"Your brother is an innocent victim of social injustice," said Lieberman. "He and your cousin and their friend will be out by tonight."

"I trust you, Rabbi," said El Perro. "Here's where you can find Madera and his old lady."

He handed Lieberman a piece of gray cardboard with an address written on it. Lieberman looked up just in time to see Mark Grace fly out to right field.

"Madera, he ain't one of my people," said El Perro with a sigh. "Too loco in the *cabeza*."

"Coming from you, that's quite a testimonial," said Lieberman evenly.

"Gracias," said El Perro. "My brother and the others are out by dark, right?"

"They'll be back looking for blood by the light of the full moon," said Lieberman.

"You look cute, Rabbi," said El Perro, getting up.

"Sit down," said a scrawny woman in the row behind them.

El Perro turned to her with a smile and said,

"The sun is shining. I'm in a good mood. I just made a deal with the Rabbi here, so I'm not gonna cut your tongue out and make you eat it."

The woman's eyes and mouth opened wide. The man at her side pretended to be completely absorbed in watching the center-field scoreboard. Lieberman turned to the woman and lifted his eyebrows to her in warning. She took the look and decided to not carry this any further. El Perro climbed the steps as André Dawson came to the plate with a man on second.

"Who was that guy?" asked Barry.

"Business," said Lieberman. "I gotta make a phone call. Be right back."

Dawson did something good. Lieberman could tell that from the sound of the crowd and the fact that people were standing and screaming, but he didn't look back. He went to a bank of phones across from a hot dog stand and called Hanrahan at the station. He gave Hanrahan the address and told him he'd meet him there at five after he dropped the kids at home. When he got back to his seat, it was the second inning and the Cubs were ahead two to nothing. Shawon Dunston bobbled a tough grounder and let the runner get to second with a throw that sailed into the left-field box seats. Barry groaned.

Lieberman took off his Cub cap and handed it to Barry, who put it on. Melisa was about to say something, but Lieberman put a finger to his lips and she nodded in a very adult way to show that she would not point out to Barry his change of heart about the cap.

This might, Lieberman thought, turn into a long afternoon.

Bill Hanrahan wasn't very early, only forty minutes early. He turned off of Ogden within earshot of the expressway and parked across the street from the address Lieberman had given him. The neighborhood was entirely *Latino*, almost entirely Mexican. Hanrahan stood out like a sore Irishman. Even then he might have sat tight if it hadn't been for the open door.

He sat for fifteen minutes thinking of Iris and last night. The day was hot and the street relatively empty. Two kids were playing catch on the sidewalk with a tennis ball. A trio of women, two fat, one thin, sat on the steps of a house near the corner. All the houses were small and from the outside looked clean. The grass, what little there was in the small fenced yards in front of each house, was crew-cut and green.

No one came in or out of the house he was watching, but the door was open and the three women on the corner were looking over at him. There were only four cars parked on the dead-end street. No place to wedge in and scrunch down.

Hanrahan got out of the car and stretched, looking around as if searching for an address. He pulled his

144

notebook from his back pocket and pretended to check it before turning to his destination, the house with the wide-open door. Hanrahan put the notebook away, crossed the street, and marched straight up the steps to the front door.

The house was a one-story, recently painted white and green. Hanrahan rang the bell and waited with a smile, looking over at the three women on the steps. One of them, the skinny one, held one hand bridged over her eyes and squinted into the sun toward him.

No one answered the door, which was not only what Hanrahan expected but what he wanted. Hanrahan said, "Hello," loud enough for the ladies of the afternoon to hear him, and stepped through the open door.

He found himself inside a living room, the furniture old, over-stuffed, clean, and flowery. A huge framed poster, a color photograph of the ruins of what looked like a castle surrounded by green-green forest, dominated the wall over the sofa. The white lettering on the poster indicated that this was Guadalajara.

"Anybody home?" asked Hanrahan, stepping in.

He had decided to identify himself as a cop if anyone answered. If no one was home and he got a look around and was caught, he'd still identify himself as a cop and say that he saw the door open and thought he saw a suspicious man enter. It wouldn't fool anyone but the chances were better than a hundred to one that no one in this neighborhood would file a complaint against a cop for walking through their open door.

"Hello," Hanrahan called.

No answer.

He moved through the living room into a small dining room with a dark wooden table and six matching chairs. There was also a sideboard with a painting of Jesus over it. Jesus was looking toward the ceiling.

"Anybody here?" Hanrahan asked once more, though not as loud as his first call.

The kitchen, like the rest of the downstairs, was clean. No dishes in the drainer. No food on the small table. The faint smell of some spice reminded Hanrahan of his Aunt Aileen, his mother's sister, the cook in the family who had come to the United States at the age of seven and gone back to Dublin at the age of seventy-five.

A drink would have been nice. A small drink. Double gin and whiskey, a Gay and Frisky, as Aunt Aileen's husband Jack used to call his favorite drink.

Hanrahan moved through the kitchen. There were three doors off of a small alcove near the back door. Two of the doors were open. One led to a bedroom, dark lace and more pictures of Jesus. A second door led to darkness and stairs, a basement. The third door was pay dirt. He stepped in. The shade was down but enough light was coming through it to show that this was a woman's room, not an old woman's room like the one next door with dark lace and Jesus. The furniture was art deco and polished. The bed was oval and covered with a pink comforter. On top of the dresser in the corner, next to which stood a floor-to-ceiling mirror, were about a dozen photographs of Estralda Valdez at different ages. In almost all of them she was with a slightly older girl. Estralda, even at seven, had her hand on her hip and a knowing smile. The photos of Estralda and the other girl stopped at about the time Estralda was twenty. Then a gap and two photos of Estralda Valdez more or less as Hanrahan had seen her. It was definitely Estralda, but a subdued sun-dressed Estralda with sunglasses, little make-up, and her arm around an older, heavy woman squinting into the sun.

Interesting, yes, but more interesting was the doll house on the table in the corner near the window.

"Under the house in my mother's house," Hanrahan said, allowing himself a very small smile.

He moved to the house, which looked familiar to him, a white mansion about two feet high. When he got close enough to touch it, Hanrahan put on his glasses.

"Tara," he said softly, reading the plate above the small door.

Hanrahan leaned over and looked into one of the windows, but there wasn't enough light coming in from the drawn shades to see the miniature furniture very clearly.

He found the corner of the house with the fingers of his left hand and started to lift. The little house was deceptively heavy. In addition, it stuck stubbornly to the table top, like a determined abalone he had pried loose from an underwater rock near Mendicino a thousand years ago when he and Maureen were on their honeymoon. That abalone had been delicious. He hoped that what he found under the house would have its own satisfying taste. Hanrahan pulled harder and the table top suddenly gave up. Tiny furniture clattered from the human earthquake.

Hanrahan held the house up and reached under with his right hand. Nothing. He groped around the edges and found it. The edges of a leather-bound book. He pulled the book out and let the house down gently. Book in hand, Hanrahan moved to the bed and sat down with his back to the open door. He opened the cover, found a withered, cracking newspaper article, looked at the photograph in the second column, read the headline, and was starting to read the article itself when he heard something behind him. Hanrahan started to turn, not at all sure of what he was going to say, when the bullet entered the back of his neck just below the skull between the two tendons which went into spasm as Hanrahan lurched forward onto the floor.

The man who had killed Estralda Valdez put the pistol in his pocket, moved around the bed, knelt, and pulled the book from William Hanrahan's fingers. Blood trickled out of the small entry hole in the policeman's neck. Blood also trickled out of the exit wound in the policeman's throat. Hanrahan's eyes were closed. The man searched the floor with his eyes and fingers. More light would have helped but he could not take a chance. It took him almost three minutes to find the spent bullet that had gone through Hanrahan.

With sweating hands the man put the bullet and small book in his pocket and left the room moving slowly, one hand on the pistol in one pocket, one hand on the book in the other. He went out the back door, through the yard, into the alley, and around to the side street where he had parked his car after following Hanrahan.

As he drove slowly down the street in front of the Madera

house, he watched a car pull up behind the other cop's. Lieberman got out. He knew Lieberman. For an instant he considered turning around, going into the alley, getting back into the house, and shooting Lieberman when he came in. What difference did it make? One cop or two. But he decided against it as he drove further watching the dwindling image of Lieberman walking up the stairs.

He had what he needed and there was a risk to going back. A small risk, that's true, but a risk. He had waited too long and there was too much at stake to take even a small risk.

Four hours later, Abe Lieberman sat in Dr. Deep's small office in the surgery wing of the University of Chicago Hospitals. Dr. Kuldip Singh Dalawal, known to his friends, who included Abe Lieberman, as Deep, had operated on Hanrahan.

"Mostly a matter of cleaning up," Deep had said outside the operating room. Deep was a short, dark Pakistani whose son had been arrested twice, both times for possession of cocaine. Lieberman had gotten the boy into a drug rehab program in California run by another former friend. That was five years ago. The boy was now a young man in his second year of medical school.

"Entry was clean," Dr. Deep went on. "Bullet was on an angle like so, to the right. Missed his esophagus, cracked the bone right here. Danger was in his choking on his blood. Your clearing of the passage was essential. Trauma is over. The danger now is from infection and we will watch that most carefully."

"He'll live?" Lieberman had asked.

"I would think so, yes," said Dr. Deep.

Deep had given Lieberman the use of his office. Lieberman had called Bess, who wanted to come to the hospital, but he had told her not to, that Bill was asleep and likely to be so for quite a while. Bess had argued, but Lieberman had changed the subject, asked her about Lisa and Todd and the kids.

"Melisa says her stomach doesn't hurt," said Bess.

"So?" asked Lieberman

"No one had asked her," said Bess. "Which led me to the conclusion that . . ."

" . . . her stomach hurt and she wanted to hide it," he concluded.

"But she also felt guilty and wanted me and her mother to know that she was hiding something. What did you give her at that ball game?"

"The illusion of restraint," said Lieberman, looking across the desk at Dr. Deep's medical degree and surgical certificates on the wall.

"Lisa and Todd are out," said Bess.

"Good," said Lieberman.

"Not with each other," said Bess.

"Ah," said Lieberman, laying the torn newspaper clipping on Dr. Deep's desk and carefully flattening it with the palm of his hand. He had taken the crumpled paper from Hanrahan's fist when the medics came to put him on the cart.

"Abe, no," said Bess. "They aren't out with other . . . I mean Lisa went to a movie with Yetta and Maish. Todd is . . . I don't know where. I tried to call him as soon as they left. I'm making late dinner for the kids. What did you give them to eat at the game?"

"Hot dogs, peanuts, victory," said Lieberman, reading the article for the fifth time. The article said that a man named Juan Hernandez De Barcelona had been murdered by two known prostitutes the night before, that the prostitutes had attempted to make it look as if another man had been shot by Barcelona, who had, in turn, shot the man. The article quoted a Detective LaSalle as saying that the intended fall guy had lived long enough to tell the police what had happened. The article pointedly neglected to name the now-deceased fall guy. The article had no date, nor the name of the paper. The article didn't even mention the city. Lieberman turned the article over as Bess said, " . . . what to do?"

"When I get home," he said.

"Get something to eat, Abe," Bess said gently. "And if you're going to sleep there, call me and let me know."

"I love you, Bess," Lieberman said.

"I love you, Abe," said Bess.

Lieberman hung up the phone and turned the article over. It was part of a supermarket ad. The address of the supermarket, but not the name, was in the ad. And across the middle of the ad were the words, "The lowest prices in Corpus . . ." The rest was missing.

Lieberman turned the article over again and looked at the picture of the Madera sisters. Hanrahan had seen a copy of that same picture less than three hours earlier, and so had Lieberman, on the dresser in Estralda's bedroom.

He made his calls slowly, calmly. First Hanrahan's wife, Maureen. He knew she wasn't listed but he was a cop. She was just getting home from work.

"Maureen, it's Abe Lieberman," said Lieberman, putting the article aside and reaching for a pencil next to the photograph of Dr. Deep's wife and four children.

"Yes, Abe," she said soberly.

"It's about Bill," he said.

"He's dead," she said flatly.

"No. He's been shot. We're in the surgical wing of the University of Chicago Hospitals on Fifty-ninth. You know where it is?"

"I know," she said and then silence.

"Maureen?" Lieberman asked.

"Sorry, it's not as . . . I thought it would come like this, but it's different in a way. You know what I mean?"

"You want me to call Michael?"

"No," she said. "I'll call him. I should tell him his father . . . I'll call him. It's odd, Abe, I thought I'd . . . but I'm just sleepy. I want to go to sleep."

"Maybe it's a good idea, Maureen," he said.

"It's running away, Abe," she said with a sigh. "I'll call Michael and be right there."

Lieberman made two more calls. One to St. Bart's Church. Father Whiz Parker was out. He left a message with the old priest who answered. The third call was to Iris Huang at the Black Moon Restaurant. She was there. He told her what had happened.

"I'll come," she said.

"He'll need you more when he knows what's going on in a day or two," said Lieberman, not wanting to deal with both Maureen and Iris.

"Yes," she said. "But I will also come to the hospital. Thank you for calling me, Detective . . ."

"Lieberman," he said.

He hung up the phone and asked the long-distance operator for the number of police headquarters in Corpus Christi, Texas.

"Police," came a voice with a distinctly Texas accent.

"Me too," said Lieberman. "You have a detective named LaSalle."

"LaSalle?" said the man. "LaSalle? Carrol LaSalle?"

"I guess," said Lieberman.

"He's the mayor," said the man. "You joking me."

"No," said Lieberman. "Thanks."

He called information again and got the number of the mayor's office in Corpus Christi. An answering machine told him that the mayor's office was closed but gave an emergency number. Lieberman dialed the emergency number and got a man who identified himself as Scott Tynan. Lieberman stated his business and Tynan got the number in Dr. Deep's office.

Five minutes later the mayor of Corpus Christi, Texas, called Abe Lieberman.

11

Carrol LaSalle was a good old boy with a vengeance, but Lieberman caught the protective edge behind the carefully chosen words. And LaSalle, Lieberman found, could choose both carefully and quickly.

"Lieberman," he said. "Chicago P.D. You got a superior officer?"

Lieberman gave him Hughes's name and number.

"You got a badge number, card number, such like?" asked Mayor LaSalle of Corpus Christi.

Lieberman gave it.

"Call you right back if I can find him," said LaSalle, who hung up.

Ten minutes later, while Lieberman sat looking out the window at another building just like the one he was in, the phone rang again.

"Ask your question, Detective," said LaSalle. "I understand it's about the whorehouse murders."

"Juan Hernandez De Barcelona and . . ." Lieberman paused, waiting for the fill-in.

"Harte," said the Mayor of Corpus Christi. "James. Also known around the state of Texas and parts of Louisiana as 'Skettle.' Prominent citizen. Uncle was once governor and old Skettle owned land bigger than most Arab states. Kept Skettle out of the papers a while but someone let it slip. Tell you the truth here, Detective Lieberman, I rode that case pretty damn hard and far. Corruption, cleanup, honest citizen murdered, framed by two whores."

Lieberman had a pretty good idea of who had let Harte's name slip to the newspapers.

"What can you tell me that wasn't in the early clips?" asked Lieberman.

"First off, I can tell you that if you find those ladies, I'd appreciate your giving some credit to Carrol LaSalle whose knowledge of the case and cooperation . . . You got the idea, Detective. I got some competition coming up in the next election. A local Negro lawyer is out to out-liberal Carrol LaSalle."

"I got it, Mayor."

"Be nice with elections coming in six short months to remind the people—"

"I get it, Mayor," Lieberman said. "The case."

"Gettin' testy here, Detective?"

"My partner's been shot. Might not make it. I'm in the hospital waiting to see. Estralda Valdez, alias Estralda Maderas, was killed here on Friday. My partner was investigating when he got shot."

"How was she killed?" asked LaSalle.

"Knife, multiple," said Lieberman.

"Partner?"

"Gunshot, pistol, close range, back of the neck. Assailant took the bullet," said Lieberman. He looked up and saw Iris and Maureen walking down the corridor, not quite together but both heading toward him.

Mayor LaSalle sighed deeply.

"Hernandez was shot back of the head," said LaSalle. "Set up to make it look like a double homicide. Those girls botched it bad. If Hernandez shot first, ole Skettle didn't have the reflexes to pull a trigger with a bullet cutting his spine. And Hernandez had a bullet in the back. Went straight down on his face away from Skettle. But hey, there's more. Gun was in Skettle's right hand. He was left-handed. We traced the ladies a bit. One, the younger one, Estralda, and I'd appreciate your sending a picture of her to—"

"She's your Estralda," Lieberman said. Maureen and Iris had both paused in front of the door looking at Lieberman, who nodded for them to enter. "Doesn't look much different from the clipping and I found the same photo in her mother's house."

"Lost her trail in San Diego anyway," said LaSalle. "Other one, older sister, left a better trail, St. Louis then Georgia. Lost her there."

Maureen entered first. Iris followed and closed the door gently.

"Some figure those girls swished out of here with a lot of Hernandez's money," said LaSalle, and then to someone on the other end, "Just finishing up, Jess. Tell the ladies and gentlemen I'm talking to George Bush."

Maureen was looking like Maureen only better. A little thinner than Lieberman had last seen her. More make-up, a yellow dress that followed her lines instead of hiding them. Her hair was redder than he remembered it and Lieberman figured that nature had some help from the pharmacy. She looked worried, but she looked good. She put her purse on the desk next to the photograph of Dr. Deep's kids and looked at Iris, who wore a longish dark blue skirt and matching blouse. Her hair was short and her eyes were red from crying, though she wasn't crying now.

"Lieberman," LaSalle went on. "Hernandez owned the Babe O'Brien bar for a lot of years. No bank accounts. Not a spender. Not a sign of the dollars. We're talking whores here, Detective, not small talk. They killed Hernandez and Skettle Harte. I got a feelin' they did it for more than fun. You know what I'm sayin'?"

"Prints?" asked Lieberman.

"Between you, me, and Southern Bell or M.C.I. or whoever is handlin' this call," said LaSalle. "First boys on the scene that night laid hands on everything. They figured it for a whorehouse double with no complications. Got to go. Got your office number and address from the cop at your station, Briggs. I'll send you copies of anything else I turn up. If you catch up with our dancin' lady, I tell you off the record what happens. We ask for extradition. We cry for priority. You do what you can to see your people up there don't give it. Carrol LaSalle claimed and will continue to claim that we got those girls nailed shut on murder one, but with all this time, evidence who knows where and a good defense lawyer, that girl could walk on the double and we want justice served."

And, Lieberman thought, we don't want the mayor embarrassed.

"I understand, Mr. Mayor," said Lieberman.

"Good talkin' to you, Detective. Ever get down our way, you look me up. Promise you the best seafood on the Gulf."

Mayor Carrol LaSalle hung up and Lieberman faced the two silent women.

"Maureen Hanrahan, this, I believe, is Iris Huang." The women did not look at each other. "Iris is a recent friend of Bill's and—"

"How is he?" asked Maureen.

"Doctor says he should probably be fine," said Lieberman.

"Probably?" asked Maureen.

"No guarantees," said Lieberman. "They don't deal in guarantees."

"Can we see him?" asked Iris.

"I'll ask the doctor," said Lieberman. "Maybe you can look in on him, but he's out."

"The doctor's name?" asked Iris.

"Dalawal," said Lieberman.

Iris got up.

"I think I'll look for him," Iris said. "The doctor."

"Sure," said Lieberman.

Iris smiled at Maureen, who smiled back, and Iris left carefully, closing the door behind her.

"Seems nice," said Maureen.

"Seems," said Lieberman.

"She should keep walking down the hall, get in the elevator, and save herself a lot of grief," said Maureen.

Lieberman got up.

"You call Michael?" he asked.

Maureen nodded.

"They're coming in the morning," she said. "They didn't want to keep Billy up all night. Only direct flight they could get here from Toronto was at nine. They can get an Air Canada . . . What's the difference?"

"He'll make it, Mo," said Lieberman, moving to her side.

"Not the point, Abe," she said, biting her lower lip. "Tell me the truth. Do you really like him?"

"He's a good partner," said Lieberman.

"When he's sober," said Maureen, the old bitterness coming back.

"He's a good partner, a good cop," said Lieberman.

"And you like him?" asked Maureen again, looking up at Lieberman.

"I like him, Mo," said Lieberman.

"You need a shave, Abe," she said. "You'll have white beard by morning."

"I'm not a kid, Mo," he said.

"I've been building up the courage to go for a divorce," said Maureen, looking away. "Got a lawyer, talked to Father Boyer at the archdiocese. They've got people looking into it."

"Might try Father Stowell at St. Nathan's," Lieberman suggested. "Used to be a lawyer and spent four years at the Vatican handling appeals like this."

"Who don't you know, Lieberman?" she asked, looking back at him.

"Probably myself," he said.

"How's Bess?" asked Maureen. "I thought a couple of times of calling her the last few years, but I didn't want it to be awkward for her, you. Did you ever tell her?"

Lieberman looked through the office window down the corridor. A black priest in his thirties stepped out of the elevator and looked around for the nursing station.

"Nothing to tell her, Mo," he said. "We never did anything."

"We thought about it," she said. "Talked about it."

"It was a tough night," he said.

"The thought is the deed where I come from," said Maureen. "Hard to believe that a few Hail Mary's will . . . I'm lying. I haven't been the Virgin Mary since I walked out on Bill and I can see that he hasn't been either." She looked over her shoulder in the direction Iris had gone.

"My sins, however, have been pathetic," she said. And then, suddenly, she stood up. "What am I talking about?"

"Guilt," said Lieberman. "I've got it too. I let Bill go to the place he was shot while I was at a baseball game with my grandchildren."

"That's it?" she said. "That's all you've got? You have nothing to feel guilty about."

She was pacing the room now. Lieberman sat down again. Both knees were warning him.

"You win," said Lieberman. "You're guiltier than I am."

"Thank you," she said angrily.

She stopped pacing and glared down at him.

"You're welcome," he said.

"What's hurting you?" she asked.

"Knees," he said. "Arthritis."

"Mine's in the shoulders," Maureen said, sighing.

"I've got to get back to work," said Lieberman, standing.

"Got time for a cup of coffee first?" Maureen asked.

"I'll take the time," he said.

She moved into his arms and he gave her a reassuring hug. Her head rested on his shoulder, her hair billowed in his face. She smelled of long ago and Lieberman was tired.

And then Maureen Hanrahan was crying.

Lieberman got back to the station a little before eleven that night. Maureen and Iris were something like friends and had gone down to the hospital dining room to drink bitter coffee and eat something made of rubber from a machine. Dr. Deep had, once again, reassured Lieberman that Hanrahan's chances were good indeed and Father Parker had promised to stay till at least morning when the hospital had a priest on duty.

"Meaning," said Lieberman, "if my partner dies, there'll be someone to give him the last rites."

"Meaning just that," said Parker.

"Bill said you're 'Whiz' Parker, that right?"

"Right," said Parker.

"How's the knee?" asked Lieberman.

Father Parker's left hand reflexively moved to his left knee.

"Forever healing," he said.

It was a call from Hughes that had drawn Lieberman from the hospital. José Madera, Estralda's brother, had been picked up returning to the house a few minutes after Hanrahan had been taken away in the ambulance. Officer Robert Shane, twenty-five years old, had been stationed at the crime scene and was waiting for the M.E. when Madera had come in and gone wild. If a massive *Chicago Tribune* photographer had not arrived and pulled Madera off, he might have killed the young cop. Now Madera was in the holding cell on Clark Street with his hands cuffed. Officer Shane had been treated for lacerations and a broken cheekbone and released.

The station on Clark Street was lit up brighter than Wendy's across the street. Wendy's, too, was still open. Lieberman stopped for a guilty double burger and an iced tea. They were out of iced tea. He settled for a diet cola and ordered two more burgers and two colas to go.

When he entered the station, Nestor Briggs was still on the job. Somewhere in the building a woman was sobbing. Lieberman carried his Wendy's bag back into the squad room. There were no squads of any kind operating out of the room. Never had been. Hadn't even been at the old station. The name dated back to the 1920s, even earlier, when squads were organized like army platoons to deal with insurrections, riots, gang wars, and labor unrest.

Hughes was sitting at one of the desks in the room, which he never did. When he saw Lieberman he stood up. At the moment, the place was empty except for the two men.

"How is Bill?" asked Hughes.

Lieberman did not remember Hughes ever calling his partner anything but Hanrahan and even that with a touch of irritation.

"Still holding on," said Lieberman. "Want a burger?"

"Sure," said Hughes. "The hell with diet."

"Diet cola," said Lieberman, handing Captain Hughes a sandwich and drink.

They moved to Lieberman's desk. Lieberman sat. Nights like this are the stuff cop dreams are made of. In the middle of a case, eating on the run, sharing thoughts on a case with the captain, half asleep, knowing you are dealing in life and death. Cops remember these nights, these moments, and it feels good, but not when your partner is shot. Then you're just tired.

"You talked to the mayor of Corpus Christi, Briggs says," said Hughes, examining his already lukewarm-at-best burger. Lieberman didn't examine his. He just ate.

Lieberman told Hughes what he had learned.

"We can keep holding Van Beeber on the Michigan warrant," said Hughes around a glob of bread, burger, mayo, and lettuce. "But counsel says we've got a weak case. No weapon, no . . . and the attack on Hanrahan—if related—makes it even murkier unless we argue for a conspiracy. Problem with that is Van Beeber would have to be part of a conspiracy. No jury would buy it."

Lieberman grunted and kept eating.

"Story of these killings in Corpus Christi, the money . . . hell," said Hughes with a deep sigh. Once again he examined the sandwich.

"Madera is in the lockup?" said Lieberman, throwing what was left of his sandwich in an already overfull wastebasket.

"Lockup," confirmed Hughes finishing his sandwich. "Don't know where the mother is."

Lieberman got up.

"I think I'll bring him a sandwich," he said.

"Suit yourself, but he won't talk. He raves. And he raves only in Spanish," said Hughes. "You want some pressure? He was armed. No permit. No way of getting one. He's only fifteen. Shouldn't even be here. Should be in Juvenile, but he looks older and he has no ID. I'd say we have about another hour before we have to turn him over."

Lieberman picked up his Wendy's bag.

"Thanks, Captain," he said.

"You want me to come with you?" asked Hughes, looking at his watch.

"I can do it," said Lieberman. "You want to take off . . ."

"Just for a few hours," said Hughes. "Wife's coming back from her mother's. I said . . . before this . . . that I'd pick her up. I'll be back in the morning. If anything breaks, call me at home."

Lieberman looked at the wall clock. Lieberman nodded. Hughes looked as if he had something else to say, changed his mind, and went out the squad room door.

Before he went into the lockup in the next room, Lieberman checked the roster to see who was on duty. Nestor would know where they were. None of the names interested Lieberman as backup.

The law said people in the lockup had to be watched round the clock, which normally was no problem since the lockup, a small mesh cell big enough for about four people with two wooden slab benches bolted to the wall, was in a space visible from the main desk, which was supposedly always manned or womaned. Supposedly. At night, the desk man often had to be called from the desk to help out with everything from cleaning up after a puking addict to trying to reassure a lost kid. The prisoners in the tank had to be watched not primarily because they might hurt someone but because they might hurt or even kill themselves and each other. It had happened. Almost always to people in on their first arrest.

Nestor Briggs had his back to the lockup. Nestor was busy answering calls that came directly to the station. Nestor didn't handle 911 calls. That went through downtown switch. Nestor was getting the calls from people who had time to check the yellow pages. Lieberman did a key-turning motion to show what he wanted. Nestor, still on the phone listening, nodded and handed over a ring with four keys. He also looked at the Wendy's bag. Lieberman pulled out the burger. Nestor smiled. Lieberman handed him the sandwich and moved toward the lockup with the cola.

There were four desks in the room with the lockup, all unoccupied. José Madera sat behind the mesh, hands in his lap, watching Lieberman approach. Madera wore a pair of faded jeans, a black T-shirt, and a stupid scowl.

"Want a Coke?" asked Lieberman.

Madera glared. Estralda Valdez's real name might have been Madera or Vegas and this kid might have been her

160

brother but their parents had gone fishing in different gene pools and God had laughed at them and given them José, a squat, flat-faced creature with very small eyes and a very thick head.

Madera didn't answer the question. Lieberman opened the door. José Madera did not move.

"Come on," said Lieberman.

Madera blinked.

"Come on," said Lieberman with a movement of his hand.

Madera stood up. His hands were cuffed. His face was sullen. Lieberman held the door open and the boy came out. Lieberman pointed to a nearby folding chair. Madera sat. Lieberman handed him the Coke and sat in a chair he pulled over across from the boy.

"Let's talk," said Lieberman.

"*No hablo* English," said Madera.

"*Bueno,*" said Lieberman. "*Entonces vamos a hablar in Español. Yo necesito a practicar.*"

"Not on me, bo," said Madera. "Your Spanish sucks."

"I know," said Lieberman. "You shoot the cop in your house?"

"No."

Madera had finished his Coke. Now he was chewing on the ice.

"Why should I believe you? You come home, find someone in your sister's bedroom, and you pop him. Makes sense."

"I didn't shoot him," said Madera. "You'll see. My gun won't match the bullets. I know about that stuff."

Madera didn't look smart enough to be playing a game. There was only a single bullet fired and that had been taken away by the person who shot it.

"Besides," said Madera, "if I shot him, I'd tell you. I'd be a name, you know? You said it. I shot a guy I find in my house. Didn't know it was a cop. But between you and me I tell 'em on the street I knew it was a cop."

"You're telling this to a cop?" Lieberman reminded him.

Madera shrugged. He had finished chewing up the ice. Now he was working on the cup, his teeth tearing off small pieces and letting them drop on the floor.

"Who you shittin'?" said Madera. "I'm Juvie. What the most I get even murder one? Three years and out. Go get me a lawyer, bo."

"I knew your sister," said Lieberman.

"Bullshit," said Madera, spitting a piece of the cup toward Lieberman.

"She gave me information from time to time. I'm trying to find whoever killed her," said Lieberman evenly.

"Bullshit," said Madera louder than before.

"Where's your other sister, Guadalupe?"

"China, dead, who knows?"

Madera was bouncing in his seat now, looking around as if the walls were closing in.

"Where's your mother?" asked Lieberman calmly.

"Where's yours?"

"OK," said Lieberman. "Back in the cage. But I've got some information for you. A fifteen-year-old can be indicted as an adult on a major felony in Illinois. My boss wants a fall guy. I want a fall guy. My partner's the guy who went down. Judges and juries don't like cop killers."

Madera was really looking trapped now. His head was bobbing, his eyes darting. He was bouncing and pulling his wrists apart. The cuffs chink-chanked. Lieberman wasn't sure whether he was witnessing madness or drugs.

"Frank," said José Madera. "Some guy named Frank. She told Lupe Frank was comin'. She was goin'. I tole her I'd tear this Frank's face off with my teeth."

José Madera showed his teeth to Lieberman. They were large, amber, and in lousy shape.

"Lupe?" asked Lieberman. "Guadalupe, your other sister. She's in Chicago?"

Madera was rocking now. Small humming sounds were coming from his closed mouth. Nestor Briggs, still on the phone, looked over. Lieberman shook his head to show he could handle it.

"I think you'd better go back in the lockup now," Lieberman said getting up.

Madera kept rocking.

"José, *levantase.*"

José Madera leaped from the chair at Lieberman. Lieberman was ready, but even then Madera almost bowled him over. Lieberman stepped to his right. His knees promised to get even later. Madera's shoulder hit his leg. Lieberman backed away as the boy tumbled into the chair headfirst and sprawled on the floor. Lieberman's gun was out now, pointed at the boy. Nestor Briggs was standing nearby, his own weapon drawn, waiting.

José Madera turned with a wail. A gash had opened where he hit the chair. Blood masked his face. It would take stitching, a lot of stitching.

"Shoot me," said Madera starting up.

Nestor Briggs started moving slowly to his right around the room.

The blood had trickled into José's mouth. His teeth were red. By the time José Madera was on his knees, Nestor Briggs had circled behind him.

"Shoot me," Madera screamed holding his cuffed hands over his head.

He was going to charge. No doubt about it. And if he did, Lieberman knew he couldn't fire. He couldn't shoot a cuffed fifteen-year-old and not do time.

"José," he said with a bored look and put his gun back in the holster. "You know what a *putz* is?" The phone on Nestor Briggs's desk began to ring. Madera hesitated. "A *putz*?" Lieberman repeated, shaking his head at the boy's stupidity. "That's what you are. Standing there like a . . . a . . . putz. I don't know. There may be no hope for you. Get back in the cage. I got to take a leak."

The phone kept ringing.

Before José Madera could make up his mind about what to do, Nestor Briggs reached up behind him, grabbed the chain on the cuffs, and pulled backward. Madera fell on his back, the wind knocked out of him. Lieberman stepped forward and grabbed Madera's legs. Briggs took his arms and they dragged him quickly into the cage, locking it.

The phone kept ringing.

"Too old for this," said Briggs, panting.

163

"You did good, Nestor," said Lieberman, refusing to listen to his knees, which were insisting on an immediate conference.

"Glad to do it," said Nestor. "I'll call for help and get him over to Edgewater for stitches. We could use one of those sleeping darts they use on rhinos for guys like this, you know that?"

Nestor shambled over to the ringing phone. Lieberman took a last look through the mesh at José Madera, who had sat up on the floor. He was spitting out the blood that dripped into his mouth.

"Yeah," said Lieberman. "I owe you one."

"One," said Nestor, moving back toward the main desk. "You owe me so damn many, you'd be paying my bills till pension day."

Nestor answered the phone.

"I'll get you something to hold on your head," said Lieberman.

"I like the taste," said Madera.

"Where's your mother?" asked Lieberman. "I'll bring her."

"She's gone," said Madera angrily. "Lupe took her away. I don't know where. They left me out there. And you know what? I don't give a shit."

"When it stops hurting, we can talk again," said Lieberman.

"Can you take this?" Nestor called holding up the phone.

"This don't hurt," said Madera, spitting blood.

"I didn't mean your head, son," said Nestor.

Lieberman moved toward Nestor, who was holding the phone out. Lieberman thought he heard an animal sob from the cage behind him, but he didn't turn. People were crying on him tonight. It was a night for crying.

"Call's for Hanrahan," said Nestor, hand over the speaker. "Doorman at the Valdez apartment."

Lieberman took the phone and said, "Hello."

"You the guy works with Hanrahan?"

"I'm the guy," said Lieberman.

"My name's Billy Tarton, the night doorman at—"

"I know," said Lieberman rubbing his eyes. It was past midnight and the day had been long.

"Hanrahan said I should call him if Nikki Morales came back," said Tarton. "She's back, but I don't think for long. She told me to get her a cab in fifteen minutes. She's going on vacation."

"Don't get the cab," said Lieberman. "I'll be there in ten minutes."

12

She was standing in front of the building, two suitcases at her side, looking down Sheridan Road for her taxi. Lieberman slowed down and pulled into the driveway, making the circle around the fountain and pulling up in front of the door. Behind the doors Billy Tarton saw Lieberman and pointed at the woman.

The woman glanced at Lieberman, who got out of his car, opened his trunk, moved to the woman's side, and picked up her suitcases.

"You a cab?" she said, looking at his car as he dropped the suitcases in and closed the trunk. Her voice was soft with too much effort. She sounded like a woman to whom the softness and accent weren't natural, but she tried hard to make them fit.

"Cab's not coming," said Lieberman, moving around to the passenger seat and opening the door.

"This is . . . I'm calling a cop," she said.

"I'm a cop," said Lieberman, still holding the door open politely.

"You stole my bags," she protested. "I can sue you, the police department, and the city of Chicago."

"Young lady," Lieberman said wearily, "my partner's been shot. My daughter's on the verge of divorce, and about fifteen minutes ago a very crazy young man tried to drive his head through my stomach. The threat of a lawsuit signifies a return to the normal world. Miss Morales, please get in the car."

Nikki Morales stood glaring at Lieberman for about ten

seconds, her hands on her hips, her ample red mouth pouting. She turned to the doorman for support but he was occupied with a phone call which, Lieberman would have bet, had no one on the other end.

Lieberman looked at the woman carefully. She was about Estralda Valdez's height and she was a looker, but not like Estralda. Nikki was fuller in the face, lighter of color, and, as Bess would describe her, full figured.

There was no way anyone could have taken her for Estralda. There was no way she could have fit into Estralda's clothes. She was also a good or not-so-good ten years older than Estralda. She was also not Guadalupe Madera, Estralda's sister.

"I'm going to the airport," she said, getting in the car.

Lieberman closed the door, went around, and got in. He had left the motor running and the radio on.

As he drove onto Sheridan, a man's voice on the radio said, "And now, on a tape delay from this morning, *Mind Talk* with psychologist Jean Kaiser. Since this is a tape delay, please do not call the toll-free number that will be announced throughout the show."

"God," sighed Nikki, "another Dr. Ruth."

"No," said Lieberman. "I know this one."

"Kaiser?" asked Nikki.

"Started in Chicago," he said.

Jean Kaiser's voice came on, and Lieberman waited just enough to hear how she sounded. She sounded healthy, sane, and strong. He turned the radio off.

"Estralda Valdez," Lieberman said, making a right turn on Foster and heading west toward O'Hare Airport.

Nikki Morales looked straight ahead out the window.

"Ever see *Detour*?" asked Lieberman. "Guy played by Tom Neal picks up a woman and she won't let him go, almost gets him killed."

"She picks him up," Nikki Morales corrected. "What's your point?"

"You've got Tom Neal's chance of getting to the airport if you don't answer some questions," said Lieberman.

They drove past Swedish Memorial Hospital and over the

bridge through River Park. Nikki was still not talking.

"When I hit Kedzie," he said, "I turn and head back to the station. You call a lawyer. We call you a hostile witness to murder. The judge—"

"Murder?" she shrieked, her soft voice not quite breaking into whatever it sounded like normally. "I don't know who killed her."

Lieberman looked at her without expression, pulled the car over, and parked across from a hot dog stand.

"No," she said. "Don't bother saying 'How did you know a woman was killed?' Columbo. I know Estralda was killed Friday. It went through the building."

"Why did you pack and run?" asked Lieberman. "Want a hot dog?"

"A kosher with ketchup and grilled onions," Nikki Morales said, shaking her head. "I want a lawyer."

"No, you don't. You want to have a hot dog and catch a plane," he said, removing the keys from the ignition and opening the car door. "Think about it while I get the dogs. What you drink?"

"Diet anything. I'm on a diet."

Lieberman crossed the street, went into the hot dog stand, and ordered two dogs from a big black guy with white hair who was alone in the place mopping up. The place smelled of Lysol, hot dogs, and grilled onions.

"Shouldn't be out this late around here, Abe" said the guy, abandoning the mop and wiping his hands on his gray-white apron to make the sandwiches. "Get yourself mugged, cop or no cop. Neighborhood's changing."

"How's life, Henry?" asked Lieberman. He looked through the window at Nikki, who was looking back at him.

"Changing," repeated the man behind the counter. "Like I said. Drinks?"

"Two Diet Pepsis."

Henry nodded and looked across the street where Lieberman was glancing.

"Can you place her, Henry?"

"I place her," said the counterman.

"She in the business?"

"Nikki," said the counterman, going back to draw the drinks. "Ain't seen her in, shit, must be five years goin'."

"Where do you know her? Grilled onions on both. One with mustard. One ketchup."

"She worked the clubs down on Oak and Rush," said Henry, pulling the steamed buns and reaching for the boiling dogs with plastic tongs. "Bartender splits. I used to fill in at Mellow's, you know? They come in, Nikki and the rest, maybe every few nights when things was slow and the out-of-town Jaspers wasn't biting."

"She moved uptown," said Lieberman. "What's her real name?"

"Nikki . . ." Henry wrapped the two dogs in thin waxed paper as he tried to remember her name. "Fries with this?"

"No."

"Last name's Hoffer," said Henry, reaching for a brown paper bag. "Memory's not good as it was, Abe. Could be like that. She done short time once for cutting a hoop trying to pull in a customer."

"Anything else?"

"She talk Baltimore?" he asked.

"Boston," said Lieberman, taking the warm bag and drinks and handing Henry a twenty-dollar bill. Henry hit the cash button on the register but pocketed the twenty.

"Wanted to be a lady, did Nikki. Always did so. Summer of eighty-six Nikki put a knife into a tricky dick who started hurting," said Henry, looking out the window. "Dick complained and your boys went looking for Jane but never found the right one. That the kind of anything?"

"The kind," said Lieberman. "See you, Henry."

"Any time," said Henry, coming around the counter and heading for the mop.

"What's your name?" asked Nikki, taking the offered hot dog, napkin, and Diet Pepsi complete with straw.

"Lieberman," he said.

"My plane's at two," she said softly. "There's a motel about—"

"Miss Hoffer," he interrupted. Nikki went silent. "Estralda Valdez was cut badly. You've got a prior for cutting. You've also got an outstanding for slicing a piece of white meat out of an out-of-town visitor."

"I didn't kill her," Nikki insisted after swallowing a bite of dog and bun.

"I think you got mine," Lieberman said. "This one's got mustard."

"I'm not trading," said Nikki. "Live with it. With AIDS and things, I'm not trading."

Lieberman considered pointing out the inconsistency but thought better of it and took another bite.

"All right," Nikki said. "Estralda was trying to set up a stable. We were the first two. Idea was we get a dozen girls, set 'em up in apartments in the neighborhood, and work the phone from Estralda's. She would send the client to the right girl. Only one who'd know the phone numbers would be Estralda. Vice would have a hell of a night finding us all if anyone got busted. And she said she had connections, cops, you and your partner."

"What happened?" asked Lieberman.

"Estralda called, said I might be getting a visitor, out-of-towner named Frank. Frank was to get a freebie. Frank was to be made nice to. Frank could fuck up the whole thing."

"Friday?"

"Friday, right," said Nikki finishing her hot dog. "I waited. Nothing. Then just before midnight, she calls, says forget it. They'll take care of Frank."

"They?" asked Lieberman.

"Estralda and her sister. Her sister was there Friday. That guy in the hot dog stand you went into, over there. That's Henry Fives. He nailed me, didn't he?"

"Why're you running?" asked Lieberman.

"Henry's a pimp," said Nikki.

"Was a pimp," said Lieberman. "Now he sells fries and cleans floors. Why'd you run?"

"Didn't want to get busted. Estralda had a book. She said I wasn't in the book, but you think I believed that? And this Frank who probably cut her up. He had my name and apartment number, remember?"

"Where does Estralda's sister live?" asked Lieberman,

170

taking the waxed paper from Nikki and stuffing it into the grease-stained brown bag.

"Don't know," she said. "Saw her in the building a couple of times."

"That's it?" asked Lieberman.

"That's all," said Nikki.

"Nikki?"

"What?"

"You bite the inside of your cheek when you lie," he said. "The word on Estralda's murder didn't get through the building that fast. You were packed and out before anybody but the police and the killer knew who got killed."

"Shit," said Nikki.

They sat quietly for a few minutes, watching the late-night trucks lumbering toward the city.

"OK," she said. "Lupe, Estralda's sister, called me, told me to clear out, said Frank was coming for me. She was crying. I didn't even know Estralda was dead. I ran, read about the murder Saturday."

"No plane tonight, Nikki, sorry," said Lieberman, turning on the ignition.

Nikki slumped back in her seat.

"You want me to ID Lupe," she said.

Lieberman made a U-turn.

"Yeah," he said. "How about another dog?"

"Why not?"

By the time Lieberman had booked Veronica Alice Hoffer as a material witness to murder and a kid from the state's attorney's office who claimed to be a lawyer had done the paperwork, it was almost three in the morning. Lieberman called the hospital and found that Hanrahan was alive and that both Maureen and Iris were still there.

A few minutes after three-thirty Lieberman went through his front door, took his shoes off, and walked slowly toward the bathroom, navigating around the sleeping bag on the floor in which Melisa lay clutching her almost bald Flower Kid doll, around the end of the day bed on which Barry lay in a near-fetal ball snoring adenoidally. He padded past the open door of the kitchen, through which a yellow night light shone on the stove. He made it to the bathroom, closed the door, turned on the light, and looked at himself in the mirror. The man in the mirror was Abraham Lieberman's grandfather, though the white beard was only stubble and not flowing. The moist, red eyes, the dark sacks under them, the curled hair.

"An observation," Lieberman told his mirror image quietly. "We do not become our parents. We become our grandparents."

He undressed slowly, took a chance and turned on the shower. He waited for it to turn hot and got in under the shower massage that Maish's son Sam, the television producer, had given Lieberman and Bess for Chanukah. He let the spray soothe his knees as he shaved, and he wondered if it was worth getting into bed.

When he found himself nodding to sleep listening to the beat of the hot water on his skin, Lieberman turned off the water, got out, dried himself, and put on his pajamas. He threw his underwear, socks, and shirt into the clothes hamper, draped his jacket, slacks, and tie over one arm and his holster and gun over the other, and opened the door. Even when his grandchildren weren't there, Lieberman put the gun and holster into the drawer of the night table on his side of the bed, locked the drawer, and hung the key on the hook in the wall below the mattress level and over his head. Lieberman turned off the light, opened the bathroom door, and stepped into the dark hallway, where the man's voice came to him softly.

Lieberman dropped his jacket, pants, and tie and let the holster fall as he leveled the weapon toward the voice in the darkness near the door to Lisa's room.

"Abe," the voice said again.

"Todd?"

Lieberman sighed and bent down to pick up the clothes and holster.

"'My thoughts are swept away and I go bewildered. Where shall I turn the brain's activity in speed when the house is falling?'" said Todd dreamily. "Agamemnon."

"What have you been drinking?" Lieberman whispered.

"What's the first bottle on the shelf over the stove?"

"Uh . . . Bailey's Irish Creme," said Lieberman softly.

"I drank a couple of glasses. Tastes good. There's a little left."

Now Todd was whispering too.

"What's going on?" asked Lieberman.

"'The lady has with courage taken and fled to distant lands because she heard the Gods tell her she should be queen,'" said Todd, moving into the hum of soft light.

"Todd, no more Greek."

"Wasn't Greek," said Todd with a small laugh. "I just . . . You're right. I can't help it. Lisa's gone. We fought some more and when I, or did she, I don't remember which, but she said I should be responsible for a while and she was going back to the house. She left. And . . . here I . . . Bess said I should stay here tonight with the kids. We played Clue. I don't remember who won."

"I'll talk to you in the morning," said Lieberman. "Go to bed."

"It is morning," said Todd.

"Go to bed, Todd."

And Todd went to bed.

It was almost four when Lieberman closed the door behind him in the bedroom, felt his way to the bed, put the gun away, locked the drawer, and got into bed.

"How is he?" asked Bess.

"Who, Bill or Todd?"

"You know Todd's here," said Bess with a sigh. "I meant Bill."

"Alive," said Lieberman, reaching out for his wife in the dark. A soft breeze blew through the window, fluttering the curtains.

"You want to know about Todd and Lisa?" Bess asked softly.

"Definitely not," said Lieberman.

A truck rumbled four blocks away on Howard Street. Lieberman found the sound reassuring.

"Rabbi Wass wants you to call in the morning," she said.

"Did he tell you why? No. Don't answer. I don't want to know that either."

"Are your knees all right, Abe?" Bess said. "I heard the shower. You took your pill?"

"I'm OK," he said. "I took my pill. Give me your hand."

He took his wife's hand. He knew her, felt her. Bess was, he was sure, considering saying something, probably about Lisa and Todd, but she changed her mind and instead turned toward him on her side. Her hand came over and he put it to his cheek.

"You shaved," she whispered.

"I was filled with passion and expectation," he said.

"Let me see," she said, running her hand down his side. "You really want to, now?"

"You?" he asked back.

And they did.

There was no morning for Lieberman. He had slept through it and Bess had not awakened him. She got up early, unplugged the bedroom phone, gave Todd breakfast, and sent him to work. When Barry and Melisa woke up, she brought them into the kitchen, told them they had to be quiet, and fed them. She also took three phone messages for Lieberman, who got up just before noon and staggered into the kitchen trying to focus.

"Where are the kids?" he asked.

"Yetta took them shopping," said Bess, handing Lieberman a cup of herbal tea. Bess was dressed, a dark skirt and yellow blouse with white pearls. He tried to smile at her, knew it came out lopsided, and put the cup to his lips. Lieberman barely tolerated herbal tea, but he made it a rule not to start the morning with coffee. Hot tea fooled his nerves and stomach for about half an hour.

Lieberman sat at the kitchen table and ran his hand through his hair.

"Forgot to comb my hair," he said.

"You look like Einstein," Bess said with a smile. The toaster popped.

"Anybody call? Or has my absence from duty gone

completely unnoticed. Has it simply been assumed that I have retired and has my mail been forwarded to the home for burned-out cops? These are questions of great pith and moment," said Lieberman.

"You want your calls or you want to feel sorry for yourself?" Bess asked, placing a plate in front of him with two pieces of white toast covered with orange marmalade.

"I'd like to spend about two or three more minutes feeling sorry for myself. Hospital call?"

He bit into a piece of toast and felt better.

"Maureen called," said Bess, sitting across from him and reaching for one of the pieces of toast.

"You don't like orange marmalade." he reminded her.

"Am I committing a felony or a misdemeanor, Dirty Harry?" she asked. "You want to hear what Maureen said or you want to complain?"

"I can do both," he said.

"She said Bill is awake, that she was at home and that Iris was with her. Who is Iris?"

"Bill's new girlfriend," explained Lieberman. "She's Chinese."

Lieberman dipped his toast into the tea. It was, he discovered, not a good idea.

"Captain Hughes called, said I should let you sleep but you should see him as soon as you come in to work."

Lieberman dropped the soggy toast onto his plate and got up. He could use, he decided, at least five days of sleep. Instead, he picked up his dishes, dumped the soggy remains into the garbage bag and the half cup of tea into the sink. Dishes and cup went into the dishwasher and Lieberman felt a minor sense of satisfaction. A domestic chore had been accomplished without mishap.

The phone rang. Lieberman looked at it. Bess reached over and picked it up.

Lieberman was on his way out of the kitchen.

"Abe," she said. "Rabbi Wass. He wants to talk to you. He called last night. I told you, remember?"

"I remember," he said, turning back into the kitchen.

Her hand was over the mouthpiece.

"What else do you remember?" she asked.

"Passion," he said. "Torrid passion unmatched by any since Gable and Harlow in *Red Dust*."

"Talk on the phone," she said with a smile, handing it to him.

"Rabbi," he said. "Do you know that my nickname is 'Rabbi'?"

"No, Abraham, I didn't," said Rabbi Wass with a hint of confusion.

"It's not relevant, Rabbi," Lieberman said. "What can I do for you?"

"A great deal," said Rabbi Wass.

This, Abraham Melvin Lieberman did not like.

"What?" asked Lieberman flatly, looking at Bess who was smiling at him.

She knows what he wants, Lieberman thought, and she likes it.

"The board," began Rabbi Wass. "That is to say the board and I and some very active members of the congregation would like you to serve as president of Temple Mir Shavot when Israel Mitkowsky moves to California in September."

"I'm overwhelmed," said Lieberman, looking at his wife and seeing the frail hand of Ida Katzman at work.

"Then you will accept?" said Rabbi Wass, sensing that victory had come too easily.

Through Lieberman's mind flashed images of himself conducting meetings, going to services every week, reading from the Torah in his halting Hebrew, cajoling Irving "Rommel" Hamel to speak to the Sunday morning men's club.

"I don't deserve the honor," said Lieberman.

"We think you do," Rabbi Wass's voice beamed.

"Irving Hamel would make a better president," said Lieberman with some despair. "He's young, wants—"

"He turned us down," said Rabbi Wass sadly. "Too busy. He's a lawyer. Avrum, we need you. There is God's work to be done."

Not only was he being pressured, Lieberman was not even first choice. And then Lieberman got an idea.

"I have a better choice," he said.

"There really is no—" Rabbi Wass began sadly, ready to tick off the reasons why Syd Levan or Herschel Rosen had turned him down.

"My wife," said Lieberman.

Bess's smile left her face. She stopped dead at the kitchen sink.

"She's a woman," Rabbi Wass said, explaining the facts of life to the obviously confused Lieberman.

"I am aware of that, Rabbi," he said.

"Being president is a great honor," countered Rabbi Wass.

"An honor my dear wife richly deserves," said Lieberman on the attack.

"We've never had a woman president," the Rabbi explained.

"There are women rabbis," said Lieberman, looking at his wife's astonished face. "I'm sure other congregations have women presidents. I'm sure Ida Katzman would love the idea."

"I really don't think—" Rabbi Wass began.

"Ari," said Lieberman softly. "I'm about to turn you down and report to the congregation that you won't consider a woman as president."

"Blackmail?" asked the rabbi incredulously.

"You've got it," said Lieberman.

Rabbi Wass laughed, a deep genuine laugh that Abe Lieberman had never heard before.

"Then what can I do?" said the rabbi. "I accept. Confidentially, Avrum, I don't think you would have made that good of a president either. As the Catholics say, I don't think you have the calling. But Bess? I like it. Ask her to come see me, today if possible. Shalom, Abe."

"Shalom, Rabbi," said Lieberman and the two men hung up.

"Abe," said Bess.

"Madame President," said Lieberman, wondering what he was going to do about his hair. "You want the job?"

"Yes," she said.

"Would that all life's problems were so easily solved."

13

Lieberman called the station where the ever-present Nestor Briggs reported that (a) José Vegas had been treated for head wounds, appeared before Judge Wilson Woolf, and been released on $50,000 bond posted by the Lewellyn Bond Agency on behalf of Vegas's mother, (b) Captain Hughes had left for a meeting with the chief of police less than twenty minutes ago. Lieberman told Briggs that he was heading for the hospital.

After reshowering, both to wake up and to tame his hair, Lieberman headed for Maish's T & L where the Alter Cockers were out in force.

"How's Bill, little brother?" asked Maish, sliding a cup of coffee across the counter. Lieberman took it.

"Alive," said Lieberman. "Should make it."

"Yetta took the kids to Toys 'R' Us," said Maish, who looked round and genuinely grieved.

"Buy you a cup?" called Rosen from the table.

"Got one," said Lieberman holding up his coffee.

"Danish?" tried Rosen.

"Why not?" said Lieberman, accepting a cherry Danish from Maish and moving to the Alter Cocker table, where Herschel Rosen was holding court. Herschel was feeling solemn today. He had taken off the yellow cap he was wearing and placed it next to his coffee cup.

"Your partner OK?" asked Howie Chen.

"He'll live," said Lieberman, who wondered whether he continued to say this because he thought that repeating it would make it true.

"God willing," said Rosen.

"God willing," agreed Howie Chen.

Bloombach and Stoltzer, the atheists, said nothing but looked at Lieberman with sympathy.

"You think it's Maish's coffee?" asked Syd Levan. "First the girl. Then the partner?"

"Not funny, Sydney," said Rosen, ruling him out of order.

"Who's being—" Levan started and then stopped.

"It's all right," said Lieberman, downing his coffee. "Cops do the same thing. You see a lot of death. You try to make jokes so it doesn't feel so real."

"Like in the books with the homicide detectives who think they're funny," said Bloombach, trying to remember the name of the books.

"All cops?" asked Howie.

"Not all," said Lieberman. He put his cup down. "Gentlemen, I must bid you adieu."

A hand touched Lieberman's sleeve. Lieberman turned.

"You'll find whoever did it?" asked Rosen gently.

"I'll find whoever did it," Lieberman assured him.

Maish waved as his brother moved to the door.

"If you get a chance, stop by later," said Maish, cleaning the counter with a sponge though Abe's coffee cup during its momentary rest had left no ring. "Let me know what's going on with Lisa and Todd."

"We think they'll work it out," said Bloombach.

Lieberman shook his head and looked at his brother, who shrugged. Lieberman went into the street, heard the distant sound of thunder, but looked up in the sky and saw no clouds.

Fifty-two minutes later he entered the University of Chicago Hospitals and went to Intensive Care. Dr. Deep was standing there in the hall talking to Maureen and her son Michael. Michael Hanrahan looked far more like his father than his mother, a clean, trim version of the way his father had probably looked a dozen years before Lieberman had met Bill Hanrahan.

Dr. Deep spotted Lieberman coming down the hall first and looked up. Maureen turned to follow Deep's eyes and saw Lieberman. Her eyes gave out a warning and Lieberman looked again at Michael and did not like what he saw.

Nurses flowed past. Somewhere down the hall and down an endless corridor a hospital transport bed with a wobbly wheel headed in their direction.

"How is he?" asked Lieberman.

"You should have been there with him," said Michael.

Lieberman looked at the young man, remembered that he was twenty-six, no, twenty-seven, his father's son, and Irish.

"He went in that house with no backup because you were eating hot dogs at a baseball game," said Michael defiantly.

"You may be right," said Lieberman.

"Michael," Maureen said. "You're not facing the—"

"You find this funny, Lieberman?" asked Michael.

"I'm not laughing," said Lieberman. "And I'm not smiling because I find the situation funny. I'm smiling because life is arranged with surprises to keep everyone but children from getting a good night's sleep."

"This," reminded Dr. Deep gently, "is an Intensive Care area. We must be quiet."

"Dad's right," said Michael, turning to his mother. "He's a bullshit artist."

Michael stalked off without looking back. He was headed for Deep's office at the end of the corridor.

"I'm sorry, Abe," said Maureen.

"I am so very glad you arrived," said Deep. "Mr. Hanrahan should have no visitation yet, but he is most agitated and insists on talking to you. I feel it would be best if you did so for just a minute. No more than a minute."

Maureen touched Lieberman's arm and he looked at her. Age had found her overnight.

"Iris had to go to work," said Maureen. "I like her."

Lieberman gave Maureen a hug and followed Deep through the white double doors, where a nurse gave him a gown, cap, and mask and waited for him to put them on.

Machines were humming and beeping. Lights and voices were dim and the carpet muffled footsteps. Lieberman followed Dr. Deep into a room with a glass window. In the bed lay William Hanrahan complete with nose tubes, IV, and the pallid skin, open mouth, and closed eyes of the critically ill.

"Thirty seconds only," Dr. Deep reminded Lieberman who advanced to the bed.

"Father Murphy?" Lieberman said, laying his hand gently on his partner's arm, careful to avoid the tube that was connected to it.

Hanrahan's eyes fluttered and opened. They sought the voice, looked in the wrong place, and slowly found Lieberman's masked face. Hanrahan's mouth formed the word "Rabbi," but no word came out. Lieberman leaned forward, his ear almost touching Hanrahan's lips, and this time, when Hanrahan repeated "Rabbi," Lieberman heard it.

"You're doing OK," said Lieberman.

"You're a bullshit artist," Hanrahan gasped.

"So your son just told me," said Lieberman.

Hanrahan's lips quivered in a smile.

"Article," Hanrahan said. "Newspa—"

"I've got it," said Lieberman.

"Sister," said Hanrahan. "Estralda's sister. Photograph in bedroom."

"Same as the one in the article," said Lieberman. "Estralda and her sister. Looks like they killed a couple of guys. Paper's from Corpus Christi, Texas."

"Detective Lieberman," Dr. Deep said. "I'm afraid we must stop for now."

"Seen her," said Hanrahan whose eyes were fluttering, fighting against drugged sleep.

"Estralda's sister?" asked Lieberman.

Hanrahan nodded.

"Where?"

And Hanrahan told him.

Before he left the hospital Lieberman went to the lobby and put in a credit card call to Mayor Carrol LaSalle of Corpus Christi. Carrol LaSalle had, according to the lady with a very heavy Texas accent, left a message with his office that any call from Detective Lieberman should be forwarded immediately, day or night. There was a click, a delay, and Patsy Cline singing something while he waited a good two minutes till LaSalle came on the line.

"Lieberman," he said. "You got my little girl with the gun?"

"Looks that way, Mayor," said Lieberman. "You might want your people to get the papers started."

"Guadalupe Madera?" said LaSalle.

"Guadalupe Madera," Lieberman agreed, watching a nurse wheel a young mother out in a wheelchair. The young woman, who looked both black and Asian, was carrying a small bundle in her arms. Lieberman couldn't see the baby's face. A nurse's aide followed with a cart of flowers. Beyond the glass doors at the entrance, Lieberman could see a waiting cab with open trunk and door.

"Best guess, Mayor. What will your people throw at her?"

"Best guess? Depends. She been a good girl? Shot any more people in the head? That sort of thing," said LaSalle. "Life maybe. Out in five depending on the judge, the climate, and the collective memory. Shoot, she may get nothing. Remember what we said about you folks giving us a hard time on extradition."

"I remember," said Lieberman.

"You plan to point out to your people and whatever press might be around that you found her with the invaluable assistance of Carrol LaSalle?"

"That's my plan," said Lieberman. "One more question. The newspaper article said a bartender named Frank was the first one on the scene after the murders. Happen to know Frank's full name and where he might be?"

Mayor LaSalle had no idea where Frank might be but he remembered him clearly and gave both a description of the man and his full name.

"Got to go now, Lieberman," said the Mayor. "Big mall opening this afternoon. Think I'll hint that some unfinished business might be wrapped up soon. Watch your back, Detective, and get yourself a new partner, hear?"

Lieberman heard. He made another call and asked the man who answered for a favor. The man didn't understand the request but he agreed.

"It's about the murder we talked about Friday, right?" said the man.

"Yeah," said Lieberman.

"Am I putting out a want ad sign?" the man said.

"I would."

And Lieberman hung up. He sat in the hospital lobby for twenty-five minutes reading the *Sun-Times*, watching patients and visitors come and go, and trying to remember if it was Ann Savage or Ann Dvorak in *Detour*.

The cab pulled up to the door and the driver looked out to see who his fare was. Lieberman came slowly through the hospital door, walked to the cab, got in the back seat, and closed the door.

"Where to?" asked the driver.

"Does it matter?" asked Lieberman.

"Guess not," the driver answered.

Lieberman removed his pistol slowly from his holster and, as the cab pulled into the street, he pointed it at the head of Francis Dupree.

14

"Frank," said Lieberman as the cab drove up Fifty-Ninth Street along the grassy Midway south of the University. "I'm seriously considering shooting you in the head."

Frank Dupree simply shrugged.

"I figured when dispatch sends me from a job on Grand Avenue here, something is not kosher," said Dupree. "But kosher, that's your area, right?"

"You shot my partner in the head, Frank," said Lieberman evenly. "I'd like to know why."

"I didn't shoot nobody, man," said Frank. "You're not sticking me with no murders cause you think you got a dumb bayou boy to close some doors."

Lieberman shot out the front window of the cab. Dupree let out a yell and swerved toward the curb, kissed a parked car, and straightened out.

"What the fuck you doin'? You crazy?"

"Turn right," said Lieberman lazily and Dupree turned right. "We are now in a neighborhood where shots are frequently heard and police do not move quickly. Park."

"Wait now," said Dupree with a laugh. "You—"

"Park," said Lieberman softly.

Dupree parked behind a rusting, abandoned Honda.

"Tell me what happened, Frank," said Lieberman. "Tell me slowly and tell me the whole thing."

"It'll all get thrown out," Dupree said, turning in his seat and leaning toward the window. "You gonna get a confession with a gun in your hand and you think it's gonna hold?"

A pair of boys, both black, both about nine, looked through

the broken front window of the cab at the two white guys just sitting there. The taller of the two was about to say something when he saw Lieberman's gun and decided to keep walking.

"That old man he got a gun," said the boy.

"She-it he does," said the other boy.

"I'm clearing away some of this glass," said Dupree, agitated.

"Your hand touches the glove compartment and your head goes through the windshield," said Lieberman.

"I'm just . . . I told you," said Dupree with a deep sigh at Lieberman's inability to understand this simple need.

"Gun's in the glove compartment Frank, right?" asked Lieberman.

Dupree slumped. A call came over the radio. Dupree flipped the voice off.

"I shoulda changed my name," he said. "But I didn't know what . . . Believe it, policeman. I came to this here city looking for work, got this cab, kissing my wandering good-by. Then one day she get into my cab."

"Which one?" asked Lieberman.

"Estralda, the younger one," he said. "She didn't change that much."

"And you blackmailed her," said Lieberman.

"Not saying I did, not saying I didn't. Just you and me in the car and you know when I get me a lawyer I'm gonna tell that judge I said nothing."

"You blackmailed her," Lieberman repeated.

"I asked her for money," he said. "Not blackmail. Old times' sake."

"Tell me about Friday," said Lieberman.

Dupree glanced at the glove compartment and turned in his seat. Lieberman leaned forward and poked him with the barrel of the gun.

"Don't turn," he said. "I can see your eyes and mouth just fine in the mirror."

"She tole me to be on the corner of Foster and Sheridan at midnight," said Frank. "She tole me she had to get out of town a while. Cops were giving her troubles.

185

She give me everything I asked for."

"Money and Nikki Morales," said Lieberman.

Dupree's eyes met Lieberman's in the mirror.

"If you know, why you ask me?"

"Continue your story," said Lieberman.

"All right, so I'm at the corner. I tell my dispatch I picked up a fare on the street, took him to Foster and Sheridan, and I'm getting a burger at the McDonald's that's two blocks from where Valdez lives. I get the call. I get back in my cab and drive over thinking, thinking."

Dupree was tapping his head with the fingers of his right hand.

"I'm thinking," he went on. "What's this? Why she don't just come out, walk two blocks, and give me the money? So, I go to the place and the door guy tells me to go up and help Miss Valdez with her luggage. Well, I know she's goin' out of town so I go up. Maybe, I think, cops are watching her and she figures this out to make it look like she's just calling a cab, but that don't make much sense. I go up to the apartment, through the door, which is open, and the place is a mess, you know? You know what happen then?"

"Someone tried to kill you," said Lieberman.

"You got that right," said Dupree. "In the living room this bum is asleep. Right in the middle of the mess. I don't know who it is."

"His name's Van Beeber," said Lieberman. "He used to have a Hallmark shop in Holland, Michigan. He killed his wife ten years ago."

"That a fact?" said Dupree. "Where was I . . . Oh, that's when she try to kill me. Estralda come out with a knife behind me. She stabbed me. I show you."

Dupree lifted his shirt. Lieberman's gun pressed into his neck.

There was a bandage on Frank Dupree's back, a big bandage.

"Self-defense," he said, letting the shirt down again. "I took the knife and there was like a little accident."

"You stabbed her eight times," said Lieberman.

"Self-defense. I threw the knife out the window into the lake and looked around. I was lookin' when the other one came in."

"Guadalupe," said Lieberman.

"Yeah. Different from Texas but her. She saw her sister and I could see she was in on it. She was gonna run but I stopped her and told her she had to get me out of the building or I'd turn her in. She got in one of Estralda's dresses and we went out."

"She did something before you went out," said Lieberman.

"Yeah, she pull up the window shade and stood looking out for a few seconds there, maybe crying. We went down the elevator, out on the street. She wave at somebody across the street. I look over and see this guy in the restaurant window."

"Hanrahan," said Lieberman. "My partner. The one you shot."

"Not me," said Dupree. "I took her where I said I took her, let her out, and tole her to come up with money or I'd turn her in."

"Why did you follow my partner?" asked Lieberman.

The two boys had returned. This time with two older boys and a girl. Both of the boys were swaggering ahead of the crowd heading for the cab.

"I didn't follow your—" Dupree began and Lieberman shot a hole into the back of the front passenger seat. The bullet went through the seat and bounced off the dashboard, leaving a dent and a ringing of metal. The swaggering boys stopped, turned, and walked back to the girl and the kids. Together, they strode anywhere but here.

"You wouldn't shoot me, Detective," said Dupree.

Lieberman could see the sweat on the man's forehead.

"You shot my partner in the back of the head, Frank. You shot a cop. I'm retiring in a few years. I shoot you and I get a medal when I go. Listen, Frank. I have arthritis, both knees."

"I'm sorry," said Dupree. "My mother had—"

"—and I've got a lot on my mind," Lieberman went on. "The easiest thing for me to do is shoot you, walk back to

187

my car, and drive north. Tell me a story, Frank."

"I don't—" Dupree began but remembered the two shots that had been fired and changed his mind. "The money. I figured he was after the money they took from, whatever was left, Juan Hernandez. You know? I followed him around a little. What happened at that house was an accident. I am no killer. I'm a musician. Things just"—Dupree was crying now—"I just followed him in," he wept. "I was gonna try to make a deal. I . . . I don' know what happened. I just . . . Next thing I know he was layin' there dead like my Uncle Dave when the gator got his leg. I got nothin' out of all this and I'm sorry what I done."

With this Dupree slumped over sobbing.

"Let's head back north to the station," said Lieberman. "You can tell your story to a public defender and complain about my brutality. Sit up and drive."

"OK, OK," said Dupree, sitting up and turning in his seat to face Lieberman. "Mind I ask you somethin'?"

"Ask," said Lieberman.

But Dupree didn't ask. He had something in his left hand. Lieberman had a glimpse of the open glove compartment and a sense of metal in Dupree's hand, the hand with the missing fingers. Dupree's hand was coming down over the top of the seat when Lieberman fired. The bullet tore through the back of the driver's seat as the knife struck, pierced Lieberman's pants, and slashed his right thigh. Dupree lifted his hand to strike again. A trickle of blood came through the hole Lieberman's gun had just made in the seat. Lieberman aimed the gun at Dupree's face.

"Frank," Lieberman warned.

"You gonna have to shoot me or let me go," answered Dupree. Lieberman shot him.

Of the five squad cars that showed up within five minutes of Lieberman leaning over Dupree's body to call the dispatcher, only one contained anyone Lieberman knew. His name was Laurel. He was black and lean with a white mustache. Laurel was the first uniform out of the cars. Six uniformed cops pointed guns at Lieberman, who was standing next to the cab with his gun holstered and his hands showing.

"Detective Lieberman," he announced.

"He is," Laurel shouted to the other officers. "What've we got, Abe?"

"The guy who shot my partner," he said. "I think the knife in his hand was the one he used to kill Estralda Valdez. You know the case? Last Friday?"

"No," said Laurel. "Wait, yeah. Hooker."

The other cops were looking at the body and keeping the curious away.

"Yeah," said Lieberman. "I think the gun that shot my partner's in the glove compartment."

Laurel took Lieberman's statement and his gun and drove him back to the hospital emergency room where Lieberman was treated for minor lacerations of the leg.

"Self-defense, no doubt," said Laurel as Lieberman rolled down his pantleg and got off the ER table. "But you'll have to go with the bullshit, Abe. You know the drill."

"I'm going to go see my captain, give him my report, and spend the evening getting sympathy from my grandchildren," said Lieberman.

And that was that. Lieberman walked to his car. His leg didn't bother him. It had been cleaned, bandaged, and taped.

He had one more stop to make and one more murder to deal with before he headed home.

15

Lieberman parked in front of a fire hydrant next to the Black Moon Restaurant and pulled down his visor to show his Chicago Police Department ID placard. The oriental blinds were up at the Black Moon but the sign in the window said "closed." Lieberman walked to the door, peered in, and knocked.

The day was bright. Sun danced on the darkened glass. Cars on Sheridan Road behind him hummed and rattled by. Inside the Black Moon, someone stirred.

"Not open," a voice croaked inside. "Dinner at six."

Lieberman knocked again.

"Not—" came the male voice again, a bit higher.

"Police," said Lieberman.

"Police. No police. Police. Not open," said the man. "Come back six."

"Mr. Huang, will you please open the door. I've just shot a man. I've been stabbed in the leg, which along with the other one, is aching with arthritis. I have to catch a killer and my daughter is giving me grief. Give me a few minutes."

The door to the Black Moon opened and Lieberman found himself facing a small, thin Chinese man with gray hair.

"Daughters give grief," said the man. "Sons too. Come in."

Lieberman entered and Huang closed the door behind him, making sure the "closed" sign was facing the street.

"Thanks," said Lieberman.

"Sit," said Iris's father, pointing to a table in the shade. The table was set for dinner for two: white tablecloth, white plate with red dragons around the rim, a red glass, and a red napkin with silverware wrapped inside.

Lieberman sat.

"You know about Iris's friend, the policeman?" asked Lieberman.

"I know," said Huang. "She called. He got shot. I got the arthritis too. Knees, arm. You know?"

"I know," said Lieberman.

"I figured. Tea?" asked Huang.

"No thanks," said Lieberman.

Huang sat.

"Sister's daughter will come tonight to help," said Huang, looking at the kitchen as if his niece were already there.

"Bill Hanrahan's my partner," said Lieberman, touching the outer rim of the plate in front of him.

"Yes," said Huang.

"He's a good man, Mr. Huang," said Lieberman.

"I don't know. Maybe yes. Maybe no. He . . . Policemen get shot, shoot, drink. He is married. I'm sorry he is hurt."

"Iris seems to be a fine woman," said Lieberman.

"Yes," said Huang. "How your daughter give you grief?"

"She's fighting with her husband," said Lieberman looking through the window at the Michigan Towers.

"Life is difficult," said Huang with a sigh.

"Life is difficult," agreed Lieberman. "You know why I'm here?"

"You keep looking across street. I think you have something to do there you don't want to do so quick. You stop here so you don't do what you don't want to do right away."

"Were you a policeman in China?" asked Lieberman, again looking out the window toward the high-rise across the street.

"No, a soldier. You have sad eyes," said Huang.

"So do you, Mr. Huang," said Lieberman.

"Chou Chin," said Huang. "Customers call me Charlie."

"You like to be called Charlie?"

"No," said Huang.

"I'll try Chou Chin," said Lieberman. "Call me Abe."

Huang got up, walked quickly into the kitchen at the rear of the restaurant, and came back with a small bottle. He handed the bottle to Lieberman.

"Knees," said Huang, moving toward a table at the rear of the small room where he poured a glass of water from a red pitcher that matched the glasses. "Take two."

The label on the bottle was in Chinese. Inside the bottle were white pills. Lieberman opened the bottle and dumped two pills in his palm as Huang handed him the water. Lieberman put the pills in his mouth and swallowed as Huang said, *"Le Chaim."*

Lieberman almost choked.

"To life," said Huang. "That's Jewish talk. You Jewish. You know."

"I know," said Lieberman. *"Le Chaim.* What's in these?"

"Herbs, ginseng, horn of a deer, things," said Huang. "Keep the bottle."

"Thanks," said Lieberman, pocketing the bottle and pulling a slightly crumpled folded sheet of paper from his shirt pocket. "I'm going across the street into that building, Chou Chin. If I'm not out in half an hour, call nine-one-one and tell them to come to the apartment on this sheet of paper."

Chou Chin looked at the paper Lieberman had handed him and nodded to show that he understood.

"Tell them an officer is in trouble. And if anything happens to me, have them read the rest of what's written there. OK?"

Huang nodded solemnly again.

"OK," said Huang.

"You know the movie *High Noon*?"

"Gary Cooper, yes. Very *dri*, the Japanese say," said Huang with a smile. "Do not forsake me oh my darling."

Lieberman rose and held out his hand. Huang rose and took it. His grip was remarkably firm for his frame, size, and age.

"Oh to be torn 'twixt love and duty," said Lieberman.

"Nearing high noon," said Huang.

"Chou Chin, this could be the start of a beautiful friendship," said Lieberman.

"Casablanca," said Huang, shaking his head.

Lieberman moved toward the door.

"Let's try a hard one," he said, looking across the street at the high-rise entrance. "Evil is. Evil does exist."

"List of Adrian Messenger," said Huang solemnly.

Lieberman opened the door.

"Bill Hanrahan's a good man, Chou Chin," he said.

Huang smiled, shrugged, and held up both hands to show that he'd be willing to consider the possibility.

And Lieberman left. Lieberman waited for a break in the traffic and crossed the street, his torn pants leg rubbing against the bandaged thigh. He went through the front door where the doorman, not Billy Tarton but a burly older white man with hair dyed too black greeted him with a false-teeth smile.

"Can I . . . ?" the doorman asked looking at Lieberman's torn pants with more than a touch of suspicion.

Lieberman showed his badge and asked the doorman to announce him to Mr. Hughes. The doorman nodded and opened the door. Lieberman entered the inner lobby as the doorman pushed a button to release the door. He moved slowly to the waiting elevator and went up. When he reached the third floor and got out, he turned to the right and found Captain Hughes's door opened and Hughes waiting for him. Hughes was wearing a suit and tie. Hughes looked concerned as he backed up to let Lieberman in and close the door behind him.

"Got a call from Briggs," said Hughes. "I put a call in to the chief of police and told him you got the guy who killed Estralda Valdez and shot Hanrahan. He wants to see us tomorrow. I think it's something good. What happened to your leg?"

"Scrape. Captain, can we sit down?" Lieberman asked.

Hughes looked at his watch, blew out some air, and said, "I'm afraid—"

"I know," said Lieberman, moving to the right into the kitchen where he sat at a small white table. "Will you ask your wife to come out for a minute?"

"What?" asked Hughes, tilting his head. "My—"

"Your wife," said Lieberman. "The woman in the picture in your hallway. Estralda's sister, Guadalupe. I can hear her in the bedroom."

Hughes was sweating, considering a lie, considering his options. He tried a quizzical, tolerant smile to indicate that Lieberman must be crazy with the heat and the rough day he had had, but when their eyes met, Dale Hughes knew it was over.

"Lupe," Hughes called. "Will you come in here for a minute?"

Lieberman was tired. He rubbed his eyes.

"I left a note with a friend telling what I know. If I don't show up at my friend's within the hour, the note goes to the chief and . . ."

Guadalupe Hughes entered the room.

She was Estralda's size and build and color, a little older, wearing a blue dress. She moved to Hughes's side. Her husband put his arm around her.

"You want to talk?" Lieberman said.

"You talk," Hughes suggested.

It was Lieberman's turn to shrug. He shifted his weight and heard the pills Huang had given him rattle in his pocket.

"Friday night was a setup that went wrong," said Lieberman. "You got Frank Dupree to come here. He was supposed to meet with you in Estralda's apartment and collect his blackmail money. Only he wasn't going to collect. You had turned Estralda's room over and pulled Van Beeber in. My guess is you gave him a bottle and let him drink till he passed out. My guess is you already checked Van Beeber out and knew about the outstanding murder against him. My guess is you planned to make it look as if the cabby had walked in on an attempted rape. My guess is you were going to stab Dupree and put the knife in Van Beeber's hand. Estralda would signal Hanrahan, who'd come running. He was supposed to be the witness. But it backfired. Dupree and Estralda had a fight. Estralda was stabbed. So far, so good?"

"Go on guessing," said Hughes softly.

"Maybe Lupe came in. Maybe Dupree saw the mess and Van Beeber and figured something was going on. Whatever

194

it was, Estralda was the one who ended up dead."

"No," said Guadalupe emphatically. "My husband knew nothing of this. Estralda and I planned it. Dupree said he'd turn us in for what we did in Texas unless I got him out of the building fast. Estralda's dress was on the floor. I put it on, went out with Dupree, waved at the policeman in the Chinese restaurant, got in Dupree's cab, and he drove off."

Lieberman shook his head and looked at Hughes.

"I can't buy it. You didn't just coincidentally answer the call on your sister-in-law's murder Friday night," said Lieberman.

"No," said Lupe at her husband's side. "Dale didn't know. Estralda and I did it. He—"

"It's all right, Lupe," Hughes said, squeezing her to his side. "Where does this put us, Lieberman? Dupree's dead. You can't even prove my wife and Estralda were sisters."

"Nikki Morales," said Lieberman. "Estralda introduced your wife as her sister to Nikki, who's willing to ID her."

"Lieberman," said Hughes. "You've got no witnesses, no crime here but suspicion of conspiracy to conceal murder."

"And a positive Texas warrant on your wife."

"I . . . We have to think," said Guadalupe.

"Nothing to think about," said Lieberman. "You used me and my partner. You got my partner shot, your sister killed, and me blowing a hole in Frank Dupree."

Hughes and Guadalupe looked at each other. Lieberman watched them.

"My wife is pregnant, Lieberman," said Hughes.

"Oh, for . . ." Lieberman said with a massive sigh. "It never comes up easy, does it?"

"It never comes up easy," Hughes agreed.

Lieberman got up from the chair. He felt slightly queasy. It could have been a lot of things. He didn't explore the feeling.

"I'm going home," said Lieberman, moving past Hughes and his wife and going back into the alcove near the front door. "You might want to seriously consider turning in your badge and finding another line of work. If you walk through the station house door the day after tomorrow, I submit a request for early retirement and a letter to the mayor and the *Chicago Tribune*."

Behind him, Hughes's voice said, "Lieberman."

Lieberman had no gun. He turned slowly ready to remind the woman and his boss about the note he had left with Chou Chin Huang but it wasn't necessary.

"Thanks," said Hughes.

Lieberman shrugged and went out the door. He crossed Sheridan Road behind a bus and headed toward the door of the Black Moon. Before he could knock Chou Chen Huang came out.

"Done?" asked Huang.

"It's never really done," said Lieberman.

Huang handed him the sheet with the note Lieberman had written. Lieberman pocketed it and held out his right hand. Huang took it.

"You like baseball?" Lieberman asked.

"Don't not like it. Don't like it. Don't understand it," said Huang.

"Want to go to a Cub game with me and my grandchildren next Saturday afternoon?" asked Lieberman.

"Yes, I think," said Huang. "Then you come here for dinner."

"It's a date," said Lieberman.

Lieberman considered going to the station but decided against it. He'd killed a man. It had happened once before in his career. Once in the winter of '72 when a cokehead known as Jumping Sport Conway had come out of the Domino Restaurant on Martin Luther King Drive with a gun in each hand shooting in the general direction of anything that moved. Lieberman and seven other cops had opened fire. They had all gunned Jumping Sport down in the street. Lieberman had an annual nightmare about that night.

It was early evening when he entered his house and called out, "Anyone here?"

No answer. Lieberman went into the dining room and called again, "Anyone home?"

Bess came out of the bedroom. She was putting on glittering earrings.

"Abe," she said. "Rabbi Wass needs me for a meeting with the board. Todd and Lisa are out with the kids for dinner. If you . . ." She looked at his face, the torn trousers, and his smile. "What happened?"

"Tore my pants, scraped my knee. Stopped at the emergency room and a nurse cleaned and bandaged it."

"You're sure?" she asked.

"Sure," he said.

Later he would tell her that he had shot the man who killed Estralda Valdez and tried to kill Bill. Later, but not now. Now he was weary.

"I'll call and tell them I can't make it," said Bess, coming to her husband and looking into his eyes.

"I'm all right," he assured her. "Go to your meeting. I'll take you out to dinner later. So my pants are torn. Big deal. How are Todd and Lisa?"

"I don't think they're going to make it," said Bess with a sigh. "Dinner with the kids or no dinner with the kids. We've got a stubborn daughter. Todd left a note for you."

"You smell good," said Lieberman.

She hugged him and her hair tickled his nose. She moved away, went to the kitchen table, and came back with a folded sheet of paper she handed to Lieberman, who had moved back to the living room. He turned on the television and found WGN. He turned off the sound and took the note. Bess leaned over and kissed him.

"I'll be sitting here when you get back," he said.

A Philadelphia left-hander Lieberman didn't recognize was stepping into the batter's box.

"I'll be back soon, Abe," Bess said and went out the door. "We'll talk about it if you want to. Sure you're all right?"

"I'm fine," he said, opening the envelope and pulling out a neatly typed sheet of paper on which was written:

"Many are the forms of what is unknown. Much that the gods achieve is surprise. What we look for does not come to pass; God finds a way for what none foresaw. Such was the end of this story. Euripides in Helen.*"*

Bess stepped in front of Abe and leaned over to touch his forehead and kiss his cheek.

"Thanks," he said. "I needed that."

"My pleasure," she said, touching his cheek.

She stepped out of his line of vision and left the house.

Lieberman folded the note, put it in his pocket, and turned his eyes to the screen. The batter had struck out. The score was four to one in favor of the Cubs in the sixth inning. Lieberman smiled, closed his eyes, and fell asleep to the distant sound of children playing somewhere outside.

Epilogue

Clarise Rogers was seventy-five years old and filled with pride.

Her son Harold was standing behind the podium on the stage of the high school auditorium. Harold was looking out at three hundred people, black and white. Her son Harold was standing tall and determined. Her son Harold had singled out his mother, thanked her for coming back from Stockton, California, to witness this moment, thanked her for supporting him through hard times and law school at the University of Texas.

"I am not just running for mayor of this city," said Harold Rogers. "I'm running for change. I'm running for the values my mother has given to me."

This time the applause was for Clarise Rogers, who acknowledged the ovation with a nod of her head. She beamed at her son and remembered the day ten years ago when she had found the cans of money in that house not ten minutes from where they sat.

"We've had enough of the Carrol LaSalles of this state," repeated Harold Rogers. "We've had enough of his cowboy stories of the past. This is now. That was then. Good-old-boy days are gone forever. The twenty-first century is on the way in. Carrol LaSalle is on the way out."

Clarise Rogers absorbed the applause, savored it. Her heart swelled with pride. She closed her eyes and remembered the past. Remembered the first cleaning store she had bought in Stockton and the one in Davis and the two in Sacramento. There were six Clarise's Cleaners now.

"The Lord works in mysterious ways," said Harold with a smile. "Mysterious ways."

"Amen to that," someone in the rear of the auditorium called.

And to herself, Clarise Rogers nodded and said her own "Amen."

About the Author

Stuart Kaminsky is the author of the Toby Peters and the Inspector Rostnikov mystery series and lives in Sarasota, Florida. His *A Cold Red Sunrise* won the prestigious Edgar Award in 1988.